DEATH IN THE SKY

Recent titles by Alan Savage from Severn House

THE RAF SERIES

BLUE YONDER
DEATH IN THE SKY

THE FRENCH RESISTANCE SERIES
RESISTANCE
THE GAME OF TREACHERY
LEGACY OF HATE
THE BRIGHTEST DAY

THE PARTISAN SERIES
PARTISAN
MURDER'S ART
BATTLEGROUND
THE KILLING GROUND

THE COMMANDO SERIES
COMMANDO
THE CAUSE
THE TIGER

THE SWORD SERIES
THE SWORD AND THE SCALPEL
THE SWORD AND THE JUNGLE
THE SWORD AND THE PRISON
STOP ROMMEL!
THE AFRIKA KORPS

DEATH IN THE SKY

Alan Savage

This first world edition published in Great Britain 2006 by
SEVERN HOUSE PUBLISHERS LTD of
9–15 High Street, Sutton, Surrey SM1 1DF.
This first world edition published in the USA 2006 by
SEVERN HOUSE PUBLISHERS INC of
595 Madison Avenue, New York, N.Y. 10022.

British Library Cataloguing in Publication Data

Savage, Alan, 1930-
  Death in the sky
  1. Great Britain. Royal Air Force. Fighter Command - Fiction
  2. Germany. Luftwaffe - Fiction
  3. Air pilots, Military - Germany - Family relationships - Fiction
  4. Air pilots, Military - Great Britain - Family relationships - Fiction
  5. World War, 1939-1945 - Participation, English - Fiction
  6. World War, 1939-1945 - Participation, German - Fiction
  7. Brothers - Fiction
  8. Domestic fiction
  I. Title
  823.9'14 [F]

  ISBN-13: 978-0-7278-6374-4
  ISBN-10: 0-7278-6374-6

Except where actual historical events and characters are being
described for the storyline of this novel, all situations in this
publication are fictitious and any resemblance to living persons
is purely coincidental.

All Severn House titles are printed on acid-free paper.

Typeset by Palimpsest Book Production Ltd.,
Polmont, Stirlingshire, Scotland.
Printed and bound in Great Britain by
MPG Books Ltd., Bodmin, Cornwall.

This is a novel. Unless historically identifiable, the characters are invented, and are not intended to resemble real persons living or dead. Much of the action is based on fact, but 833 Squadron is fiction.

'Separated for the moment by the barrier of war we shall one day be reunited by death in the air.'

Heinz Knoke, Luftwaffe pilot.

Contents

PART ONE

Waiting

'We are waiting for the long-promised invasion. So are the fishes.'

Winston Churchill.

One

Days of Triumph

Senior-Lieutenant Max Bayley lay on his back in his bed and gazed at the ceiling, just visible in the dawn light drifting through the window. As it was early June it was only just past three. And he had been awakened by . . . an aircraft landing – and it was a Messerschmitt engine. In fact, two Messerschmitt engines. He couldn't imagine who it might be. His entire squadron had been dispersed to their homes to enjoy a week's leave after their considerable endeavours, and achievements, during the past month of the invasion of France and their attempts to destroy the British Expeditionary Force on the beaches of Dunkirk. And to recover from the trauma of losing their much-loved commander. Were any of them so keen as to return to duty after only two days?

There was a tap on the door. 'Herr Lieutenant? Are you awake, sir? The Field-Marshal is here.'

'What?' Max tumbled out of bed. He was a slightly built, fair-haired young man with crisp features; despite his rank and experience, he was still only twenty-one years old. 'Come in, Heinrich. Which field-marshal?' He was still only half awake.

The orderly opened the door, helped Max into his clothes. '*The* Field-Marshal, sir.'

Max gazed at him, then buttoned his tunic as he ran for the door.

'Your cap, sir.'

Max snatched it from his hand and put it on as he went down the stairs into the mess hall. There he clicked his heels to attention. 'Heil Hitler, Herr Field-Marshal.'

Erhard Milch, Deputy-Commander of the Luftwaffe, had been standing at the window, looking out at the airfield. Through the window beyond him Max could see the twin-engined, two-seater Messerschmitt 110 in which the Field-Marshal must have arrived and whose engines had awakened him, and which was presently being refuelled. Now Milch turned and acknowledged the salute. He was a big man with strong features and an immaculate uniform, his Iron Cross First Class prominently displayed at his throat. Max had met him before, on various parades and inspections, but he had not supposed such an important man remembered a mere senior-lieutenant.

'Where is your squadron?'

'The Reich-Marshal gave the squadron a week off, Herr Field-Marshal. After we had finished with Dunkirk.'

'A week's holiday,' Milch remarked. 'Everyone seems to think that the war is over. But you are here. Have you no home to go to?'

'Ah . . . not at this time, sir.'

'I thought the Bittermans were your family.'

They were, Max thought sadly. But he said, 'Yes, sir. But down in the south of Bavaria is rather far away. I preferred to stay here.' He did not think it any of the Field-Marshal's business that the reason he no longer considered the Bittermans – his dead mother's cousins – to be his family was that Erika von Bitterman, the woman for whose love he had abandoned his English father and his English upbringing and become a German citizen, and whom he had assumed he was going to marry, had just married someone else.

Had she ever loved him? It seemed obvious that she had not, that her seduction of him had been entirely to secure his defection.

'Hm,' the Field-Marshal muttered. 'Is it possible to obtain some breakfast?'

'Of course, sir.' Max rang the bell on the bar, and a few moments later a bleary-eyed steward stumbled in, buttoning his white jacket.

'For two,' Milch said. 'But before you join me, Herr Lieutenant, I wish you to return to your quarters and shave, and then dress yourself in a fresh uniform. That one is somewhat crushed.'

Max hurried to obey, even if he did not understand the command, and fifteen minutes later was sitting opposite the Field-Marshal, drinking coffee. There was a plate of croissants, but Milch was eating sausage and bread, so Max did likewise.

4

'I am on my way to Dunkirk,' Milch remarked. 'I wish you to accompany me.'

And for this I am required to wear a fresh uniform? Max asked himself. But the comment was revealing because it indicated that, for all his pretended surprise, Milch had known he was here, and not on leave. 'There is nothing there now, Herr Field-Marshal. Only the dead.'

'I wish to look at this nothing. You have flown a 110?'

'No, sir.'

'Well, you will find it easier to handle than your 109. Would you expect any enemy activity in the area?'

'Not at this time, sir. The RAF sustained heavy casualties trying to protect the evacuation of their troops from those beaches. I think they will be resting and regrouping.'

'And you were there. That 109E outside is your machine, is it not?'

'Yes, sir.'

'It has twelve bars painted on its fuselage.'

'Two of those were gained in Poland, sir. Last September. And six were gained in France last month. Mainly against Moraines. They are not very good machines, and frankly, sir, they were not fought with any great enthusiasm.'

'But the other four were over Dunkirk.'

'Well, yes, sir. There were several sorties a day, on both sides, and thus more opportunities for combat.'

'What were they? Your kills.'

'Three were Hurricanes, sir.'

'But the other was a Spitfire. What is your opinion of those machines, vis-à-vis your 109?'

Max absent-mindedly munched a croissant while he chose his next words with care. 'There is not much in it for speed, but the British machines have greater manoeuvrability, a smaller turning circle and a faster rate of climb. We climb too slowly – at least, initially.' He grinned. 'But we dive more quickly.'

Milch nodded, and drank coffee. 'I recognized this from the beginning. Hopefully the faults will be rectified in the new machines now being produced. Do we have no compensatory advantages?'

'Of course, sir. With our cannon as well as our machine guns we have far greater firepower than either the Hurricane or the Spitfire. And there is another advantage. I have said they can turn more quickly than us, but when they do, their engines often conk out, and it takes a few seconds, losing speed, and therefore advantage, before they can be restarted. Our engines are more reliable.'

Again Milch nodded. 'It is less a question of reliability than the fact that the British are still using the same system as in a motor car: their fuel comes via the carburettor, and this is liable to flood when the engine is being thrown about. Our new fuel-injected engine is not vulnerable to this. However, I must tell you that a couple of weeks ago, before the evacuation, a 109E crash landed behind the Allied lines, and was seized virtually intact. This machine has now been transported to England, where it is undoubtedly being taken apart by experts, who will uncover all of our secrets. How long it will take them to put those secrets into their own machines . . . well, that is an open question. But it may prove a very important one. Time, Herr Lieutenant, is the essence of warfare, the decisive factor.' He finished his breakfast and put on his cap.

Max hastily did likewise.

Milch picked up his baton. 'Can you think of any other advantages, or disadvantages?'

'Yes, sir. Pilot skill.'

Milch raised his eyebrows. 'You consider our pilots to be superior to the British?'

'At this moment, yes, sir. It is a matter of experience. The Spitfire has only recently come into service, in any numbers. It is an excellent machine, as I have said, but it needs handling. Too many of their pilots are still novices. And they have not yet evolved any proper combat tactics. They come in line ahead. That is Great War stuff.'

'As you observed over Dunkirk.'

'Yes, sir.'

'And as your father no doubt told you when you were a boy.'

Max flushed. 'Yes, sir.'

'Do not be ashamed of your father, Herr Lieutenant. So he fought for England in the War. That is because he *was* English. And he was a great pilot, a famous ace. How is he, by the way?'

'I'm afraid I do not know, Herr Field-Marshal. Since I chose

German citizenship two years ago, I have heard nothing from him.'

'Did you make any attempt to contact him? Before hostilities commenced?'

'No, sir. I knew he would be unable to understand.'

'Hm. I had the great privilege of meeting your mother. It would have been eight years ago, I suppose, on one of her visits to the Fatherland.'

'That would have been two years before her death.'

'Yes,' Milch agreed sombrely. 'There was no sign of any illness when we met. What a tragedy. What a waste. I think she must have been the most beautiful woman I ever met. You must have loved her very much.'

'I did, sir.'

'As did your father, I have no doubt. Was it her death turned him against Germany?'

They walked across the apron, past a hastily assembled group of saluting mechanics.

'I do not think so, sir. As you say, he was a British fighter ace in the Great War, and although he could no longer fly because of his wound after he had been shot down, he devoted his entire life to the aircraft industry, and especially the development of a fast interceptor. He was in on the ground floor of the development of the Spitfire.'

'He did this with the full support of your mother, did he not?'

'Yes, sir. She was very much in love with him, and supported him in everything he sought to do.'

'With her money. German money. It's a tangled world, Herr Lieutenant.' He stood next to the machine. 'Let us see what you can do. I will sit in the back.'

The 110 was indeed easier to handle than the 109E, because it was slower in every way, except perhaps in its rate of climb. Max knew that it had been specifically designed with long-range tanks to enable it to escort bombers for a greater distance than the 109, which, for example – even when operating from airfields in northern France, now to be available as soon as they were repaired from the effects of German bombing and Allied demolition charges – would only have ten minutes' endurance over, say, London. The 110s were supposed to be able to last an entire raid, but Max did not feel they would do very well against a Spitfire; although they might be more heavily armed than the 109, they simply lacked the speed.

He flew at a thousand feet over the Belgian countryside, which teemed with troop movements, all heading west or south-west. There was little physical damage to be seen, until they approached the coast. The campaign, which had taken less than three weeks, had been so overwhelming that nowhere had the Allies been able to fight a pitched battle, with the resultant destruction of property and countryside that had happened the last time, as he had seen in photographs. Now they could see the huge clouds of oily black smoke still belching from the burning fuel tanks outside the seaport, and rising six thousand metres into the air. But it was not until they had crossed the border and could see the sea that there was evidence of the BEF's desperate last stand.

'Go lower,' Milch said into his intercom.

Max cast a hasty, habitual glance around himself, but the sky was clear save for a flight over the sea; they were a good distance away and he assumed they were Germans as it was still too early for the RAF to be up and about, at least over enemy territory. In any event, they had not been noticed by the distant pilots, and were even less likely to be as he pushed the stick forward and dropped down to a hundred metres. And caught his breath. Although he had overflown this area several times a day during the previous week, it had always been at height, and he had been preoccupied with looking for such things as Hurricanes and Spitfires. Now, from little more than tree-top height, he could see the apparently endless rows of burned-out tanks and trucks, blown-up guns, discarded materiel abandoned by the defeated army. He could even see dead bodies, left where they had fallen. Amidst the debris moved German soldiers, going about the task of looking for any survivors with caution, for fear of booby traps. Startled by the roar of the engines, they looked up in alarm, which changed to waves as they recognized the black crosses on the wings.

'Go round, and up and down the beach,' Milch commanded.

Max obeyed and, dropping to no more than thirty metres as there were no obstructions, flew the length of the long beach. The tide was out, and the evidence of death and destruction was even greater; here again German soldiers were only just beginning the clean-up operation.

'Was this where Squadron-Commander Maartens went down?' Milch asked.

Max swallowed. 'No, sir. The engagement actually took place a couple of kilometres inland. So we were able to recover his body.'

'And give it a hero's burial. Did you see it happen?'

Max drew a deep breath. 'Yes, sir.'

'A Spitfire?'

'Yes, sir.'

'Did you get it?'

'No one was close enough, sir.' Which was a lie. He had been immediately behind the enemy aircraft. He could in fact have fired first, and perhaps saved his squadron-commander's life. But he had not, because the English pilot had been his brother!

He had not intended to let the Spitfire escape, but as he had closed in he had realized that Maartens was unaware of the danger he was in, and instinctively had said into his radio, 'Behind you.'

The English pilot, at that moment anonymous, had heard, and John Bayley who, because of his German stepmother, spoke the language fluently, had recognized the voice. He had replied, 'Bastard!' even as he had opened fire.

For a moment, realizing he was about to kill his own brother, Max's brain had frozen. Just for a moment. But in modern aerial combat a moment was eternity. In that moment John had killed Maartens and then soared away into the clouds.

But that was a secret he must carry with him to his grave, even if he was now determined that should they ever meet again in the sky, he *would* kill John. Milch was speaking again.

'Pity. Squadron-Commander Maartens thought very highly of you, Bayley. His reports describe you as the best pilot in his squadron. That was back in September, when you were in Poland. But his regard for you grew during this campaign. That is why you now hold his position. Promotion to his rank will soon follow.'

'Thank you, sir.' He could only hope the Field-Marshal could not detect the lump in his throat.

'I have seen enough. Take her up.'

Max eased the stick back, and the Messerschmitt rose into the sky.

'So tell me, Lieutenant, how did it feel to be engaging your erstwhile comrades?'

'They were never my comrades, sir. My heart was always in Germany.' Another lie. His heart had followed his cousin Erika von Bitterman – to betrayal. But now . . .

'Well, let me put it another way, Lieutenant. You do realize that if you were ever shot down over England, and taken prisoner, you would be hanged as a traitor?'

'I understand that, sir. Thus I understand that I cannot be taken prisoner. If my aircraft goes down, I must go with it. But am I – are we – going to be engaged in combat over England? We have had no orders to prepare for that.'

'What have we just been looking at, Lieutenant?'

'Ah . . . the inevitable detritus of a retreating army, sir.'

'Would you not say it was a *defeated* army?'

'Well, sir, we never actually beat them in a pitched battle. And the majority of them got away.'

'It is not always necessary to fight a battle to gain a victory. Did not Napoleon capture an entire Austrian army at Ulm, hardly firing a shot? He simply surrounded them. As you say, a lot of the British got away. But they left all their tanks, all their transport, all their weapons heavier than a rifle, and above all, they left all their guns. That is the description of an army that has not merely been defeated, but has been utterly destroyed. They may be in England, but their morale is shattered, and they have nothing left to fight with. They are at this moment more vulnerable than the French armies south of the Somme. Take me to Sovet.'

Just as if I were some sort of chauffeur, Max thought. But he said, 'Sir? That is where the Reich-Marshal has made his headquarters.'

'I know that, Bayley. It is the Reich-Marshal we are going to see.'

Hermann Goering was a tall, heavy, florid man, who wore a liberally decorated white uniform, and could change from boisterous good humour to vicious anger in a matter of seconds. Max knew that he had been an ace in the Great War, had flown under the command of the immortal Manfred von Richtofen, the Red Baron, and had indeed taken over command of the squadron when Richtofen had been killed. He also knew that Goering was one of the Fuehrer's oldest and closest associates, and that he was reported to be a drug addict – a result of his being over-prescribed with morphine when recovering from a serious wound received during the famous Beer Hall Putsch of 1923 – which no doubt accounted for his mood swings. Today he was in the best of humours as he rose from behind his huge desk.

'Gentlemen,' he boomed as Max and Milch were shown into his office. 'I am invaded by two of Germany's most famous airmen.'

'You know Senior-Lieutenant Bayley, Herr Reich-Marshal.'

Goering sat down again. 'Of course I know him. I saw him only a couple of days ago, at poor Maartens' funeral. And I gave you a week's leave, Bayley. What are you doing here?'

'Lieutenant Bayley preferred to remain at Aachen,' Milch said, before Max could think of a reply. 'He has just accompanied me on a visit to Dunkirk. Have you been there, Herr Reich-Marshal?'

'Dunkirk? What have I got to see in Dunkirk? Dunkirk is history. A memory of a great victory, gained by my Luftwaffe. I have other things to think about now.'

'At this moment, sir, Dunkirk is a graveyard. Would you not agree, Bayley?'

'Yes, sir.'

'I am not interested in graveyards,' Goering declared.

'It is a graveyard,' Milch persisted, 'of men, and vast quantities of materiel, certainly. But it is also a graveyard of hope, of morale, of a nation's history, and high expectations of future history.'

'You will be writing poetry next,' Goering grumbled.

Milch placed his hands on the desk and leaned over it. 'Herr Reich-Marshal, at this moment the British are a defeated nation.'

'Well, someone should tell them that. That idiot Churchill has just turned down the Fuehrer's latest peace offer, and is making bellicose speeches about fighting on the beaches and in the hills and God alone knows where else.'

11

Milch straightened. 'That is the nature of the beast. They have been defeated, but they must believe that, protected by the Channel, they will be able to recover. They have always done so in the past, and why? Because they have always been given the time to recover. Because their enemies have always been afraid to challenge the Channel. But no enemy has ever had a better opportunity than us – now!'

Goering leaned back in his chair to stare at him, while Max could feel his heart pounding.

'The English may dream of the future,' Milch went on, 'but we are talking about now. At this moment, they don't have an army. So they took three hundred thousand men out of Dunkirk, but you cannot call three hundred thousand virtually unarmed and shell-shocked men an army. Canaris tells me that there is only one fully equipped division left in all of England.'

'They have the RAF.'

'The RAF has been virtually blown out of the sky this last month. They have lost something like four hundred aircraft, at least a hundred of them first-line interceptors. All right, we have lost heavily as well, but we had more planes to begin with, and we have vastly more trained pilots. I would estimate that not more than one quarter of the Spitfires and Hurricanes currently in service are being flown by pilots with any combat experience, and at least half by men with virtually no *flying* experience. Ask Bayley. He has flown against these people.'

Max gulped as Goering looked at him. 'I think the Field-Marshal's estimate is correct, Herr Reich-Marshal.'

'Now, they are going to put these things right,' Milch said. 'We know they are building planes as fast as they can, and we can be pretty certain they are training pilots as fast as they can, too. In a couple of months, who can tell? But now, right now, they have nothing.'

'So you say they have no army and no air force,' Goering remarked. 'You are not going to claim they do not have a navy either? They say it is the best navy in the world. Well, I should think the Americans and the Japanese would have something to say about that. But it is the best navy in Europe, and it is certainly better than anything we have to offer right this minute.'

'I do not dispute that the Royal Navy can stop any large force from crossing the Channel, Herr Reich-Marshal. But even the Royal Navy can do nothing to stop us once we are across.'

Goering looked at him, then at Max. 'Is this some game, some riddle I am supposed to solve? The navy can stop us crossing, but it cannot stop us once we are there. Quite a conundrum. I am defeated. I surrender. Give me the answer.'

'The air, Herr Reich-Marshal. The air! We, the Luftwaffe – *your* Luftwaffe – have at this moment complete air superiority over a beaten and demoralized enemy. They have one combat-ready division. We have our airborne divisions, fully armed and ready to go, and we have innumerable other divisions to back them. We would not have any panzers in the first instance, but then, they have hardly any tanks at all. See!' He went to the huge map of England on the wall. 'We use every aircraft we have to blanket bomb the entire south-east of England in the biggest blitzkrieg there has ever been. Under this cover we put down our airborne troops. Forget London, or any big cities. We occupy the airfields, such as Manston and Hornchurch and Biggin. Every airfield in south-eastern England. Once we have occupied the airfields, the RAF cannot fly. The sky is ours. Oh, they will counterattack, savagely, but with what? Rifles?'

'You seriously think you can conquer England with a few brigades of paratroops?'

'No, sir. Of course not. The paratroops are our spearhead. Their job is to seize and hold the airfields. Once they have been dropped, the planes will return here to take on more troops. They will have to fly round the clock, but without interceptor opposition this should not be a problem. I estimate that we should have four fully equipped divisions on the ground within a week, with more troops arriving every hour. Let the Royal Navy control the Channel; we will simply ignore them.'

Goering gazed at him for several seconds, while Max held his breath, then the Reich-Marshal said, 'I have never heard such a load of rubbish in my life.' Milch's face stiffened, and Goering hurried on. 'Forgive me, my dear fellow, I did not mean to be rude. But surely you must see that such a scheme as you propose would be virtually suicidal, and does not take into account the realities of the situation.'

'I am aware that there is a certain risk involved,' Milch said coldly. 'But everything in war is a risk, and in this case the prize is worth the risk.'

'Worth it? The scheme is absolutely harebrained. Let me tell you why. There are still the French armies south of the Somme. They have to be defeated, and the Wehrmacht will need maximum support from us to do that. But that also means there are going to be no spare divisions, as you put it, to be flown across the Channel on a suicide mission.'

'Do you seriously believe, Reich-Marshal, that the French are going to hold out for very much longer?'

'No I do not, if we bring all our strength to bear upon them, as we will do.'

'Then there may still be time, after they have surrendered.'

'Time! Why are you so obsessed with time? All the time is on our side, Herr Field-Marshal. You say the British are building planes as fast as they can. Are we not doing the same, and we have more to start with. As for experienced pilots, we have so many we no longer need huge training programmes. We did that before the war ever started. But the main reason why an airborne invasion of Britain – even if it were successful – would be a total waste of men and materiel is that once the French surrender, the war will be over. As you say, the British are shattered. They are only hanging on in the hopes that the French will continue fighting. Once that hope is gone, all hope is gone. We have it on first-hand authority, from Ribbentrop himself –' Milch snorted in contempt, but Goering continued with the utmost confidence – 'supported by our agents in contact with the Abwehr, that a large part of the British aristocracy is against this war. They call themselves the Establishment, and they are hostile to Churchill, who they regard as an adventurer. They are just waiting for the opportunity to throw him out and accept the Fuehrer's peace terms. They even have a king, this fellow they now call the Duke of Windsor, who is known to be pro-Nazi, waiting in Lisbon to retake the throne. This will all happen by the end of this month. Why should we waste a single life, a single aircraft, to win a war that is already won?'

Milch continued to stare at him in disbelief, and Goering

smiled. 'Believe me, Milch, I respect and admire your keen-
ness to get on with the job. But I also know that you, Bayley
here, all of your pilots, have been under an immense strain
for the past month. You are wound up like a child's clockwork toy, and you cannot wind down without being activated,
as it were. But you must wind down. Now, I am going to
Berlin this afternoon. I suggest you do so as well. Get amongst
friends. Have a few drinks. Have a few ladies as well, eh?
That is what I am going to do. As for you, Bayley, three days
ago I gave you a week's leave, which you have decided not
to take. I am giving you another week's leave now, and this
time I am ordering you to take it. I will give you the same
instructions as I have given the Field-Marshal. Only in your
case it will be more basic. Find yourself a woman, and spend
the week in bed, eh? That will wind you down. I have enjoyed
talking to you gentlemen. Good morning.'

Max did not dare speak as they walked back to their aircraft.
Milch did not speak either until they were airborne. Then he
said, 'You do realize, Lieutenant, that we may just have lost
this war?'

'Sir?'

'You think I am being melodramatic? You were educated
in England. Was it not an English playwright, Shakespeare,
who wrote, "There is a tide in the affairs of men which, taken
at the flood, leads on to fortune; omitted, all the voyage of
their life is bound in shallows and in miseries."'

Max concentrated on flying the Messerschmitt. He had never
suspected his commanding officer could be so well read.

'Do you know that quotation, Lieutenant?'

'Yes, sir. It comes from the play *Julius Caesar.*'

'But you do not agree with it?'

'I am sure it is right in many cases, sir. But . . .'

'Would you not agree that Nazi Germany is at this moment
at the peak of its flood tide? Our armies have proved invin-
cible, our air force not less so. We are about to complete the
conquest of mainland Europe west of Russia. Italy supports
us; the Balkans and Scandinavia are there to be plucked should
we ever wish to do so. But all of that is nothing, and cannot
be considered permanent, until England is beaten, and in the
meanwhile, soon enough and inevitably, the ebb will set in.'

'But if England is about to make peace anyway, which will virtually be a surrender . . .'

'Because Ribbentrop says so? I would not have you repeat this, Bayley, but anyone who believes anything Ribbentrop says needs his head examined. He exists by telling people, principally the Fuehrer, what he thinks they would like to be told. He has not the intelligence to realize that all the so-called friends and contacts he made when he was Ambassador to Britain spent their time telling *him* what they thought *he* wanted to be told.' He sighed into the intercom. 'Time, Bayley, time. Every second that passes, wasted, can never be recalled.'

They landed at Aachen, and shook hands before Milch took the control.

'Thank you for your company, Captain. And your support, even if we accomplished nothing.'

'Captain, sir?'

Milch smiled. 'I will have it gazetted when I return to Berlin. I am also recommending you for an Iron Cross. You should have had one long ago. Enjoy your week's leave.'

Max saluted and remained at attention as the 110 climbed into the late-morning sky. It was barely lunchtime, and it had already been a very long day. And a disturbing one. Was the war really over? He didn't know whether to believe that or not. Because he didn't know whether he *wanted* to believe it or not.

He had abandoned England for his mother's homeland two years previously, when war between England and Germany had seemed a remote possibility – Prime Minister Chamberlain had seemed determined to keep the peace no matter what the provocation. It was a move Max had considered for some time. It had been Mother's habit to return to Schloss Bitterman every year for a holiday, and she had taken her two sons with her. Germany in the Twenties had been a chaotic, hedonistic place, but he had only been a small boy then, and had found it very exciting, especially the fact that his family lived in a castle – not a great deal larger than the house in Sussex, but far more romantic, complete with suits of armour, turrets and crenellated battlements. He had appreciated it more in the early Thirties, when he had been a teenager, old enough to understand the remaking of the country under the auspices of the Nazi Party. Of which Mother, wholly influenced by Father, of course, had strongly disapproved. Max knew now, if he had not recognized it then, that there had slowly been building inside him a deep resentment as he began to realize just what his position was. He was Mother's only son, just as he was his father's only legitimate son, at least from birth. But he remained the junior.

Mother, again undoubtedly influenced by her love for Father, had adopted the love child of one of Father's wartime flings entirely as her own, sharing her love equally between the two boys. John had been legitimized, established after the event as the first-born. That he had always been bigger and stronger, even when they had both become young men, had not helped. But as long as Mother had lived, their looming rivalry had been kept in check by their mutual adoration of the beautiful woman who ruled their lives.

Her tragically early death from cancer had been cataclysmic, even if none of them had really understood it at the time. Max knew that Father had been most affected of all, but that knowledge had not brought them closer together, principally because Father had quarrelled with the Bitterman cousins – partly due to their resentment that he should have been left in sole control of his wife's fortune, and partly because they had adopted the Nazi philosophy. As of then the summer visits to Bavaria had ceased.

Max had still been at an English public school, and in any event, Father was not a man who allowed his decisions to be questioned. But the resentment had grown, and reached a crescendo when, on reaching the age of eighteen, he had been informed that he was to go to Cranwell, to train to be an RAF pilot. John had passed through the training school, and had already been flying Harvards as he prepared for the real thing. No one expected anything less than aerial skill from the son of one of Britain's greatest World War I aces. No one had expected anything less of his younger brother.

Max knew that, having been brought up with the strictest English middle-class principles of patriotism and obedience to authority, he would almost certainly have accepted his father's decision, and would probably now be flying Spitfires . . . but for Erika. His German cousin's visit had altered his life irrevocably. She had taught him how to enjoy every breath; how to take, rather than merely respond. Two years older than himself, she had taught him the joys of sex, such a taboo subject in a refined English household; she had laughed both at his gaucheness and at his fear that sex with a cousin, even if she was only a second cousin, must be a mortal sin.

Above all, she had told him of Germany, a Germany more brilliantly exciting than he even remembered, a Germany being led to greatness by the Fuehrer, a future in which he, with his German Aryan blood, could and should play a full part – if he had the courage to do so. And she had promised him a future in which the immediate reward would be herself!

That had been the final, irresistible inducement. He had understood that to acquiesce in what had appeared to be her desire would alienate him from Father, both on moral grounds and because of his deep-seated dislike of Nazism, but the pull of possessing so much ardent beauty had been too strong for Max. Besides, he had no doubt that Father would forgive him in time, when a reconciliation would become possible. It had never crossed his mind that hardly more than a year after he had fled to Germany, the two countries would be at war. That was the last moment at which he could have returned home to beg forgiveness.

But it had already been too late. He had been welcomed in Germany with open arms by the Bittermans, immediately introduced into German society, always with Erika, beautiful and sophisticated, on his arm. He had even met the Fuehrer!

And he had been inducted into the Luftwaffe, with breath-taking speed and encouragement. Most recruits had to spend something like two years training to become a fighter pilot. He had been placed in the personal care of one of the Reich's greatest aviators, Major Klaus Maartens. Maartens had not only taught him how to fly in record time, but had taken him into his own squadron and led him into his first action, and to his first kill, over Poland. He had found himself living on an unbelievable high, with the world at his feet. Although it had seemed inevitable that he would one day have to fly against the RAF – against his own brother – he had treated the fact as a bridge to cross when he came to it. Well, he had come to it, even if only he knew of it. And John, to be sure.

18

He was still not certain when exactly he had realized that it was all a sham, that he had been lured to Germany for the purpose of propaganda. The son of the great Mark Bayley flying for the Luftwaffe!

But by then it had not really mattered. With the two thick black stripes painted on his aircraft – no matter that they had been obsolete Polish biplanes – he was already a hero. He was flying what everyone in Germany believed was the finest interceptor in the world, he belonged to the best fighter squadron in the Luftwaffe with the finest commander, he was on the winning side, and he would soon be marrying the most beautiful woman in the world – his world, certainly.

And then had come Dunkirk. It had followed the most exhilarating three weeks of his life, when he had added another six bars to his tally – mostly French Moraines and English medium bombers such as the Blenheim and the Battle – and had become a genuine ace himself. He had even engaged Spitfires for the first time over the beaches, and brought down one of them. But on the last day of the evacuation had come that fateful meeting with John, when his moment's hesitation had cost the life of his friend and mentor. He had been shattered, the burden the harder to bear because it could not be shared. He could have no doubt how the admission that he had been unable to shoot down an enemy just because of their relationship would be received by his comrades – or indeed by the regime.

And then there was Erika. When Goering, like everyone else quite ignorant of the truth, had promoted him to Senior-Lieutenant and given him command of the squadron, and then a week's leave, he had telephoned Max von Bitterman, his mother's first cousin – and since her death the head of the German family – and who was also Erika's father, and had indeed become his own de facto father since his arrival in Germany, to give him the good news. He had been roundly congratulated on his promotion before he asked if it would be possible for his marriage to Erika to be arranged for during his week at home. There had been an amazed silence on the end of the line, and then Bitterman had said, 'But, my dear boy, Erika was married a fortnight ago. Did you not know?'

* * *

Max remembered staring at the telephone in utter disbelief. 'But,' he had said, 'we were engaged.'

'Engaged?' Bitterman had asked. 'No, no, my dear boy, that cannot be. Erika was very fond of you, I know, but she has had an understanding with Paul Haussmann for years. Ever since they were children.'

And therefore long before she ever visited England and seduced me, Max had thought. She had been acting a role the whole time. A role dictated by who, or what? The regime, certainly: she was a dedicated Nazi. The regime which was about to give him a medal.

'Will you be in for dinner, Herr Lieutenant?' Heinrich enquired now.

'It is Herr Captain now, Heinrich.'

'Oh, Herr Captain! My best congratulations.'

'Thank you, Heinrich. No, I shall not be in for dinner. But I will have lunch now. Then I would like you to pack me a bag, and have my machine fuelled. I am going to Berlin for a week.'

Max radioed ahead, and re-fuelled at Hanover before landing at Tempelhof. Berlin glowed with light in the summer evening. It was impossible to suppose there was a war on, anywhere. But of course, it was equally impossible to suppose that any British bomber could ever get this far into Germany without being shot down.

A car was waiting for him, and he was driven into the city centre, through streets that were thronged with people, enjoying some late shopping, enjoying an early evening drink at the pavement cafes, enjoying being German at this time of the greatest achievement in their nation's history.

Before leaving Aachen he had telephoned to book himself into the Albert, where the Bittermans usually stayed when in Berlin, and where he had stayed with them. He was remembered, and shown to his room by an attentive under-manager, followed by the porter with his one bag.

'If there is anything we can get for you, Herr Lieutenant . . .?'

'Yes,' Max said. 'I would like a woman for the night.'

'Sir?'

'I'm acting on the orders of Reich-Marshal Goering. I had lunch with him today – ' he had learned always to bring overwhelming fire power to bear, even if it meant stretching a point – 'and he told me that I had been overworking and that I needed a good woman to relax me. The woman I have in mind will be young, pretty, willing, and above all clean. And not talkative. What are you going to do about that?'

'Ah. Well, in the circumstances, Herr Lieutenant . . . leave it with me.'

'Thank you. As soon as I have had a bath I will be going down to dinner. I would like to hear from you when I have finished my meal. I will leave the negotiating of a price with you, and will settle with you after.'

'Of course, sir.' The under-manager folded the two notes into his pocket and left.

Well, Max thought as he stepped into the shower stall, now I am to be as hedonistic as anyone, and let the war go hang. He found that a curiously attractive thought.

The dining room was as crowded as the streets outside, and everyone was in the same boisterous good humour. The maitre d' escorted him to a table at the side of the room, where he ordered his meal and a bottle of good wine, as well as a glass of schnapps as an aperitif, leaned back with his drink . . . and found himself looking at Erika Haussmann.

Max stood up so suddenly he nearly spilled his drink. She was as radiantly beautiful as ever, her long, silky black hair shrouding her slightly bold features, and she wore a slinky black evening gown, off the shoulder, to enhance both her figure and the whiteness of her skin.

Nor was she the least embarrassed to be standing before him. 'I saw you come in,' she said. 'What a happy chance.'

'Is it?'

She sat down, uninvited, and snapped her fingers. Immediately a waiter hurried forward with another glass of schnapps. Of course, he realized, she was far better known here than he; he should have gone to a less high-profile hotel. But . . . 'I thought you were at Bitterman.'

'I was, last week. But when you never turned up, I got bored.'

'Why did you wish to see me? To tell me about your honeymoon?'

'Oh, you are in a grouch. You are angry with me.'

'Angry? By God! I never wished to see you again.'

'But I am here. What would you like to do to me?'

His first course arrived.

'I think you would like to beat me,' she said. 'Well, we will talk about that.' She finished her drink and stood up. 'Enjoy your meal, and join us for coffee and brandy in the lounge afterwards. There is someone I so wish you to meet.'

'Erika, I have not the slightest desire to meet your husband.'

She smiled. 'But this is not my husband, darling.'

He watched her cross the room, but could not see where she was sitting through the throng of diners, and did not wish to be conspicuous by standing up and peering. Anyway, he didn't have to obey her, however often it had happened in the past. But he knew he was going to. It was not just a question of habit. The sight of her . . . She had bewitched him, seduced him, ruined his life, and then betrayed him, and she was still the only woman in the world he wanted to hold in his arms.

He finished his meal, drank his wine, signed the bill, and left the dining room. The under-manager waited in the foyer. 'I have taken the liberty, Herr Lieutenant, of placing the young woman in your room.'

'Eh?'

'The woman you requested, sir.'

'Ah. Yes. I had forgotten. I'm afraid I have changed my mind. Would you remove her again? Pay her fee, by all means. But get her out of my room. Thank you.'

The under-manager stared after him in consternation as he made his way towards the lounge. Well, Max thought, if I am damned in any event, I may as well travel to Hell in first class.

Two

Secrets

The three Spitfires sank out of the clear-blue June sky to land, one after the other, and taxi to the side of the field to join the other parked machines.

'Well, sir?' asked Sergeant Mowbray, as Flight Lieutenant John Bayley climbed out of his cockpit.

'Well, indeed, Sergeant,' John said. 'The Channel is like a mill pond.'

But then, the Channel had been like a mill pond for a fortnight, fortunately for the British Army trying to get off the beach at Dunkirk. John Bayley did not expect ever to be able to forget the last day of the evacuation when, hurriedly placed in command of a fledgling squadron, he had led his inexperienced pilots into battle against the Messerschmitt 109s. They had given as good as they had got, and he had earned instant fame for shooting down one of Germany's leading airmen, Squadron-Commander Klaus Maartens. He had not known it was Maartens when he had picked on him as an opponent, although he had been able to determine that it was a successful pilot in his sights from the twenty-plus black bars, each bar denoting a kill, painted on the German fuselage. But after his experiences in France a few weeks earlier, when he had watched his comrades, like himself flying obsolete Boulton-Paul Defiants, cut to ribbons by the same 109s, or some of their sisters, the mere fact of shooting one down had given him great satisfaction.

John Bayley had been the only survivor of that doomed flight, and even he had had to parachute to safety as his machine had broken up beneath him. To be given the chance to avenge those friends, even after only a few hours' training on Spitfires, but already recognizing it as the finest interceptor in the world, had left him wanting only to engage the enemy, at the highest

23

possible level. And he had again been lucky to survive, as while he had been closing in behind the Squadron-Commander, the Messerschmitt on *his* tail had miraculously refused, or been unable, to fire.

Had it been Max? He knew that his defecting half-brother was serving with the Luftwaffe, and was in 109s, but he had not encountered him during the campaign in France, which was hardly surprising, as the Luftwaffe disposed of several hundred of the deadly little planes. But on that day over Dunkirk, he was sure he had heard Max's voice on the radio, shouting a warning to his commander. That indicated he had been close enough to see what was happening. He had responded with an instinctive shout of his own – 'Bastard!' – and the plane behind him had not fired. Because the German pilot had in turn recognized *his* voice? He supposed he would never know; the situation was hardly likely to occur again.

But suppose it did, in reverse, as it were?

John Bayley was a taller, generally bigger version of his half-brother. He had the same aquiline features, but his hair was dark. He moved now with easy athleticism, the sergeant hurrying at his side.

'Think they'll be coming now, sir?' Mowbray asked.

'Well, as they haven't come for the past week . . . God knows what they're waiting for.'

'But now the Frogs have packed it in . . .'

'Eh?'

'Fact, sir. Came through on the radio this morning. This chap Pétain has asked for an armistice.'

'Holy shit!' exclaimed Pilot-Officer Newman.

'It is that, sir,' the sergeant agreed.

'You'd better fuel them up,' John said, striding towards Dispersal.

'Saw you come in,' said the officer on the desk. Yardley was an old hand, and wore the handlebar moustache that was becoming fashionable. 'Any activity?'

'Nothing,' John told him. 'What's this about France packing it in?'

'Afraid it's true. Lucky Dowding refused to send any more squadrons over there, eh? The old man wants to see you.'

'I'll bet we're going to be moved further east,' Pilot-Officer Rigg said. 'Maybe Biggin. Closer to the action, eh?'

'I'll let you know.' John made his way to the Wing-Commander's office and knocked on the door.

'Come. Ah, John. That'll be all, Corporal.'

The WAAF who had been taking dictation hastily stood up and hurried past John with a quick smile.

'Sit!' Hawkins invited.

John sank into the chair the woman had just vacated. 'Bit of a bad show across the Channel, isn't it, sir?'

'Well, I suppose we all knew it was going to happen.' Hawkins was a short, round-faced man, who wore a moustache and bristled with energy. 'So I suppose we're next in line.'

'What surprises me is that there's been absolutely no activity so far. You'd have thought after Dunkirk . . .'

'I imagine they have quite a bit of re-arranging to do, and they need to have their newly captured airfields in full working order. Actually, it's not true to say there has been *no* activity. There have been some attacks on our convoys in the Straits of Dover.'

'Is that where we're going, sir?' John was eager.

'Who said you were going anywhere?'

'Well . . . Ops said you wanted to see me immediately. I thought it was urgent.'

'Important, John, not urgent. I have two pieces of information for you. The first is that you have been confirmed as Squadron-Leader, 833.' He frowned at John's expression. 'Weren't you expecting that?'

'Well, I had hoped, of course, sir. But . . . not so immediately.'

'I imagine for a little while to come everything is going to be immediate. The second thing I have to tell you is that as of now you, and the entire squadron, are grounded.'

'Sir?' John straightened.

Hawkins grinned. 'You're not on the mat. Your engines are to be remade.'

'Sir?' This was even more alarming.

'You, and everyone else, have been complaining that when in combat and forced to make tight turns, or rolls, which your Spitfires do better than any other machines, you lose much of your advantage because your engines conk out, and it takes a second or two to restart.'

'Well, yes. It's the nature of the beast, I suppose. It will happen with any petrol engine. When it gets thrown around the float chamber floods.'

'It doesn't happen in a Messerschmitt.'

'Well . . .' John grinned. 'They don't turn or roll as quickly as us.'

'They're not that much slower. The reason their carburettors or float chambers do not flood is that they do not have carburettors or float chambers.'

'Eh?'

'We've suspected it for some time, but couldn't be sure. Nor could we work out how it was done. But about a month ago a 109 came down behind our lines, virtually intact. The machine was taken to pieces and shipped over here for examination, and we found the answer: fuel injection.'

John frowned. 'I've heard of that. It's used in some racing cars, isn't it?'

'That's right.'

'But never in ordinary petrol-driven engines.'

'We can't afford to have *ordinary* petrol-driven engines, John, if Jerry does not. We are going to convert every Spitfire and Hurricane engine to fuel injection.'

'Holy smoke. But . . .'

'Quite. It's expensive, and it'll take time. But it has to be done. If it isn't, you chaps will be fighting the rest of the war at a serious disadvantage. So 833 Squadron is one of the first to be withdrawn for engine refurbishment. We have also discovered that a Messerschmitt pilot is partially protected from the rear by a steel plate in his seat. So we're going to fix those as well. It'll take about a week, so you and your boys can have a week's leave. And frankly, John, I think you need it. You've been looking extremely tense these last few days.'

'What happens if Jerry comes while we're out? I mean, if France has really surrendered . . .'

'The rest of the Wing will have to cope. Only one squadron from each wing is being withdrawn at a time.'

'That still vastly increases the odds in Jerry's favour. He has almost twice as many planes as us, anyway.'

'Agreed. But we have an ace up our sleeve. What do you know about radar?'

26

'Well . . . I've seen those towers scattered about the south coast. But it's all pretty hush-hush, isn't it?'

'It needs to be. It's our secret weapon. It's based on the discovery that solid objects reflect radio waves. That is, if we send out radio waves from a station here in England, and those waves encounter something in the sky, it will bounce back as what the pundits call a blip.'

'So we can tell something's coming. How far away?'

'Oh, up to a hundred and fifty miles.'

'Right,' John said. 'So we may know there is an enemy force approaching. But are we that much further ahead?'

'Certainly. The signals have been so refined that they can tell us almost exactly how many planes are coming towards us.'

'Great. I still don't see how that is going to help us. I mean, suppose we get a message that eight hundred enemy planes are on their way, and we still have only four hundred to put up against them, that's going to dampen morale rather than improve it.'

'Ah, but it can also tell us height, speed, and course, and therefore probable target. So, you see, instead of having you chaps floating back and forth looking for the enemy, burning fuel which will have to be replaced every hour or so, we can work out just where Jerry is heading, and just when he is going to arrive. Which means you won't have to be scrambled until he is just where it is most convenient to hit him. More importantly, we can hit him with all our strength in one place, instead of having to keep other flights up looking out for any other attacking forces there may be. We'll *know* where they all are, and we'll be able to decide who can be attacked, with overwhelming force, and exactly when.'

'Sounds fantastic, in theory. If it works!'

'It works. I have seen a demonstration.'

'And Jerry doesn't know about it?'

'We think he does. He must do. But there is no evidence that he is making any use of it. The point is that it is an essentially defensive weapon, certainly at the moment. And up till now, Jerry has operated entirely on the basis of overwhelming aggression. And I would say that, having neglected to develop it for that reason, he hasn't yet realized just how useful – vital, in fact – it can be for a defending force.'

27

'Well, let's hope the boffins are right. But the fact remains, sir, that even if we know where he is and in what strength, we still have to get planes into the air to meet him, and if he comes over the next week, my squadron isn't going to be one of them.'

'Have you seen any evidence that he's coming next week?'

'Well . . . no.'

'Neither has anyone else. Maybe he has just been waiting for the French to pack it in. Not that there's any evidence that more than a fraction of his available air force has been employed in that battle. God knows what he's at. But my guess is that you'll be back in time to take him on. Have a fun week.'

'John?' Joan Bayley herself opened the front door; she had heard the roar of his Harley-Davidson – a present from his father – on the drive, followed by the enthusiastic barking of Rufus, the family Newfoundland, who was now eagerly rubbing himself against John's pants. 'Good to see you. But . . . is there a problem?'

'I've been grounded.' But he grinned as he spoke, and took her in his arms for a hug and a kiss. His aunt was one of his very favourite people, and she was so very attractive. Still in her early forties, she had crisp features and a splendidly full figure, and wore her straight yellow hair fashionably short, in a bob just below her ears. Her blue eyes were as vivacious as her personality, and it was an ongoing mystery to him why such a lovely woman had never married. He suspected there was some tragedy in her background, but neither his father nor his aunt encouraged probing into skeletons in the family closet, principally, he supposed, because he was the biggest skeleton of them all. Now he added, 'Temporarily. They're doing things to my engine.'

'Ah.' Although, because so close to her brother, Joan had spent her entire adult life virtually in the air force, she had always refused to become too closely involved in the technicalities of the business. John knew she reckoned at least one member of the family needed to maintain a sense of proportion as regards civilized living.

'Dad around?'

'He's in London at a conference. He should be back

tomorrow, or certainly the day after. How long have you got?'

'A week, they say.'

'Well, then, you'll certainly see him.' She held his arm as they went into the hall, Rufus padding at their heels, while Clements the butler hurried forward to take his overnight bag and cap; most of John's clothes were in his room upstairs.

'Welcome home, Mr John.'

'Thank you, Clements.' John's acknowledgement had genuine warmth; Clements knew, and had always kept, too many of his secrets.

'Now come and have a drink.' Still holding his arm, Joan escorted him through the drawing room and into the book-lined study, where she released him to pour two whiskies.

'I've been confirmed as squadron-leader,' John said.

'Oh, my darling! Then we'll put these aside, and have some bubbly.' She opened the icebox and took out a bottle of champagne, handed it to him to uncork. 'Your father will be so proud. Squadron-Leader was his final rank.'

John handed back the open bottle. 'But that was because he had to give up flying after being wounded. If he'd been able to stay in the RAF he'd be a marshal by now. He was senior to Air-Commodore Hargreaves.' John knew that Cecil Hargreaves, his father's oldest friend, and his own ultimate commander, had served under Mark Bayley on the Western Front in 1917.

'Probably.' Joan poured, gave him his glass, raised her own. 'Here's to your next stripe.' She sat in one of the comfortable armchairs.

John drank. 'Was he very bitter about that?'

Joan considered. 'I think he was bitter when he came home from the German prison camp and discovered there was no future for him in the RAF. He already knew he couldn't go on flying with a crippled leg. But he had hoped for at least an administrative position.'

'Instead they gave him a medal and sacked him.'

Joan made a moue. 'It was a very difficult time. The war was over, Britain was virtually bankrupt; it was economy, economy and economy, especially in the services. Do you know that Trenchard was told he had to reduce his establishment of a hundred and eighty-five squadrons to thirty-

29

five within a year? Anyway, Mark didn't stay bitter too long.'

'Because he had Karolina to support him and finance his future.'

Joan finished her drink, then got up to refill her glass. 'Are you still bitter about that? She always treated you as if you were her own son.'

'But I wasn't.' He held up his glass for a refill. 'I'm not bitter about that any more, Aunt Joan.'

'But you wish it could have been different.'

'Did you know my mother?'

'I think I saw her, once. I never met her.'

'Do you think she was mad?'

'Because she killed herself?'

'After trying to kill Dad.'

'Well, you know, women – some women – do strange things when they feel they have been rejected.'

'She *was* rejected.'

'What did you expect your father to do? He was already married, and Karolina was pregnant. Even if she hadn't been, do you think he could possibly have considered divorcing her for a woman with whom he had had a one-night stand? Don't bother to look at me like that, Johnnie. If you're old enough to fly a Spitfire in combat and kill an enemy, you have to be old enough to look fact in the face. Your mother and your father got together by accident just before he was sent back to France in 1917. Her husband had been killed a couple of years earlier, and, yes, you have to face it, she was a little unbalanced. Your father was seventeen years old. You know he lied about his age to get into the services. He had just qualified as a pilot at a time when the average life expectancy in the air over the Western Front was three months. As far as he was concerned, he had just been handed a death sentence. So he's wandering around Tunbridge Wells on embarkation leave and he bumps into this beautiful – because she was beautiful, you know, well, you only need to look into the mirror to know that – apparently sophisticated, wealthy woman looking for physical love. They had met before, at the funeral of her younger brother when he was killed in a flying accident. So they spent the night together. One night! So he asked her to marry him. What do you expect, of a seventeen-year-old boy with no experience of either sex or women, but with a sense of honour? He was simply overwhelmed by what had happened. So she laughed at him, and turned him down. Again, what do you expect? She was nine years older, and he was a hick from the sticks who had happened to give her a good night. So he went to France, became famous, and survived. Just. And met a woman with whom he genuinely fell in love, and who genuinely loved him back. And no sooner is he back in England, with his bride, than Patricia arrives on his doorstep and presents him with you, and says, "this is your son."'

John refilled their empty glasses. 'Are you saying I'm not Father's son?'

'Oh, for God's sake, of course you're Mark's son. Again, you just have to look in the mirror to know that. But that doesn't alter the fact that he didn't know you existed, until that day.' She rested her hand on his. 'John, that's history. It's bad, tragic history, but it's still history. You have to forget it, and start looking to tomorrow, not yesterday.'

'And how am I supposed to do that, Aunt Joan, in my circumstances? When I'm living that history over again every day?'

'You know your father and I have promised to give you all the support we can, even if we have to get some kind of legal dispensation. Have you told her yet?'

'I haven't seen Avril for a month.'

'Oh! But . . .'

'There just wasn't time. After our . . . well, night together, I told her I'd be in touch as soon as I'd spoken to Father. And you, of course. And the next day I began training on Spits, twelve hours a day. Then I was thrown into action over Dunkirk. And after that, it's been round the clock patrols for the past fortnight. Not that we've seen anything remotely resembling an enemy aircraft, at least in our area. But up to today there's been no leave.'

'There is such a thing as a telephone.'

'I tried that. I called the barracks, and was told that Private Pope had been transferred to another camp.'

'Shoot! Where?'

'They wouldn't tell me. These people have gone completely paranoid. They seem to think that releasing the whereabouts of a single ATS private is going to cost us the war.'

'I agree, that's ridiculous. However . . . what exactly is the situation? You asked her to marry you . . .'

'After a one-night stand. Just like Dad. Talk about history repeating.'

'I think we need to stick to facts. Unlike her aunt, Avril said yes. And you said you'd just have to ask your father's permission. And having done that, and got our permission, you haven't been in touch since? Four weeks? Jesus! She must be going mad.'

'What do you think I'm doing? Even the CO is noticing that I have things apart from flying on my mind.'

'And she still doesn't know she's . . . well . . .'

'My first cousin? No.'

'But you knew when you proposed.'

'No, I did not. We . . . well, we had sex . . .' He gave his aunt a quick glance. 'Do you . . . well . . .'

'I've had sex,' Joan told him.

'Oh. Right. Well, I just knew she was the girl for me, so I proposed, and she said yes.'

'Didn't you have any suspicions? You knew her name, didn't you?'

'I knew her name was Pope, yes. But I also knew that her father was a bank clerk. Well, I have always been told that Mother's parents were wealthy people, that her father was an industrialist who owned several factories. That didn't relate to a son working as a bank clerk. At least, I didn't think so.'

'So when *did* you find out?'

'Well, you know I brought her here for dinner. She was impressed, realized for the first time that I could be a bit out of her class. Maybe that was the reason she went along with me, that night.'

'Was she a virgin?'

'I don't think so. I mean, she's a grown woman. And an ATS. But anyway, when we were, well . . .'

'Sharing a cigarette,' Joan suggested.

'Neither of us smokes. But we were lying there, and I think she felt she had to compete, in some way. So she told me that her grandfather had been a very wealthy man who had lost all his money in the Crash, which was why her dad had to

32

give up the good life and go out to work, and while that was still sinking in – I was half asleep – she added that she felt I should know that she had an aunt who had committed suicide because of an unhappy love affair . . . shit! I beg your pardon, Aunt Joan.'

'I'm inclined to say snap.'

'So I took her back to her barracks.'

'Without another word?'

'Well, of course we had other words. But not on that subject. I needed to think. As I said, I told her I would have to clear the idea of marriage with my father, and that I would get back to her as soon as I could. I had only just told Dad, and you, what had happened, but as I said, I hadn't got back to her when the war got in the way.'

'So the poor girl still doesn't know anything more than that she thinks she's engaged.'

'She *is* engaged.'

'Do you love her?'

'Yes, I do. Of course I do. I love her desperately.'

The way he spoke made Joan wonder if he was trying to convince himself. 'And she loves you.'

'Yes, she does.'

'And you reckon she'll go on loving even when she discovers you've committed incest.'

'I . . . yes. Yes, she will.'

'Well, I think both she, and her family, need to be informed of the situation. There are some secrets which have to be shared.'

'Um.' He brooded into his now empty champagne glass, and stroked Rufus's head.

'Look, it'll wait until your father gets back. He'll tell you what to do. I mean, as this has been hanging fire for just about a month, another day or so isn't going to matter.'

'Ahem,' said Clements from the doorway. 'Dinner is served, Miss Joan.'

'Thank you, Clements.' Joan stood up. 'Let's eat.'

John stood also. 'Secrets, secrets. Don't you have any secrets, Aunt Joan?'

'Everyone has secrets, Johnnie. But, thank God, mine aren't for sharing.'

* * *

Secrets, she thought, as she undressed. If only he knew. But he could never know; knowledge would only pile another intolerable weight on those already overburdened, and so youthful, shoulders. But her secrets were known only to her brother, and they would carry them to their graves.

She sank into bed, throwing back the covers; the June evening was still and warm. She closed her eyes, and almost immediately saw his face, dancing before her, smiling that little smile he had worn when making love to her. A very special smile for a very special occasion. In the long ago and very heady days of the Great War, when she had been no more than a girl, but able to earn money for the first time in her life by working in an aircraft factory, she could seek pleasure wherever it was available and had had several affairs. But ever since Karolina had come into her life, so cool, calm, composed and utterly civilized, those wild days had been abandoned forever.

Karolina had been the elder sister she had never had, a dominating yet always loving personality. Had Karolina lived, Klaus Maartens would never have happened to her. For had Karolina lived, Max would never have turned traitor and fled to Germany. Thus she would not have gone to Germany to get him back . . . and found herself arrested as a spy!

Johnnie did not even know that secret. Nor should he. Those weeks in a Gestapo cell, subjected to constant beatings and humiliation, and then the two months in a concentration camp, subjected to even more beatings and humiliation, were a recurring nightmare, which would, no doubt, accompany her to her grave. Yet out of it had come Klaus, arriving out of the blue at Ravensbrück with an order for her release.

By then she had almost begun to despair, however certain she had been that Mark would be moving heaven and earth to rescue her. But Mark was persona non grata in Germany, and she could not doubt that his efforts through the Embassy would be met by a simple denial – as had indeed been the case – that they or anyone in Germany knew anything about this strange Englishwoman who was supposed to have disappeared somewhere in central Europe.

But Mark had sought Maartens, who he had met, and liked, at Karolina's funeral. Joan had also met Maartens then, and liked him, but it had not occurred to her that the handsome young Luftwaffe pilot might have taken more than a liking to her: she was several years the elder. But there he was, her knight in shining armour, about to perform a miracle: no inmate ever left Ravensbrück on her feet, unless she had an admirer who was also Hermann Goering's favourite pilot. With that power behind him, anyone could perform miracles in Nazi Germany.

She had accepted his help gratefully, but suspiciously. Britain and Germany had not been at war, but as far as she was concerned Germany had made war on her, and besides, Klaus spoke of the coming war as if it were already decided. Additionally, she could immediately tell that his apparent determination to help her was based on something far deeper than mere friendship.

She had had no intention of accommodating him. Quite apart from the fact that he was a potential enemy and so much younger than her, she had not had sex with anyone for fifteen years, and was virtually a virgin again, at least in her mind. But she had been unable to resist his invitation to spend a few weeks in the old family home of Schloss Bitterman before returning to England. She needed the time to allow her scars to heal, her shaven scalp to regain some semblance of normality, and above all, to achieve some mental stability, to resist her continuing desire to shrink away from any physical contact, to scream at any sudden noise.

But he remained an attractive and attentive man, and while she felt she had to resent and regret it, she could not help but appreciate the way he was caring for young Max, even if he was training him to fly for another country. She had not had to meet the Bittermans at all; she thought that if she had come face to face with Erika she would have scratched her eyes out, even if it had entailed an immediate return to Ravensbrück.

So she supposed what had happened had been inevitable. It had been the night before she was due to leave for England, fully restored to physical health, with a head of fashionably cropped hair, and at least superficially restored to mental health as well. She had not been, of course. She was not sure she would ever be fully in control of her mind again in her life. Thus a distaste for the idea of sex, with anyone, much less a potential enemy, had become combined with an urgent desire

35

for the warmth and comfort of a man's arms before she had to face the business of returning to a normal life, to Mark, and to John.

Klaus had come to say farewell. It had not, of course, been final; at the time there had been no reason why they should not meet again. Or perhaps something deep in her mind, some feminine instinct, told her that this *was* the last time she would ever see him. It had been the best night of her life, even if for the first time it had left her feeling guilty. Mark had understood, of course; they had no secrets from each other. He had not offered an opinion on whether or not he approved, or wished the brief romance to continue. In any event, within six months of her return to England the two countries had been at war.

Joan had known then that their abortive romance was over. But she had not expected it to be over so finally and irrevocably, that her lover should be shot down by her own nephew. She remembered the shock of real pain the day John had come home, only three weeks ago, on top of the world. 'My first kill!' he had announced. 'A chap with twenty-three bars on his fuselage. They tell me he was Germany's leading ace, fellow called Maartens. Do you know, I'm certain I – we – met him once. At Stepmother Karolina's funeral. Do you remember him, Dad?'

Mark Bayley had looked at his sister, and then at his son. 'Yes,' he had said. 'I remember him. He was indeed Germany's best. You are to be congratulated.'

'I'm to get a gong.'

'Well then, again, congratulations.'

He had shaken John's hand. And she had gone forward for a hug and a kiss.

Secrets, she thought. And now she had another.

She had been walking the Downs below the house with Rufus, as she liked to do. Her trouble was that she had too much time on her hands; Clements ran the house like a clockwork machine, and all she had to do was approve the daily menus. This made her feel very guilty. She had several times suggested to Mark that she should join up. But he had always refused to consider it. He knew how vulnerable she really was, and he doubted she would be able to survive having to share a barracks or even an office with several other women of totally different class, background and outlook.

He would jokingly remind her that she had absolutely no skills apart from social graces and a distant memory of how to make wooden propellers for out-of-date flying machines. She did not even drive a car, and had absolutely no idea of what went on under the bonnet of one.

She knew he was right, but the feeling of non-participation in the immense events going on around her, and in which her brother and her nephew were so heavily involved, gave her a terrible sense of isolation. Her only real companion was Rufus, who accompanied her everywhere. And it was Rufus who had suddenly growled.

Joan had turned and watched a man walking down the slope behind her. She was not the least afraid. Quite apart from the formidable presence of Rufus, she was herself a big, strong woman. But she was irritated. Irrationally, she supposed, she regarded these Downs as her very own, an extension of the house gardens.

'Are you following me?' she enquired.

The man raised his bowler hat. Incongruously, for walking on the Downs on a summer's day, he was wearing a belted raincoat over a dark suit, black shoes and a tie. 'Forgive me,' he said, coming closer. 'You're Miss Bayley, aren't you? From the house?'

He was now quite near her, and she saw that while not very tall he was well built, and his features, if reminiscent of granite, were not unhandsome. 'I am Joan Bayley. Will you answer my question?'

He smiled, and some of the hardness left his face. 'Or you'd set the dog on me?'

He did not seem apprehensive of that. 'I might report you to the police. This close to the sea, they're not too keen on strangers,' she warned.

He looked past her at the distant waters of the Channel. 'Quite. I have been following you, since you left the house. I would like a word, if it's convenient.'

'Couldn't you have rung the bell?'

'I felt that might be *in*convenient.'

'You are not encouraging me to wish to continue this conversation. I will be returning to the house now, and I suggest you walk the other way. If seeing me is urgent, you may telephone for an appointment, which I will grant you, when my brother can be present. Come along, Rufe.'

'I wanted to speak with you about Germany,' he said.

She had already passed him. Now she stopped and turned, feeling a peculiar tingle spreading through her body.

'I know,' he said, 'something of what happened.'

Joan peered at him. 'I don't even know your name.'

'Jim Carling, Miss Bayley.'

'And you wish me to talk to you about what happened to me in Germany? Who are you, some kind of a reporter?'

'No, ma'am, I work for the government.'

She frowned, suspicions not the least abated. 'Can you prove that?'

'I'm not supposed to do that. But I will tell you that I work for the Ministry of Propaganda.'

'And the Ministry of Propaganda is interested in me?'

'In your experiences, Miss Bayley.'

'Why?'

'We are building up a dossier, several dossiers, on what is actually going on inside Germany. One hears rumours – refugees bring out with them virtually unbelievable tales of what has happened to their friends and relatives – but none of them have any first-hand experience of what *did* happen. You are one of the very few people who has actually been arrested by the Gestapo, been inside a concentration camp, and have not only lived to tell the tale, but have *escaped* to tell the tale.'

'How do you know this?'

'The British Secret Service has agents inside Germany. They pick up various bits of information which eventually filters through to us.'

And I thought my secrets were secure, Joan thought. But she retained her composure. 'And what will you do with my tale, if I decide to tell you what really happened?'

'With your permission, of course, we could use it as a formidable propaganda weapon against the Nazi regime. No less important, the dossier will be part of the indictment we will bring against the Nazi leaders when the war is over.'

'Would anyone believe what I have to say?'

'You would make the statement under oath, and although

at this moment the enemy would undoubtedly dismiss it as the ravings of a demented woman, such a statement, if supported in person, would be totally acceptable in a court of law.'

'If this is all on the up,' Joan said, 'why are you behaving so secretively?'

'We do not know how much your family know of what happened.'

'I have no secrets from my brother. But, yes, I would not wish to involve him at this time. He finds the memory of it very disturbing, especially as he had some idea of what might be happening to me, and was unable to do anything about it. But he is not at the house now. Would you like a cup of tea?'

She had not been sure how to proceed, how far she wanted to go. She did know that she did not wish to become a public figure on such a subject, at such a time, and Carling seemed prepared to accept this.

Equally, she did not know how much she would be able to tell him about such a terrible and essentially intimate experience; she wondered why they had sent a man and not a woman. But when she started talking to him, the words just flowed. She realized that for over a year she had wanted desperately to talk to someone: having heard the story once, Mark had not ever wanted to discuss it again.

The only thing she omitted was any mention of Klaus Maartens, leaving Carling with the impression that the strings Mark had been able to pull, through his connection with Bitterman Manufacturing, had at last been successful.

Carling had listened, his face expressionless, but when she had finished her story, he said, 'I can see why your brother's blood boils every time he thinks of it. How about yours?'

'I feel like a drink.' Joan stood up. 'How about you?'

He glanced at his empty teacup. 'Thank you. Scotch?'

'I think I can manage that.' She poured two measures, gave him his, stood above him. 'I hate them, Mr Carling. I would like to see all of the men, and women, who laid their hands on me hang. Is that very uncivilized of me?'

He closed his notebook and found himself staring at her

skirt. 'I think that is very human of you, Miss Bayley. I will have this typed up and then, if I may, I will bring it back for you to sign.' He stood up.

'Surely you have time to finish your drink,' she had suggested.

She was strangely anticipatory. She had moved, almost inadvertently, into an intensely intimate relationship with another human being – and for how long, she was realizing more and more, had she wanted that? Needed that?

So he was a complete stranger. Perhaps that was necessary. She knew absolutely nothing about him, although she did suspect that he was not exactly Eton and Balliol. But then, however successful and wealthy he now was, neither was Mark. She did not even know if this man was married. Even less did she know how she wanted this so sudden, and so strange, relationship to develop. But then, she had felt exactly the same way about Klaus. At least, she reflected, there was no possibility of Jim Carling being shot down by her own nephew.

But for the time being he remained her private pleasure. She did not tell Mark of the visit. Or of the next one, when Jim brought the statement down for her signature.

'I suppose everyone in the Ministry of Propaganda has read this?' she asked.

'Only my secretary and my boss. It will now go into the dossier and remain there until you give us permission to use it.'

'I apologize. I am still a little sensitive.'

'Who wouldn't be?'

'You see, you, your secretary, and your boss are the only people, apart from my brother, I have ever told the truth of what happened.' She signed the paper, got up and poured two drinks. 'Will I see you again?'

'Do you want to?'

She gave him his glass, and their fingers remained in contact for some time. 'Yes,' she said. 'I would like that very much.'

'Secrets,' Mark Bayley said, sinking gratefully into an armchair while his sister hovered with a scotch and water. Two years the younger of the pair, he was forty-one; he remained a surprisingly youthful-looking man – big, strong, his hatchet features always striking. But his hair was entirely grey, and his crippled leg still trailed awkwardly; he used a stick as he refused crutches, but even getting from the car, across the house to the study was an exhausting business. Now he drank with obvious relish. 'Sometimes they are better left as secrets.'

'But . . .'

Mark raised a finger, and John checked what he was going to say. 'I gather you are genuinely in love with this girl and want to marry her.'

'Yes, I am.'

'Very good. Now, her aunt was your mother. But nobody outside this room knows that.'

'Eh?' Even Joan was taken aback.

'Fact. When Patricia discovered she was pregnant, going on what she told me during our admittedly brief exchange before things got out of hand, she told her parents, and there was the most tremendous row. Well brought-up young ladies didn't do that sort of thing in 1917.'

'I don't think they do now,' Joan suggested.

'Perhaps not. But it is a later generation. Anyway, there was a frightful quarrel, and she moved out. She could do this because she was quite wealthy in her own right from her dead husband, which is why, if you'll excuse me, John, she was able to be footloose and fancy free, why she was able to get together with me in the first place, and no questions asked. The point is that she apparently refused to tell her parents who the father was. So after the quarrel, she moved out, took a flat in Tunbridge Wells, and devoted her time to trying to get hold of me. Only by then I had been shot down and posted missing, believed killed. It was some time before it was learned that I was actually alive and in a German prison camp. It was even longer before your mother discovered that. Then again she tried to get in touch with me. But as you can imagine, the mails were pretty chaotic, and she never did manage to find me, until I returned home and found a letter waiting for me.'

'And by then you were already in love with Stepmama.'

'I was, yes. And your mother did not specify why she was so anxious to see me. She just said she wanted us to get together again. Had she told me she had borne my child . . . But I had no idea, and I was about to return to Germany to marry Karolina. So I ignored her letter.'

'Hold on,' Joan said. 'You showed me Patricia's letter, and I advised you not to follow it up.'

'All right, so you did. But I was happy to accept your advice. So I went to Germany, married Karo, and did not see or hear from your mother again until that dreadful day when she turned up here. We have explained all this to you.'

'Yes, you have,' John acknowledged.

'But to return to my point, no one knew who you were. You were just a baby in a carrycot in the back of Patricia's car. Karo insisted upon taking you in and adopting you. The police obviously had to inform Patricia's parents what had happened, and that there was a child, but that if they did not wish to be involved, the natural father was prepared to take on the responsibility. Your grandparents did not wish to be involved. They did not even attend your mother's funeral. You mustn't be too hard on them. Back in the early Twenties suicide was even more of an ethically unacceptable crime than it is today. They never even enquired after the father, and the police, very discreetly, did not offer the information. So the fact is that no one outside this room knows the truth.'

'And Beerman,' Joan said. 'He was there. Patricia shot him before turning the gun on you.'

'Jim is absolutely reliable,' Mark insisted. Jim Beerman had been his mechanic during the Great War, and his chauffeur for the past twenty years. 'So there it is, Johnnie. If you really love this girl, go for it and forget the legalities. You'll have our hundred per cent support.'

John finished his drink. 'And you feel, if I marry her, it will somehow atone for what happened to Mother.'

Joan gulped, but Mark Bayley neither flushed nor lowered his gaze. 'Nothing can atone for what happened to your mother, Johnnie. It's what happens to you, and Avril, that matters. I look forward to meeting her.'

John got up and went to the door, but hesitated. 'May I ask a question, Dad?'

'Of course.'

'If, in the letter that was waiting for you when you came

back from Germany, before you had actually married Stepmama, my mother had told you that she had borne your child, would you have married her?'

Mark sighed. 'I won't lie to you, Johnnie. The answer is no. Karo was the most wonderful woman I ever met, and I think that most people who knew her, including you before she died and you found out the truth, felt that as well. No, listen. I promised you my fullest support, so here's what I'll do. I know a lot of the big boys. I'll find out where Avril is now posted for you, and you'll be able to get in touch. OK?'

John considered for a moment, then said, 'Thanks, Dad.' He closed the door behind himself.

'Woof!' Joan said. 'I think we could both do with another drink.' She took their glasses to the sideboard. 'I really thought all this was behind us after that heart to heart talk you had with him four years ago.'

'I thought so too,' Mark said. 'And it would have been, but for his meeting that girl. Would you believe that out of all the women in England he has to run into Patricia's niece and fall in love with her?'

'But you're still going to welcome her into the family.'

'Yes. And so must you. It's John's happiness we're concerned about. We just have to pray that he hasn't made a mistake.'

She refilled their glasses. 'I'm peripheral.'

'You are the mainspring that keeps this family going.'

She blew him a kiss as she handed him his glass. 'I can't be that forever.'

'Were you planning to go somewhere?' He frowned as she sat down without replying. 'What's happened?'

Joan knew he still had a severe mental hang-up regarding women who suddenly told him they had a problem. That was exactly what Karolina had told him, with her invariable bright smile, and sitting in this very chair, as she recalled. So she didn't smile. 'There's nothing wrong with me.'

He released his breath in a long, slow sigh.

'At least physically,' she added.

Immediately he was watchful again.

Joan drew a deep breath. 'What would you say if I told you that I also would like to get married?'

43

Mark stared at her with his mouth open, and she flushed. 'So I'm a forty-three-year-old spinster of this parish. Not everyone feels that's too old to stop being a spinster, if you follow me. I mean, all my bits are in the right places.'

'You are a beautiful woman.'

Joan went on as if he hadn't spoken. 'I suppose you can blame Klaus Maartens. He . . . well, he sort of awakened my senses. Well, reawakened, I suppose. Made me realize how sterile my life had been. It was all right while Karo was alive. The house was so full of fun and laughter and "what shall we do next" that there was no time, and certainly no inclination, to indulge in too much speculation.'

'But since her death we've rather flown apart.'

'Well, we have, you know. Oh, some of it was going to happen anyway. But in a different way. I mean, the boys would have grown up anyway, and wanted to do their own things, but it would have been different were Karo still here.'

'Oh, certainly. Max wouldn't have gone flying off to Germany in search of his "roots", you wouldn't have gone after him to get him back, and so you wouldn't have been arrested by the Gestapo . . . God, what would I give to get my hands on that bastard Luttmann.'

'It wasn't all bad, Mark. If it hadn't happened, I wouldn't have met Klaus again, and, well . . . But it isn't only that. Johnnie now definitely feels estranged. Oh, I'm sure he'll come back, but . . . And then you're away for so much of the time . . . Did this conference turn up anything important? When are the Germans coming?'

'Probably any day, now that the French have quit. It's a miracle they haven't come yet; they must know how weak we are. I suppose they have some deep scheme up their sleeves.'

'And when they do come, are we ready?'

'God, no. But every day they don't come, we're getting stronger. We're producing Spitfires and Hurricanes as fast as we can, and perhaps even more importantly, we're training pilots as fast as we can, too. We're also improving the performance of the aircraft we already have in commission. That's why Johnnie is home on leave; the engines of his squadron are being changed from the float system to fuel injection. It's planned to re-engine the entire Spitfire fleet.'

44

'How long will that take?'

'A couple of months.'

'And until then?'

He grinned. 'We do the best with what we have, and we pray. It's not all doom and gloom. We have radar. It hasn't been properly tested in battle yet. We did send one to France, but the French didn't understand it and got no worthwhile use from it. But if what our boffins claim is true, we should be able to meet the Luftwaffe on our terms, not theirs. And then – this is top secret, but the lads at Bletchley Manor claim to have broken the code being used by the Luftwaffe. It's something called Enigma, brought to us by some Polish refugees. Don't ask me how it works. I know absolutely nothing about ciphers. We didn't use them in the RFC, because we didn't have radios, just a telephone call in plain English from HQ to the squadron adjutant telling us where to go next. And of course, like radar, it hasn't been tested in battle conditions yet. But if it works it could give us some advance information on what Jerry is planning next.'

'As you say, not all gloom and doom. You've made me feel a whole lot better.'

'*Nil desperandum*, eh? But just remember that when push comes to shove, for all the extra information about what Jerry is doing or wants to do, it's going to come down to the quality of our machines, and the men who fly them . . . and for a while yet most of them are going to be pilots with very little flying time behind them, and no combat time at all.'

'Now you are making me feel like another drink.'

'There's no point in getting tight. You still haven't told me about this chap you want to marry.'

Secrets and lies, Mark thought as he sat in the back of the Rolls being driven to the factory in Southampton. Joan and John both supposed he had no secrets, at least from them. And in a purely objective sense they were right. Neither, not even Joan, knew the turmoil that roamed through his mind whenever he was not actually working.

They didn't know the obsessive guilt that shrouded his personality. They considered him to be a dominating figure, an enormously successful man, who had overcome the psychological catastrophe of being crippled in the prime of his youthful vigour, to become one of the most successful of men. That it really was a sham, in that none of it had been planned, or indeed worked for, they could never know.

Logic told him that for Patricia Pope to have agreed to his absurd proposal of marriage would have been a disaster for both of them. She had been nine years older, with a background of wealth and privilege; he had been the son of a sub-postmaster and a seventeen-year-old virgin. But to watch a woman, the first woman he had ever slept with, blow her brains out in front of his eyes, had been a far more traumatic event than being shot down over the Western Front. Had Karo not been there to support him he did not think he could have coped.

And then, Karo herself. He had gone to France in a mood of almost manic aggression, a compound of Patricia, the death of his elder brother at sea, and the resultant stroke suffered by his father. He had thrown himself into combat with an utter disregard for his life and, as was so often the case, had been brilliantly successful at shooting down German aircraft, until being brought down himself. And then, the leg. He had pleaded with the German doctors not to take it, even after they had explained that he would be crippled for life; the idea of having to spend the rest of his life on crutches had terrified him. He did not suppose they would have paid any heed to his appeals but for Manfred von Richtofen. The German hero had come to visit him the moment his name had been released, as one ace to another; they had never met in aerial combat. Richtofen had observed his distress and had promised to speak with the doctors. So he still had his leg.

But by then his life had changed irrevocably. It had been a face leaning over his bed, separating an enormous, starched white headdress from an equally starched white uniform. The face of an angel. Perhaps his immediate opinion was borne of his half-delirious state, but even when he had regained full possession of his faculties, he had never doubted she was the most beautiful woman he had ever seen.

That she, a German nurse, should, after an initial period of suspicion, have fallen in love with a badly wounded English airman, had been incomprehensible. That she, a German nurse, should have turned out to be the daughter of Germany's leading industrialist, doing her bit for the Fatherland, had induced total consternation. That such an aristocrat, on becoming a millionaire after her father's sudden death – she had been an only child – had been prepared to grant her husband complete control over her widespread fortune, had been nothing less than a miracle.

His entire life from that moment had been devoted to attempting to measure up to her estimation of him. But it had been Karo who had pulled every string, opened every door. He knew he had not recovered from her death, and would never do so. With her death the world she had so lovingly created had come to an end. The fact was that he and John, for all their mutual endeavours, had begun to drift apart the moment John had learned the truth of his parentage. That truth had had to come out at some time, but had Karo lived it would certainly have been handled both differently and more success-fully. Equally, he had not been able to cope with Max's perhaps natural preference for the glamour of Nazi Germany over what he had seen as the bowler-hatted stuffiness of his father's England.

That had left him only Joan. Although she was his older sister, she had always, like everyone else, regarded him as someone on whose shoulder she could cry or rest her head whenever necessary. Now she too was leaving. He did not know, and perhaps he did not wish even to consider, what life might be like alone in that huge house. Karo's house.

'Hello?' the voice on the phone said. 'Hello?'

'Avril?'

'John?' The woman's voice rose an octave. 'Oh, John! Where are you?'

'I can't tell you that. But I'm not all that far from you. Listen, I may be able to get up to see you. Can you get some time off?'

'It's so sudden. After so long . . .'

'I know. I've been trying to get hold of you for the past couple of weeks, but you're always out or something. What exactly do you do?'

'I'm in the motor pool. I drive a car, for colonels and things. Sometimes a general.'

'But you do have some time off?'

'Oh, yes.'

'Well, listen. I've been having some work done on my engine, but it's due back the day after tomorrow. Then it'll have to be tested. As part of my test I could fly up. There's an airfield near where your camp is. Can you get the day off? The day after tomorrow?'

'Probably.'

'Do it, and I'll see you then.'

'Oh, John . . . It's been so long. You were going to speak with your father . . .'

'I did speak with my father, and it's going to be all right. I couldn't get back to you before because I got caught up in the fighting over Dunkirk.'

'Oh, Lord! Are you all right?'

'I'm fine. I even got a kill. My first! And then, when that was done I tried to get in touch with you, but you'd been transferred away from Didcot, and no one would tell me where you were.'

'But you've managed to find out.'

'I put my dad on it.'

'Gosh. He really is a big wheel. Is he a general or something?'

'No, he only has one workable leg. But his firm played a big part in developing the Spitfire, so he has a lot of friends in high places.'

'Gosh,' she said again. 'And he's happy about us?'

'Yes. Yes he is. He can't wait to meet you.'

'And we can get married?'

'Yes.'

'When?'

'Well, whenever we can both get leave at the same time.'

'They're saying the Germans are going to invade at any moment.'

'Well, they haven't come yet, have they? Listen, the first thing we have to do is get together and make some plans.'

'Oh, yes. Does your father . . . well . . . know . . .'

'That we've slept together? Yes. I told you that we had no secrets from each other.' Not one, he thought.

'Wow!'

'Have you told your father and mother yet?'

'Well, no. I haven't had a chance to see them, and it's not

48

the sort of thing you can put in a letter, just out of the blue, like. And I wasn't sure . . .'

'Of course you weren't. I'm so sorry I couldn't reach you before. Now stop worrying. It's going to be all right. I'll see you in two days' time.'

'I love you, Johnnie.'

'And I love you too, Avril.'

He hung up, and leaned against the wall beside the phone. He found that he was sweating. Secrets, he thought. Secrets and lies. But what had he lied about? Avril had been, and remained, the most attractive girl he had ever met, save for that German girl, Erika von Bitterman, and she had turned out to be an utter bitch. But did he love her? He had certainly loved her body, and he dreamed of getting his hands on it again. And everything else about her was delightful. He could think of no one he would rather spend the rest of his life with. But when, having proposed, she had told him her family background and he had realized that she was actually his first cousin, he had honestly thought that, young and strong and fit as he was, he might have a heart attack.

That had been followed by an urgent desire to be away from her, to give himself time to think. But as he was an officer and a gentleman – and a Bayley – he had not considered ending the evening with tears and recriminations. Besides, he had known he would be going into combat in the very near future, and having already been shot down once – and well remembering the dreadful feeling of impotence and despair as he had realized he would have to bale out or die that time – that future had seemed uncertain to say the least. Shades of Father and Mother in 1917!

So he had returned Avril to her barracks and fled back to his own. He had known he had to tell Father and get things straight, but the war had got in the way and he had not had the opportunity until after Dunkirk. By then what had happened was already a memory. That night had been about sheer lust, the culmination of an on-off romance that had begun on that fateful night in the pub nearly a year previously, before the war had even started.

If only he could be certain of his feelings, towards so many things. He knew in his heart that his father had done nothing wrong, had acted in the only possible way, and yet he could

49

not stop himself resenting the fact that his father had found such happiness, albeit for a brief fifteen years, while his mother had gone to a forgotten grave. So how much of what he felt for Avril was sheer guilt, a desire to atone for his family's destruction of her aunt?

Was that a sound basis for the enormous risk he was taking in marrying her, without her knowing the truth? Could he maintain that secret for the rest of his life? At least Father had had Aunt Joan to share it with. He had no one.

But in two days' time he would be holding Avril in his arms again. Perhaps that would resolve everything.

Joan kissed her nephew and Mark shook hands as John prepared to leave. 'Did you manage to get in touch?'

'Yes, I did. I never thanked you properly for arranging it.'

'What are fathers for? And is all well?'

'Oh, yes. I'm hoping to see her in a couple of days.'

'Well, that's great. And now you have a virtually new aircraft waiting for you.'

'Hopefully. I'll be in touch.'

He mounted his motorbike and went roaring down the drive.

'What do you reckon?' Joan asked.

'I think we just have to wait and see, and keep our fingers crossed. Now, what time is this young man of yours arriving?'

'He's coming for lunch,' Joan said. 'And he's not all that young. Oh, by the way, Helen's coming as well.'

'Oh, God! Is that necessary?'

'I thought it would make Jim feel less isolated in the Bayleys' den. Don't you like her? She's very fond of you.'

'I know,' Mark said grimly.

'And that bothers you?'

'She is not really my idea of the sort of woman I want around. I mean to say, she's no beauty, and she's overweight, and, well . . .'

'Is that all you men think about? She may be overweight, but that means there's a whole lot of her to get hold of. You are absolutely amoral. Anyway, she has a husband, for the time being.'

'He's not coming, is he?'

'That bounder? No way! Anyway, she's actually divorced

him. It's a matter of waiting for the nisi to be completed.'

'I find that rather ominous.'

'Oh, you great twit. I'm sure she has no desire to get married again. Although, she'd do you good, you know.'

'Brrrr,' Mark retorted.

'What do you think?' Hawkins asked. But he already knew the answer, from the enthusiasm on John's face, on the faces of all the pilots in the squadron, and they had only done a couple of brief circuits.

'I think it's tremendous,' John said. 'The lads want to know if we can go into combat upside down from now on. Almost makes you believe that old Winston could be right.'

'Oh, inspiring stuff. Our finest hour, what? However, when the old boy talks about shooting down four Jerries for one of ours he is, how shall I put it, being creative with the truth. As you well know.'

'Of course,' John said, as nonchalantly as he could, 'we really need to put them through their paces. If you agree, I thought we'd go on a prolonged exercise tomorrow, make sure the new system is as good as it seems.'

'Makes sense. But you need to pack up your gear and take it with you.'

'Sir?'

'There's no time for trial runs. This afternoon we move down to Biggin. You can do some exercises on the way. Our heavy gear will be following by truck.'

John stared at him. If lumps of lead seemed to be gathering in his brain, his heart was soaring. 'You mean the balloon has gone up? Jerry is actually coming?'

'No, I do not mean that. At least, we have no concrete proof of it. But this could be a preliminary step on his part. He has greatly upped his attacks on our coastal shipping, and the ports on the south-east – Dover and Newhaven and places like that. We've taken some heavy casualties, mainly Defiants. I imagine you understand that.'

'Yes, sir,' John said grimly. 'I was flying a Defiant when I was shot down in France. They're simply not in the same class as a 109. But do you mean Jerry is using fighters to attack our shipping?'

'Not in so many words. He's using his fighters to protect

the bombers who are attacking our shipping, and our chaps need help. That is what we are going to provide. So pack up your gear and be ready to leave at fourteen hundred.'

Shit! John thought. Shit, shit, shit! 'Will it be possible to make a telephone call, sir?'

'Sorry, John. Not even to your dad. That we are putting Spits into the defence of the Channel ports has to be top secret.'

'Jerry will recognize what he's up against, quickly enough.'

'No doubt he will. But it's not our business to tell him in advance. Now brief your pilots and prepare to go.'

Three

First Blood

Max wondered if he would ever cease waking up at dawn, even if the dawn was just the slightest sliver of light peeping round the drawn bedroom curtains. But it was there, the start of another day.

It would be a day of endless pleasure, as had been the past four days, in which he would hardly leave this bed except to bathe, use the toilet, and eat – and even the eating took place close to the bed. He looked down to his right, at the naked woman beside him, long black hair scattered across her face, breathing slowly and evenly, breasts inflating enchantingly, and then subsiding again, no less enchantingly.

But then he looked down to his left, at long golden hair also scattered across the face, slender body wedged against his. Her lips moved slightly. She was dreaming. Her name, apparently, was Heidi. Neither she nor Erika had offered more than that, and he had had no desire to pry. He knew absolutely nothing about her, apart from the estimation that even from his point of view – and he was not yet twenty-one – she was younger than himself. And that she was extremely pretty in a slight fashion, so unlike Erika's bold voluptuousness. And of course her prowess in bed, which was considerable. And that she was quite definitely Erika's lover.

52

And for the past four days she had given him her all. That while doing this she had also played with Erika did not disturb him – at least, not at the moment. It fitted what he was doing, what he had become, over the past four days. Goering had told him to get himself a woman and relax. Well, he had got himself two, and without spending a mark. That they had actually got him was also not relevant, at this moment. That one of them was a woman he knew to be as treacherously self-centred as it was possible to imagine, who was now adding adultery, as she had clearly long added lesbianism, to her other moral crimes, was of no concern to him. He had finally accepted the ideology that the strong shall inherit the earth, that the strong meant the Aryan master race, and that they inherited the earth by taking what they wanted from their inferiors . . . or from their fellows, if offered the opportunity.

After two years of lip service, he had finally become a Nazi.

To get out of bed he had to straddle one of the women. He chose Heidi, who was normally the heavier sleeper. But as his weight rested for a moment on her thighs, she stirred, and instinctively reached for him.

'I must go to the toilet first,' she muttered.

'So must I.' Gently he disengaged her fingers.

After a few seconds she followed him, leaned against the wall to watch him, and then took his place. 'What time is it?'

Max looked at his watch. 'Just gone four.'

'Jesus! We've only been asleep four hours. And you are ready again?'

'Not really. I'm always awake at this hour. Hadn't you noticed?'

'I prefer not to notice bad habits. However, as we're both up . . .' She peered at him. 'Well, sort of . . .'

'He can wait.' He got back into bed, carefully. Erika was now snoring faintly.

Heidi lay beside him, and reached for him again. 'I do not think I can.' She sighed. 'I was having a dream.'

'About me?'

'I was taken prisoner by pirates, who made me strip naked and then forced me to have sex with them, one after the other.'

'But surely they were all men?'

'Of course. But their captain was a woman. A pirate queen, eh? She stood above me while they were raping me, watching, and I knew—'

The telephone jangled.

'Shit!' Heidi cried. 'I was just about getting myself off.'

Erika sat up, hair flailing. 'What in the name of God . . .?'

Max was already out of bed and standing at the table beneath the window. 'Yes?'

'Captain Bayley?'

'This is he.'

'Good morning, Captain. You are to report immediately to your station. You will know where that is.'

'Yes,' Max said. 'Can you tell me . . .?'

'I can tell you nothing more, Herr Captain. Except to repeat the word immediately.'

'Understood.' Max replaced the receiver.

'Does that person know what time it is?' Erika demanded.

'I suspect he does.' Max picked up the phone again. 'Reception? I wish a taxi in fifteen minutes. For Tempelhof. Thank you.'

He dashed into the bathroom, began to shave.

'What the fuck is going on?' Erika enquired, getting out of bed to join him and use the toilet.

'I have absolutely no idea.' He dried his face, returned to the bedroom and began to dress, watched by Heidi with enormous eyes.

'You have two more days' leave,' Erika pointed out.

'My leave appears to have been terminated.'

'But we have paid for a week.'

'So you can enjoy the other two days without me.'

'But what are we to *do*?'

Max knotted his tie, put on his tunic, picked up his cap, took her into his arms to kiss her. 'I'm sure you'll think of something.' Heidi had also got out of bed and was sitting at the desk. He bent over to kiss her as well.

She squeezed his hand. 'I would like to see you again,' she whispered, and pressed a folded piece of paper into his palm.

He opened it in the taxi; as he had expected, it was a telephone number. She was a sweet little thing. But the phone number, and the woman herself, were for the distant future, if he ever got there. Only the immediate future mattered now.

His entire body was tingling. Could Milch have got his way after all?

Aachen was a long way away, but he followed the same pattern as before, fuelled at Hanover, and landed just before noon, to be immediately surrounded by his pilots.

'Do you know what is happening, Herr Captain?'

'No. But I think we are about to find out.'

He had spotted the 110 on the parking apron, and this was confirmed by his next in command, Senior-Lieutenant Gunther Langholm.

'He arrived half an hour ago. I think he is waiting for you.'

Max nodded and hurried into the briefing office, where an anxious flight-sergeant was watching the Field-Marshal, who was standing at the window looking out at the runway. Max saluted. 'Heil Hitler!'

'Heil!' Milch turned to face his protégé. 'You look tired. Was it a difficult flight?'

'No, sir. I had a late night, and an early morning.'

'The exigencies of war. I am sorry to have terminated your furlough so abruptly, but we are getting some action, at last.'

'We are going to invade?'

'Sadly, no. That is apparently still under consideration. But the Luftwaffe has been instructed to disrupt the Channel traffic, which is proceeding up and down under our noses as if there was no war on at all.'

'Yes, sir,' Max said without enthusiasm.

'Absolutely,' Milch agreed. 'It is hardly work for our interceptors, which is why you were not called upon immediately. However, as you may imagine, the British are responding to this, quite strongly. This is to the good, of course, as it is bringing the RAF out of its lairs, but they have been quite effective, and over the past week several of our bombers have been shot down. You will therefore take your squadron down to Ostend this afternoon, and as of dawn tomorrow you will provide cover for the bombers. It will be the battle for control of the Channel: the Kanalkampf! Obviously, even from Ostend, your flying time will be limited, but you will be relieved on a regular basis, just as you will relieve your sister squadrons in turn. A duty roster is also waiting for you in Ostend. Now

I want you to understand, very clearly, Max, that you are not to risk either pilots or planes unnecessarily. Any plane that runs out of fuel, any pilot who has to bale out over the Channel will be lost. If the RAF comes out, engage them, destroy as many of them as possible, but only maintain the engagement within the limits of your fuel range.'

'Understood, sir.'

'Very good. Your investiture will be in three weeks' time. I'd like you to be still around at that time.'

Ostend was clearly going to be an improvement on Aachen, and the airstrip was only a mile outside the town, but obviously enjoying it was going to have to wait. By the time the squadron was down, and the roster for the following day had been studied, Max was exhausted: he had been flying for some twelve hours.

Heinrich had already come down by truck, with his gear, and he awakened his boss just before dawn. 'It is calm, Herr Captain. But there is mist. The met office says it will burn off.'

'By which time we'll be home again.' Max shaved and dressed. 'Breakfast at eight, Heinrich.'

'It will be ready, sir.'

His pilots were waiting beside their planes. 'I understand the Dorniers are going in pretty low, in . . .' He looked at his watch. 'Fifteen minutes. So we will take three thousand metres. But that is not a satisfactory combat height. Gunther, you and A Flight will maintain station at six thousand, and let us know if the Tommies are coming. Now, gentlemen, there are to be no false heroics. We have a job to do, to protect the bombers – and, just as important, to return to base. It is not merely a matter of men and machines. It is morale. Every German plane that goes down, whether it is shot down or runs out of fuel, will be trumpeted as an English victory. Right now they do not have many of these to shout about. We must keep it that way. Listen to my radio. When I say we go home, we go home. At oh-seven-thirty we will be relieved by JG 47. Understood?' He looked around their faces. They were certainly eager. 'Well, then, I will see you at breakfast.'

*　　*　　*

Within seconds of taking off, the ground was lost to sight, and even the last plane in the squadron was no more than a shadow.

'How do we shoot at what we can't see?' someone complained.

'It'll lift,' Max promised.

In fact, they were through the mist at two thousand metres, into a magnificent clear blue sky. 'Taking position,' Gunther said, his flight continuing to climb.

Max thumbed his mike. 'JG 36 to KG 17,' he said. 'Your position, please.'

'We are at map reference AK 20,' the bomber commander said. 'Fifteen hundred metres.'

Max hastily checked his marked map.

'I see them,' Zeitel said.

Max looked down at the dozen Dorniers, easily identifiable by their long, slender bodies.

'We see you,' the bomber commander said. 'The target is sixteen kilometres ahead of us, just entering the strait. In those narrow waters they will find evasion difficult. Going down.'

There was still mist on the water, but it was thinning very rapidly as the sun came up. A few seconds later Max could see the white of the ships' wakes. And only a minute after-wards he saw the red flash of the first explosion. Now he could see the ships themselves, several freighters. They were certainly moving to and fro, their wakes criss-crossing each other, but as the bomber commander had said, they did not have much room to manoeuvre: he could see the coasts of both England and France to his right and left.

One of the ships was already on fire. The others were surrounded by the huge white splashes of exploding bombs, and then another suffered a gush of red flame followed by billowing black smoke.

'That is like shooting fish in a barrel,' someone commented.

But at that moment Gunther said, quietly, 'Babies one o'clock. Distance ten kilometres, height estimated three thou-sand metres.'

'Numbers?' Max asked.

'Twelve.'

'Maintain your position until we engage. Climb,' he told his pilots.

The 109s rose quickly.

'Identification,' Max requested.

'They are not Spitfires. Or Hurricanes. I can see the rear gunner's cupola. They are Defiants!'

'I didn't think there were any of those left. Very good. Maintain your position, and keep looking out. We will deal with this lot.'

'Some people,' Gunther said, 'have all the fun.'

'Boulton-Paul Defiants,' Max told his pilots. 'We saw some in France. They are two-seaters and the pilot is not armed. The gunner has three-hundred-and-sixty-degree manoeuvrability, but he is obviously strongest facing aft. We attack from the side. We are faster and more heavily armed.'

They levelled off at four thousand metres; the gap was now down to a kilometre or less.

'They have seen us,' someone said.

The British squadron was dividing. Six of them were climbing to take on the Messerschmitts, the remaining six maintained course to attack the bombers.

'All right, Gunther,' Max said. 'You may have those fellows.'

He put his plane into a steep dive, followed by the rest of the squadron.

'They are in line ahead,' someone said incredulously.

It did seem suicidal, but no doubt they felt that their gunners could cover their flanks. The Messerschmitts descended like a swarm of bees. One thousand metres, Max calculated, staring into his sights as he set his guns. Seven hundred metres. He had picked the leader, and now he saw the turret revolving to bring its guns to bear. Five hundred metres, and he saw the red tracers coming towards him. But they passed beneath him; the gunner seemed to have miscalculated his speed. He pressed his own trigger, aiming now forward of the gunner, watched the tracers passing very close, but just above the fuselage. Then he was above the enemy. The gunner swung his electrically controlled turret through 180 degrees to keep firing, but Max was still too fast for him, and he brought his machine round in a tight turn that had the blood draining from behind his eyes. His number two, Hans Bleymans, struck the now undefended flank. As vision returned Max saw the gunner slumped in his seat, his plexiglass cupola torn to ribbons, while the pilot was trying frantically to gain height. Bleymans was now beside Max, but he had done the hard work. Max gave him the thumbs-up to finish the job and claim his kill, while he went after the third plane in the line.

He now played the role of killer, this gunner in turn having been distracted by another plane. Max ignored him and went for the pilot, using his Oerlikon cannon to send several 20mm shells into the forward compartment, watched the pilot's body jerking, while almost immediately a stream of smoke issued from the engine. He soared past it as the gunner baled out; whether he drowned or not would depend on how quickly the recovery launches could get to him.

He looked around. The British flight had disintegrated, and the three survivors were heading for home. Above him Gunther had similarly dispersed the other section. There were three parachutes floating downwards, and he reckoned half of the twelve Defiants had gone down. His squadron had not lost a plane.

He looked at his fuel gauge and then at his watch. It was just 0720, and he was below half. He hoped JG 47 was on time, but they were not really needed. The Dorniers had now completed their assault and were turning for home. He merely had to escort them. 'Five thousand,' he said. 'Course north-east.'

Gunther's flight was already above him. 'I see 47,' the lieutenant said.

'Well, there's not much for them to do,' Max commented.

Bleymans broke in. 'Babies, eleven o'clock.'

'Don't say they're coming back for more,' someone said. 'I'm almost out of ammo.'

Max checked his own position. Because of his experience, he had held his fire until close enough to make it effective, and so he still had more than fifty of his 120 20mm cannon shells left; but the 109 only carried a thousand rounds for its two machine guns, which really amounted to two five-second bursts, and even his were nearly all gone. The temptation to inflict another heavy blow to the enemy was enormous, even if he would be cutting it fine. Then Gunther said, from his vantage point above him, 'Spitfires. Four flights.'

'Shit,' someone commented.

The decision had to be instantaneous, but to engage an equal number of Spitfires, who would only just have left their base and therefore be fully fuelled and armed, would be fool-hardy in the extreme, and he had Milch's orders always in his mind. And, as if to confirm his decision, a new voice came on the radio.

'Leave them to us, 36. You've had your fun.'

'As you say,' Max replied. 'Squadron will return to base.'

'But, sir . . .'

'That is an order, Bleymans.' Max levelled off at five thousand metres and flew towards the still rising sun.

'Bandits,' Newman said, 'Half past four.'

'I see them,' John acknowledged.

'You think those are the ones we want, sir?'

'I'm sure of it. Follow me.'

He swung his machine towards the distant cluster, the squadron falling into line behind him. He was in a mood of angry desperation. They had been slow getting off the ground after the order to scramble, and to that had been added the sight, and the sound, of the half-destroyed squadron of Defiants returning from their gallantly futile attempt to protect the convoy.

John had only flown Defiants in France in May for two days before being shot down on the twelfth. He could remember as if it were yesterday the feeling of angry despair as he had gone into action for the first time in his life and realized immediately that his machine was utterly outclassed – for speed, manoeuvrability and armament – by the Messerschmitts that had been buzzing around him.

In that sickening moment he had known he was about to die, just as his rear gunner had already died. Miraculously he had found some cloud cover and escaped immediate destruc-tion, but his aircraft had been shot to pieces, and he had been forced to bale out. Fortunately he had been over the Allied lines, but the wounds he had sustained had ended his part in the war in France. He knew now that it had been a fortunate escape; thanks to his father's influence, once he had recov-ered he had been transferred to Spitfires. But that had not mitigated the bitterness he had felt on learning that the entire squadron, men with whom he had messed and served and drunk for over a year, had been destroyed. Rather, the fact that he was now out of action while he retrained to fly the superior machine had increased his feelings of angst.

Those feelings had been, to a certain extent, relieved when he had at last got back into action, on that final day of the Dunkirk evacuation. He had been flying a Spitfire and actually leading a hastily assembled squadron of tyros, thrown into the breach because after four days of unceasing combat the RAF had been running out of pilots who were not utterly exhausted. Simply because they had *been* tyros, not yet completely familiar with the accepted conventions of how aerial combat should be conducted, they had scored a success. The Germans had by then spent three weeks fighting the RAF, and had worked out its strengths – and, more importantly, its weaknesses, its tendency to cling to out-of-date tactics such as attacking in line ahead. They had undoubtedly been surprised at being assailed by a swarm of fighters, after their own fashion, not realizing that the attack was being carried out in such a way by ignorance rather than design.

He had lost two planes, but the Germans had lost three, including the crushing downing of their flight-commander, and had broken off the engagement. That day had earned him fame and promotion, even if he knew there were whispers of nepotism. But the bitter anger remained. He knew it went deeper than the memory of his comrades being destroyed on that first day of battle. There was also the desire to equal Father – *surpass* him – and in doing so in some small way atone both for what had happened to his mother, and what he knew he was about to do to Avril.

The sight of the battered Defiants deepened John's mood, especially as the leader asked, 'What kept you?'

He preferred not to reply, looked down instead at the sparkling waters of the Channel, and the remains of the convoy. One ship was definitely sinking, two others were on fire. But the bombers were gone.

'Over there,' Rigg called.

'Those are single-engined,' someone else countered.

'109s,' John said.

'And running like hell,' Newman commented.

'Out of fuel or ammo or both, I reckon,' John said. 'Well . . .'

'Bandits,' Anderson the wingman said. 'Eleven o'clock and twenty thousand.'

'Climb, climb, climb!' John snapped.

The Spitfires soared upwards, while John studied the approaching machines. These were also single-engined, and he had no doubt that they were also 109s, but fresh off the tarmac. 'It's one-to-one,' he said.

'Formation, sir?'

John considered, briefly. There were three basic attack formations regarded as the correct way to enter battle. Number one was line ahead in flights of three. Number two was two planes to attack one target, from the rear. Number three was for three aircraft to attack together, one from the rear and one from each side. But all of those were designed for coping with bombers which, being far slower and less manoeuvrable, could do nothing better than keep flying and put their trust in their own defences. Against fighters during the battles in France those tactics had proved disastrous.

In any event, the Messerschmitts were above them, equal in numbers, and at least as fast. He had either to give the command to run like hell, which he was not going to do, or . . . 'I think it has to be up boys and at 'em,' he said. 'Remember to hold your fire to five hundred yards maximum. That's when they fill your sights. When they overlap, front and rear, they're point blank.'

The pale-blue machines were now swooping fast. Several opened fire at maximum range, and the tracers disappeared into the air. The ether was filled with excited chatter, both English and German, but although John was fluent in High German he had no time to decipher any of the gabble.

He concentrated on the plane immediately in front of him. Seven hundred yards, he reckoned; it was in his sights but only occupied the very centre. There was a flash of light and his machine trembled. He knew that the Messerschmitt had fired its wing cannon, and that the little shells hadn't missed by much. But the range was closing with the speed of light; the 109 was filling his sights and overlapping. He pressed the trigger, but had no time to follow the tracers; the two planes were too close.

He pulled back the stick and went upwards, knowing that

if the German did the same they stood a strong chance of colliding. But the enemy had gone beneath him. He rolled and looped, the blood draining from his brain even as he instinctively waited for the engine to cut out. But this time it didn't, thanks to the fuel injection, and he was now on the tail of his opponent. There was already a thin stream of smoke issuing from the 109's engine where his first burst had struck, but it was still capable of fighting, and the pilot was twisting his head to and fro, looking for him. John was again close, and fired a prolonged burst. He could see fabric ripping apart, and a moment later the machine went into a spin.

He stayed with it for a few seconds, saw the pilot push back the cockpit canopy and climb out. As he left the plane, the German looked back at him and raised his hand. John touched his own helmet. His opponent's war was over; he was too close to the English coast to be rescued by his own people. If he didn't drown he'd be picked up by one of the British recovery vessels down there. Then his parachute opened and he disappeared beneath the white silk.

John climbed back up to rejoin the still raging fight, and saw to his distress a Spitfire spiralling downwards, trailing a plume of smoke. There was no parachute to be seen and when he looked again he could see that the cockpit was engulfed in flame. 'Shit!' he muttered. And was then in combat once more.

The battle lasted a further ten minutes before the Messerschmitts broke off and went for home. 'No pursuit,' John said, as one or two of his planes made to follow. 'Or you could wind up in the drink.'

His gauge was under half full, and he reckoned he was virtually out of ammunition as well; the Spitfire carried only 2500 rounds for its eight machine guns, a matter of hardly more than fifteen seconds' firing. He looked around him, counted nine aircraft.

'We got three of them,' Newman said.

'And they got three of us,' John replied sombrely. 'Let's go home.'

'Anderson, Blythe and Richards,' John said, slumping into the chair before Hawkins' desk. 'There's a chance Blythe and Richards were picked up; they managed to bale out. But

Anderson is definitely dead.' He sighed. 'The only good thing about this morning is that we got three of theirs.'

'And that is not a good thing either,' Hawkins said. 'As Jerry has approximately twice the number of planes that we do, there is no way we can match him loss for loss. We have to shoot down two of his for every one of ours.'

'There is the point that all three of his men are definitely lost or prisoners. If we get Blythe and Richards back, it'll be three to one.'

'In men, not machines. And we're ignoring the Defiants. Whether we like it or not, they are part of our front-line strength, and they lost six planes today. That was a massacre, and it means that Jerry scored at the rate of three to one. What happened?'

John sighed. 'We got there about five minutes too late.'

Hawkins nodded. 'I was watching, and timing. It took you three minutes to get airborne after being scrambled. That is not acceptable, John. It has to be under two.'

'Yes, sir.'

'So what are you going to do about it?'

'Plenty. If you'll excuse me, sir.' He went outside. It was mid morning and a bright early summer's day. The pilots had just finished their debriefing with the inevitable overlap of more than one man claiming a kill, and were lounging in chairs in front of Dispersal drinking coffee and discussing the morning's adventure, principally as regards the three missing pilots. Their machines were lined up on the apron, the petrol bowsers just pulling away. John went towards the group of mechanics. 'Refuelling completed?'

'Yes, sir.'

'Very good.' He turned to face his pilots, who were watching him a trifle anxiously. 'Scramble!' he shouted.

They stared at him.

'Now!' he snapped. 'Follow me, line ahead.'

He was still carrying his helmet and life jacket. These he put on, climbed into the cockpit, fastened his parachute and belts. His engine was still warm, and kicked immediately. He swung on to the runway and gunned the engine. Airborne, he looked over his shoulder, watched his men taking off. He waited for the last one, checked his watch, allowed them to form line behind him, led them in a circuit, and then said,

'Land.' He taxied to a halt, got out, waited for them. 'All right, gentlemen, sit down and relax.'

They exchanged mystified glances, took off their gear, and slowly returned to their seats. John stood in front of them. 'That took two minutes and forty seconds – to get airborne, I mean. That is forty seconds too long. So . . . Scramble!'

This time the response was quicker, out of the chairs at least, and they were up in two minutes thirty.

'Whew!' Newman said when they got down. 'My head is spinning.'

'I've been thinking,' John said. 'Putting on your life jackets is taking a good five seconds. As of now, every pilot on stand-by will wear his life jacket all the time. Understood?'

They nodded.

'So fetch them.'

They trailed out to the planes and returned with their jackets.

'Very good,' John said. 'Now put them on, sit down, and relax.'

'Don't tell me we have to do it again, now?' Rigg asked.

'Why, yes. You're going to do it again, now, and then again, and then for the rest of the day, if need be.'

'What do we have to do?'

'Be airborne in under two minutes.' John said. 'So . . . Scramble!'

By four o'clock they had scrambled a dozen times and were down to just over two minutes. Even John was exhausted, and he was quite relieved when Hawkins, who had been watching from the office window, and had also been timing them, joined him on the tarmac.

'That was quite something, John,' the WingCo said. 'But I think you should call it a day. I'm sure you'll get it down to under two tomorrow, and the lads are pretty well played out. If you keep them at it much longer there could be an accident.'

'Yes, sir.'

'So, give them the evening off. And take it off yourself.'

'Yes, sir. Thank you.'

He dismissed his much-relieved squadron and headed for the telephone.

'Private Pope?' the woman asked. 'Who is speaking, please?'

'John Bayley. I'm her fiancé.'

'Ah. Would you hold the line, please, Mr Bayley.'

John waited for a good ten minutes, listening to various background noises at the other end of the line. But at last the woman returned. 'I am sorry, Squadron-Leader, but I'm afraid Private Pope is not available right now.'

'I see. May I ask how, in the past few minutes, you have learned I am a squadron-leader?'

'Ah. Well . . .'

'Listen, I quite understand that Avril is upset because I stood her up today. But she's been in the army long enough to know that these things happen. The squadron was reassigned yesterday and I was unable to call her until now. Will you tell her that, please, and tell her that I really would like to speak with her. I'll hold.'

'Yes, sir,' the woman said doubtfully.

Again John waited.

'I'm sorry, sir,' the woman said. 'But . . .'

'I'd like her exact words, please.'

The woman drew a deep breath. 'She said . . . that she did not wish to speak to you ever again.'

'Oh, for God's sake,' John said.

'She is very upset, sir,' the woman attempted to explain. 'You see, she asked for, and obtained, leave for yesterday. The entire barracks was buzzing. Now she feels not only let down but humiliated. I'm sure she'll get over it.'

'Yes. Well, if she does, tell her to be in touch.'

'Ah . . . get in touch where, sir?'

'You know I can't tell you that, Private.'

'I am a sergeant, sir.'

'I apologize. But I can't even tell a sergeant that. She can write to me care of my father's house – she has the address – and the letter will get to me pretty quickly. Thank you for trying to help.'

He knew he was being a little hard, but at that moment he was not only tired but despondent over the day's events. Certainly he was not in the mood to put up with female tantrums, his mood exacerbated by the sheer desire for her. He should have been holding her in his arms. Instead he telephoned Air-Sea Rescue.

'Pilot Officer Blythe, and Flying Officer Richards,' the operator said. 'Yes, sir, we picked them both up . . .'

66

'Thank God for that,' John said. But he had caught the hesitation in the man's voice. 'But?'

'Well, sir, they're both in hospital. Flying Officer Richards is rather badly wounded. I don't believe it's life threatening, but I understand he may be out of action for some time.'

'I see. And Pilot Officer Blythe?'

'It took us some time to find him. He was suffering severely from exposure, and also from smoke inhalation due to his aircraft being on fire before he managed to bale out. The medics are concerned about possible lung damage.'

'Shit!' John muttered. 'Thank you.'

He hung up, gazed at the wall. He didn't know about the Defiant crews that had gone in, but it did look very much as if Jerry had indeed got nine pilots and six gunners for three of his own – quite apart from the personal catastrophes to both Blythe and Richards.

Newman was waiting for him. 'You don't look too happy.'

'They managed to recover both Blythe and Richards.'

'Well, isn't that great news?'

'We're not likely to see either of them again for a while.'

'Shit! Well . . . we're off to the pub. We'd really like you to come along.'

'I think I'd rather do my own thing tonight, Bobby. But thanks all the same. I appreciate it.'

Newman hesitated, then nodded and went to join the others.

John mounted his Harley-Davidson and took the road to Hillside, which actually wasn't all that far from the airfield. He supposed this was hypocritical of him; he resented so much about the house, about the money that had created it and maintained it, and yet he always turned back to it as the ultimate place of refuge.

He arrived just after seven, noting that the Rolls was missing from the garage, which indicated that Dad at least was not at home. But there was a car, an Austin Seven, parked before the front steps, and also a woman's bicycle leaning against the wall just beyond it.

Rufus came bounding up to greet him with his usual enthusiasm. He fondled the dog for a few moments, and then went up the steps.

'Mr John!' Clements opened the front door.

'Hello, Clements. Aunt Joan entertaining?'

'Well, sir. Mr Carling is here . . .' He paused, as if expecting John to know the name, and also that Mr Carling was a regular visitor.

'You've lost me, old son. Will I be interrupting anything if I go in?'

'Oh, no, sir. I shouldn't think so. Miss Hargreaves is with them.'

'The fog is growing thicker. Would Miss Hargreaves be anything to do with Air-Commodore Hargreaves?'

'His daughter Jolinda, sir.'

'Ah.' The name was vaguely familiar but, although the Hargreaves and Mark and Joan had exchanged dinner parties from time to time, that had been quite a few years ago before the Hargreaves had split up. Their children had never been involved. John also knew that it was Hargreaves who, having been approached by Dad, had had him transferred to Spitfires when he had recovered from the wounds he had suffered on 12th May. It had also been Hargreaves, as overall commander of the training squadrons that had included his own, who had chosen him to lead the newly formed combat squadron into action during the desperate days over Dunkirk, and had effectively relaunched his career. For which reason he was one of John's favourite people. But he could not recall meeting a daughter.

He straightened his tie, went into the drawing room and heard voices from the study beyond. 'Anyone home?' he called.

'John!' Joan came to the door to greet him and kiss him. 'I wasn't expecting you.'

'I have the night off, so I thought I'd see how the other half live.'

'Splendid.' She held his arm and escorted him into the room. 'You haven't met Jim Carling.'

Carling was on his feet. 'The hero,' he commented. 'I've been looking forward to meeting you, Squadron-Leader.'

John did not much care for the over-effusive greeting, but he shook hands.

'Jimmy and I are, well, engaged,' Joan explained, flushing, and added, 'Your father knows about it.'

It was Carling's turn to look slightly put out, but John

reckoned he must know that nothing happened in the Bayley household without the knowledge and consent of Mark.

'And Jolinda, of course, you know,' Joan said.

John turned to the young woman. She was tall and slender, with shoulder-length yellow hair. He thought he might be looking at a picture of his aunt, perhaps twenty years ago, except for the exquisite delicacy of the features, which clearly indicated that she was Hargreaves' daughter.

'You don't remember me,' she said. Her voice was low and husky, a delightful match to her face, and the gentle American accent seemed to enhance it. 'We used to play together as kids.'

'And I've forgotten that? I need my head examined.'

'Well!' Joan said. 'Then, Jolinda Hargreaves, I'd like you to meet my nephew, John. Again.'

'Hi,' Jolinda said, shaking hands. 'I've been hearing a lot about you recently.'

John was still trying to get his mind under control. He had only ever felt like this on first meeting one woman before in his life – and he was supposed to be in love with that woman. Engaged to her. Or was he? He shot his aunt a glance.

'From Dad,' Jolinda added. 'He seems to think you're going places.'

Relief flooded John's mind. 'I can't imagine how we've missed each other all these years.'

'That's because I live in the States,' Jolinda explained. 'I went over there with Mom, when she and Dad fell out.'

'I suspect John has forgotten about that, too,' Joan remarked. 'John, I can see that your tongue is hanging out. And I think we could all do with a freshener as well.'

'Right.' John went to the sideboard.

'I'll pass,' Jolinda said. 'I'd like to be home before dark.'

'If you stayed a bit longer,' John said, 'I could run you home on my bike. It's a Harley-Davidson,' he added winningly, remembering the effect that announcement had had on Avril and her ATS friends at their first meeting, two years ago.

But Jolinda had obviously never heard of the famous model. 'And what would I do with my bike?'

'Well . . .' John looked at his aunt, who was regarding him with a quizzical expression. 'I'm sure Beerman would run it over in the boot of the Rolls, when Dad gets home.'

'Sorry,' Jolinda said, the decisive quality of her tone leaving absolutely no possible chance that she could be persuaded otherwise. 'It's an awfully sweet idea, but I'd be lost without my bike. Thanks for everything, Joan. See you around, Mr Carling.' She looked at John.

'I'll see you out.' He avoided his aunt's gaze, escorted Jolinda into the hall. 'May I ask a personal question?'

'I guess you're going to. So shoot.'

'Well, you live in the States.'

'Right.'

'And I understand that you like to see your dad from time to time. But England isn't exactly flavour of the month as regards holiday resorts right now, is it?'

'What exactly is it you were going to ask me, Mr Bayley?'

'John, please. Our families have been friends for years.'

'OK, John. So?'

'Well . . . how long are you here for?'

'The duration, I guess.'

'Eh?'

'I have dual nationality; I'm half English. So I reckon I should do my bit. I've only been over here a couple of weeks, but Dad's organizing it so that I can become a WAAF or something. I get to wear a uniform, like you.'

'That's terrific.'

'Heck, I've just thought: I'll have to call you sir.'

'Only in public. Now may I ask you another question?'

She waited.

'Where did you get a name like Jolinda?'

'God knows. Mom dreamed it up.'

'So do I call you Jolly?'

'The last person who called me Jolly is still in hospital. I accept Joly from close friends.'

'I'll remember that.'

'When we're close friends, perhaps.' She eased herself on to her seat. 'Maybe I'll see you around. Bye.'

He watched her pedal off, hair and skirt fluttering. Oh, yes, he thought. You are going to see me around.

'You really going to marry that character?' John asked, when Joan returned inside after seeing Carling off; he had stayed to dinner.

'That is my intention, yes,' Joan said, peering into the mirror over the fireplace. She was somewhat breathless, and her lipstick was smudged.

'And Dad is happy with that?'

She turned to face him. 'He is, yes. It really isn't any business of yours, you know, Johnnie. Although I hope you'll come to the wedding. But you can tell me why you don't like him.'

John considered. As far as he was concerned, the list was endless. But he decided it would be safest to keep it simple. 'Shouldn't he be in uniform? He can't be that old.'

'Well, presumably you and I have different interpretations of the meaning of the word old. Jimmy is a year younger than I.'

'Oh, Aunt Joan, I did not mean . . .'

'Of course you did not. Port?'

'Thank you. And then I'm for bed. It's been a very long day.'

Joan went to the sideboard, poured. 'Jimmy is in a reserved occupation. I'm not going to tell you what it is.' She gave him his glass, sipped from her own. 'And before you rush off, I think you owe me an explanation. Or at least tell me something of your plans.'

'To shoot down as many Germans as I can before they shoot me down.'

'I was, as I am sure you know, referring to the fact that, like me, you are engaged to be married.'

'Ah. Well . . . Avril and I were never actually engaged, you know.'

'"Were", not "are",' she mused. 'You've broken it off?'

He shrugged. 'It's a point of view. Avril doesn't seem to realize that there's a war on.'

'When did this happen?'

'This afternoon.'

'And an hour later you are making advances to Jolinda Hargreaves. You really are the limit.'

'She doesn't know about Avril, does she?'

'As I didn't know you were coming here this evening, your name was never mentioned until you turned up.'

'Thank God for that. Now tell me straight, Aunt Joan. Wouldn't you and Dad breathe an almighty sigh of relief if I were to marry someone like Jolinda Hargreaves instead of committing incest?'

'Well . . . perhaps we would. But Avril . . .'

'Knows nothing about that, remember? No one knows anything about it, except you, me and Dad. From Avril's point of view, I'm someone with whom she's had an affair, and with whom marriage was discussed. Now it appears it's not on. It's more her decision than mine.'

'But you've slept with her.'

'She wasn't a virgin. And anyway, haven't you slept with your Jimmy?'

'Certainly not. He's my fiancé, not my husband yet.'

'Well, I suppose one grows wiser, or maybe more patient, as one grows older. Now I really must be off. I can hardly stay on my feet. If you'd like the truth, Aunt Joan, I took off after that girl because I have an excess of adrenaline rushing about.'

Instantly she was solicitous. 'Combat?'

'I killed two men this morning, before breakfast. And watched several others die.'

'Oh, Johnnie!' She was in his arms, hugging him tightly. 'How puerile you must think me. Think us all.'

'Without people like you, Aunt Joan, to remind us what real life is about, we'd become monsters.' He kissed her and went to the door, looked over his shoulder. 'But I would like to see Jolinda again, some time.'

'Come in, Herr Captain,' Colonel Hartmann invited.

Max entered the room, saluted. 'Heil Hitler!'

'Heil! Have a seat and tell me what is bothering you.' He looked at the notes on his desk. 'I would say you have had a successful fortnight.'

'It has not been quite as good as it reads, Herr Colonel.'

'Indeed? The figures have been confirmed. You should be proud of them. Your squadron has shot down twelve enemy aircraft in the past two weeks, and you personally have accounted for four. That makes your total sixteen kills. That is magnificent. The entire record is good. But for that unfortunate fellow Hassinger . . .'

'Hassinger is symptomatic of the problem, sir.'

'Oh, come now, Max. You cannot possibly feel responsible

72

for that. His people were inexperienced, and it was bad luck to run into a squadron of Spitfires.'

'We should have been there to assist them.'

'But you were running low on fuel.'

'Yes, sir. That is the point. The same thing happened yesterday. We had been patrolling the Channel for no more than fifteen minutes, and saw a flight of Hurricanes doing the same. I was about to give the order for an attack when I realized that my fuel was dangerously low, and so we aborted. The Hurricanes gave chase but, thanks to our superior speed, we were able to get away. If a squadron of Spitfires had turned up at that moment, we could have been annihilated. And if we ever have to escort our bombers over the English mainland, even the south-eastern corner, well, we will have to turn back the moment we cross the cliffs of Dover. Or commit suicide.'

'You are taking this too seriously, Max. In the first place, the 109E was never designed for long-range bomber protection. Your planes are interceptors. Your business is to shoot down *enemy* bombers – and fighters too. That you are being used at this time as escorts is merely to give your pilots experience in actual combat. The task of escorting our bombers is the business of our 110s, with their long-range tanks.'

'With respect, sir, I do not believe a 110 can engage a Spitfire with any hope of success. It is simply too slow.'

'But it is far better armed.'

'It is speed that matters in the air. The faster plane, armed with a pea-shooter, will defeat the slower, armed with a howitzer.'

Hartmann stared at him for several seconds. Then he said, 'You need a rest, Captain. And as it happens, I have an order here for you to go to Berlin.'

'I cannot leave the squadron, sir. We are fighting a war.'

'Not very decisively, at this moment. The squadron can spare you for three days. You are to receive your medal, from the Fuehrer himself. Go and be feted, and have a good time. You will return to us refreshed. That is an order, Captain Bayley.'

'Captain Bayley!' said the under-manager at the Albert. 'This is an honour.'

'Thank you, Gottfried. Have you a room for me?'

'Of course, sir.' He snapped his fingers and a bellboy picked up Max's bag while Gottfried led the way up the stairs.

'Would anyone I know happen to be in residence at the moment?' Max asked.

'I'm afraid not, sir.' Gottfried opened the door and drew the drapes over the windows. 'But . . . ah . . .' He gazed at Max.

'I'll let you know. Just reserve me a table for dinner.' Max tipped both men, and the door was closed. He took off his boots and jacket and stretched out on the bed, so much softer than his cot at Ostend. It was, of course, absurd to suppose that he could again run into Erika: the last time had been the most utter coincidence. But while he refused even to think of women when on duty, to him a holiday had always meant sex – with Erika. Much of his bitterness at her marriage had been the certainty that he would never share her bed again. But then had come that stupendous week . . . Was it only three weeks ago?

So what now – one of Gottfried's women? But again, thanks to Erika, he had never actually paid for sex in his life. So then . . . He frowned as he started to remember, then swung his legs off the bed and picked up his tunic. The slip of paper was still there; he had not thought to feel in his pockets before. He sat at the table and gave the number to the switchboard girl.

'Yes?' asked the female voice.

'Would it be possible to speak with Fraulein Heidi Stumpff?'

There was a moment's hesitation while he had a fleeting panic that she might actually be a Frau. There had been no evidence of a wedding band, but as she was a friend of Erika's she might well regard adultery as an irrelevance. Then the voice said, 'I am she. And you are Captain Bayley! I would have recognized your voice anywhere.'

He couldn't be certain whether she was pleased to hear from him or not. 'You asked me to call you when next I was in Berlin.'

'And you are coming to Berlin soon?'

'I am here now. I am at the Albert. I would like you to have dinner with me.'

'When?'

'Well, tonight.'

74

'Oh! I cannot tonight.'

Shit!

'I could tomorrow,' she said.

One night, instead of the two he had been hoping for. But perhaps . . . 'Yes. Yes, I would like that.'

'So would I.'

Just twenty-four hours away. He had a bath and went downstairs. 'A word, Gottfried,' he said at reception.

'The Cross suits you,' Milch said, as the several newly decorated officers and their superiors milled about and drank champagne following the investiture.

'Thank you, Herr Field-Marshal.'

'What exactly did the Fuehrer say to you? He seemed to hold your hand for longer than usual.'

'He actually said very little, sir, with his voice. He said, "Congratulations, Captain Bayley. I am sure this is but the first of many." But with his eyes . . . he stared at me, as if trying to convey a message to my brain. It was hypnotic.'

Milch nodded. 'He knows your background, of course.'

'*My* background, sir? We did meet once, two years ago, but he cannot possibly have remembered me.'

'He knows the background of every officer in the Luftwaffe, or the Wehrmacht, or the Navy, who has ever been brought to his attention. He has quite the most remarkable memory I have ever known.' The Field-Marshal gave one of his quick smiles. 'It is not always an asset, as he sometimes recalls facts or details given to him perhaps years ago, and reckons they are still valid when they may have been overtaken by new developments. However . . . When do you return to Ostend?'

'Tomorrow morning, sir.'

'I would like you to stay another day.'

'Sir?'

'There is to be a meeting of all the senior Luftwaffe officers. You are not one of those, but you are a protégé of the Reich-Marshal and I know he will be pleased to see you and have you hear what he has to say.'

Max's heart was thumping, and no longer at the prospect of another day in Berlin. 'May I speculate . . .?'

Milch smiled. 'The meeting is top secret. But I can tell you that since Great Britain has refused the Fuehrer's latest peace offer, the Fuehrer has finally lost patience and has given the go ahead for the invasion. It won't be as easy as it should have been; we have allowed them a month to improve their defences. However, Captain Bayley, we can safely say that the balloon is about to go up.'

PART TWO

Engagement

'The terrible grumble, and rumble, and roar,
Telling the battle was on once more.'

Thomas Buchanan Read

Four

The Ace

Back in the privacy of his bedroom at the Albert, Max could allow the mixture of excitement and apprehension to flood in. He desperately felt like getting drunk, but did not wish to blur a moment of Heidi's visit. But that visit was totally insignificant compared with what he had just been told.

He did not believe he was afraid. He had never been afraid in the air, had always believed himself to be a superior pilot to anyone he was likely to meet – even his own brother. But the thought of coming down in England and being captured, and then tried for treason, and perhaps hanged, made his skin crawl. Just as the thought of ever having to face his father again was a recurring nightmare.

Six o'clock. He bathed and dressed, went down to the bar, ordered champagne, and caught a whiff of a familiar scent. He turned, looked at her, and seemed to be seeing her for the first time. Because on the previous occasion, however often she had lain naked in his arms, she had been an appendage of Erika. Tonight she stood alone, and he realized that she was actually the more lovely of the two women, with her soft yellow hair floating past her shoulders, her crisply handsome features, her slender, long-legged body so entrancingly crowned by the surprisingly large bust, so perfectly delineated by the décolletage of her pale-blue evening gown.

'It is me,' she said.

'Oh, please forgive me. I had forgotten how beautiful you are.'

She raised her eyebrows. 'You forgot what I looked like, in three weeks? But that was a very nice thing to say.'

'Drink?'

79

'If it's from that bottle, yes, please.' She sipped appreciatively. 'I had not expected to see you again so soon.'

'But you remembered what I look like.'

'Oh, yes. I remember every part of you. Or do you not like direct women?'

'I like you,' he said. 'Shall we dine?'

They ordered.

'And have you come all the way to Berlin just to see me?' she asked.

'I'm sorry, but the answer is no. I came to collect this.' He touched his Cross.

'Oh, good lord!' she said. 'And I never noticed. The fact is, almost every officer in town nowadays has one of those . . .' She paused, her mouth making an O. 'I have done it again. Would you like to beat me?'

'I find that a most attractive idea. But it can keep until after dinner.' He tasted the wine, nodded.

'Actually,' she said, 'I suspect the reason so many officers in Berlin sport Iron Crosses is that the men who do not have them are doing the actual fighting. Except that we are not doing any fighting right now, are we? There is no one left to fight.'

'There is still the English.'

'Ah, yes. The English. But they are hiding behind their water wall.'

'They come out from time to time.' He suddenly felt an intense dislike for this gorgeous creature, who knew so little about anything beyond the narrow limits of her sexual morality. 'But I did not invite you here to discuss the war. I would like you to spend the night.'

'Just like that?'

'Isn't that what you do? Or do you only do it with your girlfriends, and any company they may happen to accumulate?'

She gazed at him for several seconds. 'In normal circumstances, I would slap your face and throw this glass of wine into it. But I think that in the mood you are in, you might hit me back, and I do not wish there to be a scene. Why do you not tell me why you are in this mood? You should be on top of the world. You have just been decorated – was it by the Fuehrer himself?'

'Yes.'

'Well, then, you have been honoured above most men. I assume he shook your hand?'

'Yes. Have you ever met him?'

'Sadly, no.'

'Well, maybe the whole thing made me too introspective. I apologize for what I said just now.'

She shrugged, delightfully, and finished her meal. 'I understand your mood. Erika has often spoken of you.'

He frowned. 'Regarding what?'

'Regarding everything.'

'Shit! I beg your pardon. But she really is a . . . well . . .'

'What you just said.'

'It's her I ought to beat.'

Heidi drank the last of her wine. 'But I am the one who is here.'

By the time he had locked the bedroom door she had already stepped out of her gown. She wore only knickers underneath, and these she discarded immediately, while he merely gazed at her; he had also forgotten how exciting she was.

'How would you like me?' she asked.

'I wasn't serious, you know. I mean about beating you.'

'You do not enjoy beating women?'

'I have never hit a woman in my life.'

'Good lord! You will probably find that you enjoy it.'

'You mean you actually wish me to beat you?'

'I think it would do you good. There are rules. You must not touch my face, and you must leave no permanent marks on my flesh. It would be best for you to spank me. I think you would find that most stimulating.'

'And you think I need stimulating?'

'It would stimulate me, as well,' she explained.

'Gentlemen,' Reich-Marshal Goering said. 'Be seated.'

His gaze drifted over the twenty-odd men in front of him as they took their places. With one exception they were all at least colonels. All much decorated men and, in some cases, famous men. But Max wondered if any of them had ever had a night such as he had enjoyed – had indeed continued to enjoy well into this morning. And she would be there, waiting

81

for him, when he returned from this meeting! All of that pink and white flesh, growing pinker and whiter with each slap of his hand, while her glorious buttocks had seemed to move separately as she had wriggled and given little whimpers.

But when he had stopped, for fear of really hurting her, she had risen from his lap and given a deliciously wicked, throaty gurgle of laughter. 'Now,' she had said, 'let's have fun.'

She had utterly debauched him, removed the very last vestiges of the moral upbringing he had received from his mother and father. Of course, Erika had begun the process two years ago, and equally it was possible to say that that kind of Christian morality had no place in a war, when his business was to kill, quickly, efficiently, and as often as possible. But would it have any place in a country ruled by Nazi Germany, to which he had now devoted his life, even when the war was over?

Max had carefully remained at the very back of the room, but the Reich-Marshal's eye picked him out and he felt a pang of apprehension, although Milch was also present, but Goering merely gave a brief nod and completed his survey of the room.

'I am sure you will all be pleased to learn that, as the British have again refused to accept the Fuehrer's peace terms, it has been decided that they will have to be forced to surrender. This of course means that the islands will have to be occupied. I can tell you this process has already begun; as a first step what might be called the fringes of England – the Channel Islands of Jersey, Guernsey, Sark and Alderney – are now part of the Reich. However, the real business is now to begin. The code name is Operation Sea Lion.

'Now, gentlemen, no one should suppose that this is going to be a simple campaign, as it was in Poland, or even in France. It is not just a matter of crossing a few rivers, of launching pincer movements to encircle the enemy. This is going to have to be a frontal assault on a bold and determined foe protected by a very wide and dangerous stretch of water. And the task, once commenced, must be completed by the onset of winter. It must again be blitzkrieg, on a bigger scale than ever before.

'Now, there can be no doubt that once we put a few divisions of the Wehrmacht ashore, the battle is as good as won.

The British Army has not yet recovered, either in men, morale or weaponry, from the catastrophe of Dunkirk. The problem we have to overcome is in getting our men ashore. The Royal Navy is still a powerful force, and we do not yet have the ships to defeat it. That task is ours in the Luftwaffe.'

He looked round at their faces. 'I have no doubt that we can do this. But the Royal Navy will be protected by the RAF, operating virtually in its home waters. Our first task, therefore, is the elimination of the RAF as a viable fighting force. This will be accomplished in two ways. The first is to draw it into continuous battle against superior numbers. A war of attrition, if you like, which we must win, because we have those superior numbers. The second way is equally important. It is to deprive the RAF of its bases – and the Navy also. This is the task of our bombers. They will strike at selected ports along the south and east coasts of England, and at the RAF aerodromes in those areas as well. The elimination of their airfields will force them to withdraw further into the country to refuel and rearm, and thus be less able to get at our bombers.

'However, make no mistake, they will attack our bombers. But that is all part of our plan, as that means they will have to engage our fighter escorts, our 110s and 109s.'

There was a rustle of unease. Goering spread his hands and beamed at them. 'I know there have been questions asked about both these machines as escorts rather than interceptors. It has been suggested that the 110 is not good enough. Gentlemen, that is rubbish, completely negated by our experiences during the battles in France, when the 110 was every bit as effective as the 109.'

'Against Hurricanes, not Spitfires,' someone said.

Goering looked at him, but the scowl was quickly replaced by another beaming smile. 'What is the difference? A few miles an hour? A slightly quicker turn? The Hurricane is actually more difficult to shoot down because of its fabric body; too many bullets go straight through it without damaging anything vital, whereas the Spitfire's metal fuselage is ripped apart by any hit. I cannot accept that it is an inferior machine. As for the 109s, there can be no argument that it is a match for any aircraft in the world. However, it is the concern of its pilots that it lacks the range to carry out sustained operations at any distance from its base, and certainly over Britain.' His gaze drifted round the room and came to rest on Max.

'I can tell you that problem has been addressed and has been solved. The solution was perfectly simple. An extra fuel tank has been devised that will be fitted to each aircraft. This tank is detachable at the flick of a switch, and can be jettisoned as required and replaced upon return to base. This will double the range of each aircraft, permitting it to remain over southern England for up to half an hour longer than is at present possible. Will that satisfy you, Captain Bayley?'

Heads turned to look at Max, who, taken by surprise at the direct question, took a moment to collect his thoughts. Then he said, 'Yes, Herr Reich-Marshal, it will.'

'Excellent. Well, gentlemen, you have it. I will just confirm your dispositions and your battle plan. Air Fleet Three, operating from Normandy, will attack the south and west of England. Its area includes important targets such as the Solent and the naval bases of Portsmouth, Portland and Plymouth, but in the context of the overall battle, its prime duty is to lure the RAF interceptors to that area and destroy as many of them as possible. Air Fleet Five will operate from Norway, and attack Scotland and the north-east. Again, while there are targets up there, such as the naval base of Rosyth in the Firth of Forth, its principal purpose will be to force the RAF to maintain an adequate force of interceptors in that area, thus weakening its resources in the south.'

He gave another of his beams as he picked out the relevant faces. 'To Air Fleet Two, operating out of Belgium, Holland and north-western France, falls the prize of south-east England. This contains the vital airfields that the RAF needs to maintain its fighters in the air, but also important ports such as Dover and Newhaven, and on the east coast such as Harwich and Great Yarmouth. Air Fleet Two has at its disposal one thousand, one hundred and thirty-one bombers, of which seven hundred and sixty-nine are always available. It has three hundred and sixteen dive-bombers, of which two hundred and forty-eight are in constant service. It has eight hundred and nine 109s, with six hundred and fifty-six always available. It has two hundred and forty-six 110s, with one hundred and sixty-eight always ready for action. It also has sixty-seven long-range reconnaissance machines. The capacity, gentlemen, in this single air fleet, is far greater than that available to the entire RAF.

'Now, the battle will be carried out in three stages. The first will be that war of attrition I mentioned, but will also be a gigantic reconnaissance in force. The targets I have listed will be attacked from Day One, but initially your main effort will be against Dover and the Channel traffic. We have observed that the RAF come out in force to defend their convoys. We must hope they continue to do so, because that gives us the greater opportunity to shoot them down. A big early victory here will be bad for their morale, and good for ours, eh? I have allowed a fortnight for this stage. Stage Two, when they have been suitably softened up, will be the attack on their airfields. This will take us into August. Stage Three, when we will have gained total air superiority, will be the strategic pounding of their military units and defensive capability on the ground, and also, of course, the systematic destruction of the Royal Navy. Once those three stages have been completed, which will be before the end of August, we may leave the rest to the Wehrmacht. Now, are there any questions?'

One of the colonels stood up. 'Herr Reich-Marshal, you have said that Air Fleet Two is to attack the south-east corner of England, and also East Anglia. But you have made no mention of London, which lies between these two areas.'

'I have not mentioned London, because London is not a target.'

'Is it not the capital of England? Of the British Empire?'

'Yes, it is. But it is not the Fuehrer's intention to destroy England, or the British Empire. He merely wishes them to admit defeat and cease opposing us. Due to the insane stubbornness of this man Churchill, it appears that we will have to occupy the country to force them to accept the reality of the situation, but it is certainly not our intention to destroy the infrastructure of the country, and London is the very heart of that.'

'We must hope that the RAF feel the same way about Berlin,' someone else muttered.

85

'Berlin?' Goering gave a shout of laughter. 'Do you seriously think any RAF bomber could ever even reach Berlin? I will tell you this, gentlemen: if a single bomb is ever dropped on this city, you may call me "*meier*".'

There was a ripple of amusement; '*meier*' was a slang word meaning dimwit.

'So, now, gentlemen,' the Reich-Marshal said, 'it but remains to name the day. It is to be a week today: Wednesday, 10th July. I wish you good hunting.'

Field-Marshal Milch caught up with Max in the lobby. 'How do you feel?'

'Exhilarated, sir. And you must be very pleased.'

'I am not as pleased as if we had been given the go-ahead a month ago. But better late than never, eh? Tell me, are your doubts resolved?'

'Certainly, sir. If these extra tanks work.'

Milch nodded. 'They do. I have seen the tests. And you must take some of the credit. If you had not raised the matter, I would not have put the experiments in hand.'

'Thank you, sir.'

'Well, enjoy the rest of your leave. I will be in Ostend before the campaign commences, and will see you then. When do you return?'

'I was due to leave tomorrow morning. But . . . do these reserve tanks take a lot of fitting?'

'Good lord, no. They can be fitted in half an hour. That is the beauty of the idea. You can be totally refitted between sorties.'

'Yes, sir. May I ask you a question?'

'Certainly.'

'Does the name Stumpff mean anything to you?'

'I know several people named Stumpff. To which are you referring?'

'I don't know, sir. But the one I have in mind has an extremely attractive daughter.'

'Ah. I would say you are referring to Helmuth Stumpff.'

'Is he a friend of yours, sir?'

'A friend? We meet socially from time to time. He is an industrialist, and a fervent supporter of the Party. May I assume that you have met the beautiful Heidi?'

She is lying, probably naked, in my bed at this moment, Max thought. 'Yes, sir,' he said. 'I was hoping to see her tomorrow, if I may have another day's leave.'

'Aha,' Milch said. 'You have more than just met her, I suspect. So you know of her?'

'Sir?'

Milch regarded him for some moments. 'It would be incorrect of me to discuss a lady's morals, Herr Captain. But it may be of interest to you to know that not everyone approves of Heidi's lifestyle. She is what you might call a free spirit. It is a case of too much money, and too much time in which to spend it. But there it is. She is Helmuth's only daughter and he can refuse her nothing.'

Max drew a deep breath. 'I was going to ask your permission to marry her, sir.'

For a moment Milch looked as dumbfounded as when Goering had trashed his plan for an immediate invasion of England. 'In that case, my dear boy, I owe you an unreserved apology. You mean that she has agreed to this?'

'Well, no, sir. I haven't yet proposed. But I would like to do so today.'

'You said you were seeing her tomorrow.'

'I am also seeing her today, sir. But I thought that if I could have tomorrow off as well, we could obtain a special licence and get married before I return to Ostend.'

'Ah, the romantic impulses of youth,' Milch remarked, somewhat ruefully. 'You are assuming that she will say yes.'

'I believe she will, sir.'

'Have you spoken with her father?'

'I did not know who he was, until you told me.'

'You appear to have had a rather peripheral relationship with this young woman. You will have to speak with Helmuth, but I imagine he will be happy to see his daughter married to one of our leading air aces, and marriage to you may make her more responsible. You do not mind me speaking like this?'

'I appreciate it, sir.'

Milch nodded. 'Then there is something you must promise me you will do, before you even propose. I do not wish you to give away any military secrets, but you must convey to Heidi that you are about to embark on a campaign which may well involve your death. You are aware of this?'

'Yes, sir.'

'Well, I am not suggesting for a moment that this know-ledge has influenced your wish to get married so suddenly, as you seem to have already formed the idea, but I think it would be highly improper for you to proceed without telling your intended wife the facts. You will only have the briefest time together before you return to duty, after which she may never see you again.'

'I will do that, sir.'

'Very good. Then you may have an extra two days off. I will inform the field-commandant. Report for duty on Saturday.' He held out his hand. 'Good luck.'

Heidi was up and dressed. 'I am starving,' she announced. 'Where are we lunching?'

'I thought we'd use room service.'

'Oh! If you're short, I . . .'

'I know. But I want to talk to you.'

'Shit!' She sat on the bed. 'Something has happened.'

He sat beside her. 'Yes. I want to marry you.'

She stared at him for several seconds. Then she said, 'If we are not going out, we should order. I really am hungry.'

'In a moment. Didn't you hear what I said? Listen, I have an extra two days' leave. We can go and see your father this afternoon, get a special licence and be married tomorrow morning, and honeymoon tomorrow and Friday.'

She continued to stare at him. 'You really are serious.'

'I am. And we have the blessing of Field-Marshal Milch.'

'You told Milch you wanted to marry me? What did he say?'

'I just told you. He gave us his blessing.'

'He said nothing else?'

'Well . . . he muttered something about not everyone approving of your lifestyle . . . But then he said that marriage to one of Germany's leading air aces would probably change that lifestyle.'

She got up, moved restlessly around the room. 'Are you really an ace?'

'The Field-Marshal seems to think so.'

'So you must go on leading the fight until you are shot down.'

'I haven't been shot down yet.'

'Um. *Do* you think we could order lunch?'

'I'm sorry. I have been very selfish.' He picked up the phone. 'Shall I include a bottle of champagne?'

'Yes,' she said. 'I think that would be rather nice.'

Heidi placed her left hand flat on the counter of the somewhat crowded bar at which they were seated. 'I know it's not much, but there was not a lot of time, and, well, I couldn't offer to buy my own wedding ring. He's not that well off.'

'I know he's not well off,' Erika said. 'He has only his salary. But a wedding band is a wedding band. What I can't understand is how it happened. And *why* it happened, before you had informed me. I would have come to the ceremony.'

'I couldn't inform you,' Heidi explained. 'Because there was no time. Max had to rejoin his squadron. As for why . . . that's the main part of it, I suppose. He goes to war next week, and he's convinced he's going to die.'

'Oh, really? Who is he going to war with? There is no war at the moment. We have won.'

'There is still England.'

Erika blew a raspberry.

'It is true,' Heidi insisted. 'The Fuehrer has determined that England is to be invaded. Max told me this.'

'And the Fuehrer told Max, personally,' Erika suggested contemptuously.

'On Wednesday morning Max attended a top-level meeting of the Luftwaffe. All the brass were there. Max was included because he had just been decorated, and because he is a protégé of Field-Marshal Milch. They were all given their orders, their targets and the date: next Wednesday.'

'And Max hurried away from this meeting to your home and proposed?'

'Well, it was not actually like that.' Heidi flushed, finished her drink, and pushed the glass across the counter to be refilled by the barman. 'I was actually in his bed upstairs at the Albert, waiting for him to come back.'

'You beast!' Erika also summoned a refill.

'He invited me to dinner,' Heidi pointed out.

'And having slept with you all night he proposed marriage.

89

Did he really suppose it was a one-off for you? Mad, passionate love at first sight?'

'Well, of course he did not. We spent that week with him last month, remember?'

'Good lord, yes. I'd forgotten.'

'Actually,' Heidi said, 'I fancied him even then. He's so . . . well, I suppose innocent would be the word. There is something fascinating, don't you think, about a man who has killed God alone knows how many people – because apart from his kills in the air he has also done a lot of strafing – who can at the same time be so ignorant of the important things in life.'

'Then he must know about us,' Erika muttered thoughtfully.

'Well, of course he knows about us,' Heidi snapped. 'He spent a week in bed with us, remember? Watching, when he wasn't trying to muscle in on the action. Anyway, I found him, or the idea of him, attractive. So I gave him my telephone number and told him to call me next time he was in Berlin. I didn't expect him to follow up – well, not so soon. But he did, and . . .' She shrugged, 'Here we are.'

'You need your head examined,' Erika remarked. 'How much else does he know about you? Does he know about Heinz?'

'There is no necessity for him to know about Heinz.'

'So what are you going to do about him? Heinz?'

'I think I will have to drop him. At least for a while. I don't want any rumours getting back to Max, at least before he is killed. Isn't that an exciting thought? I will be the widow of one of Germany's leading fighter pilots. I shall be invited *everywhere*.'

'And are you also going to drop me, for a while?' Erika asked.

'I don't think that will be necessary. I would like you to come home with me now. I am in the mood for some *real* sex.'

'Snap.' Erika finished her drink.

'Excuse me.'

Both women turned their heads, sharply, to look at the man who had been sitting on Heidi's other side all evening, drinking by himself, somewhat morosely. 'I am terribly sorry,' he said. 'I really did not mean to eavesdrop. But I could not help overhearing your conversation. Well, some of it. Do I gather that one of you beautiful young ladies has just got married?'

'That's me,' Heidi said.

'And your husband has had to go rushing off to war. That is very sad. I would be honoured if you would permit me to buy you a drink.'

'Well . . .' Heidi looked at Erika.

He was quite a good-looking man, and although, unusually in Berlin in 1940, he was not in uniform, his suit was very well cut, and both his tie and his shirt were obviously silk, while he was certainly not yet forty.

'Why not,' Erika said. 'If you'll buy me one as well.'

Joan peered into the hall mirror as she adjusted her hat, and then pulled on her gloves. 'How do I look?'

'As always, superb,' Mark said, and looked at his watch. 'We'd better make a move.'

'Just a moment . . . Ah.'

Rufus was barking, and now they could hear the clip-clopping of hooves. 'Oh my God!' Mark said.

'She asked if she could come. And I said yes.'

'It's not as if she were family,' Mark grumbled.

'She's very fond—'

'Don't say it.'

'Of John, is what I was going to say. And this is his big day.'

Clements was opening the door to allow both Rufus and Helen Stanton to enter; the pony and trap waited behind them, watched by Beerman, today wearing his livery.

'Sorry I'm late,' Helen said. 'Do I look all right?'

'We'll have to do something about your hair,' Joan pointed out.

Helen was releasing her headscarf; she carried her large, floppy-brimmed hat in her hand. Now she peered into the mirror. 'I do look a sight.'

'We'll fix that.' Joan opened her handbag and took out a comb.

'You do realize that we have to be there before HM,' Mark reminded them.

'I know,' Helen said. 'It's all my fault.'

'He's just a fusspot,' Joan said, doing things with her comb. 'There we are. Now the hat.' She placed it on Helen's head and moved it a little to get exactly the right angle. 'I'll just pin it. There, you look tremendous. Doesn't she look tremendous, Mark?'

'Ah . . . Yes, she does.' Mark realized, to his surprise, that he was telling the truth. There might be perhaps a shade too much of Helen, but then he based his estimate of feminine beauty on his memory of Karolina, who many had always considered a shade too thin. Helen certainly had good legs, to go with her somewhat large bust, and when she was wearing a smart summer frock and high heels, in place of her habitual tweeds and brogues, she was an extremely attractive woman.

Clements was still holding the door. 'Do keep an eye on Willow,' Helen requested.

'And don't let her eat the roses,' Joan admonished.

The two women sat in the back, and Mark was in front beside Beerman. 'Are you excited?' Helen asked. 'But of course you have done this sort of thing before.'

'A long time ago.' Mark turned to smile.

'Were you there the first time?' Helen asked Joan.

'Yes. I was terrified out of my wits. The old king was so frighteningly gruff.'

'Was Queen Mary present?'

'She was more frightening than him.'

'You're giving me goose pimples.'

'Well, relax,' Mark recommended. 'You won't have to meet this one; I'm not actually getting a medal. I would put your foot down, Jim.'

'I do believe you are nervous, Johnnie,' Wing-Commander Hawkins remarked. 'You are sweating.'

'It's a warm day,' John said. 'But I wish Dad would get here.'

The station was *en fête*, with flags flying, the aircraft lined up in neat rows, both pilots and aircraftsmen wearing full dress uniform, and already a fair-sized crowd of spectators gathered beyond the ropes. If Jerry were to come over now, John thought, it could be a catastrophe.

'Here is the boss,' Hawkins muttered, and looked along the line of pilots. 'Squadron, attention.'

Heels clicked and shoulders were squared. Air-Commodore Hargreaves was invariably good-humoured, and looked more pleased than ever this afternoon.

'At ease,' he told his men. 'All set, Wing-Commander?'

'I hope so, sir.'

'And you, Squadron-Leader?'

'I think so, sir.' But John's attention had been caught by the WAAF private who had accompanied her father to the beginning of the parade and remained there while he went down the ranks. 'Is that Jolinda, sir?'

'Why, yes. Brilliant of you to remember her.'

'We met again the other day, sir. But she hadn't yet joined up.'

'She's dead keen. We'll make a Limey, as they say, of her yet. Ah, here's your father.' He went off to greet the Bayleys as they got out of the Rolls.

John was just happy to have them there. And Jolinda? But she was on her way to join her father. She wore her uniform as if she had done so all of her life, and moved with a military precision. He felt there was some knowledge of her that he was lacking. But now everyone's attention was taken by the arrival of the King. The band struck up the National Anthem and the crowd cheered.

There were eight officers from the various squadrons waiting to be invested. King George, wearing the full dress uniform of an air-marshal, accompanied by Hargreaves and his various equerries – but not, on this occasion, the Queen – passed slowly down their ranks, fixing the black and white diagonally striped ribbon from which hung the silver Distinguished Flying Cross to each breast in turn. He spoke a few words with each of the men. John was last in the line. There remained a single cross on the cushion, and an aide-de-camp read John's name and the citation.

'John Bayley,' the King said. 'I know your father.' He spoke with only the slightest hesitation, a legacy of the boyhood stammer he had worked so hard to overcome. Of course, John remembered, King George had served in the RAF after having been a sailor, in the tradition of his family; he had actually been present at the Battle of Jutland, and was thus no stranger to shot and shell. Now he continued, 'Is he well?'

'He is here today, sir.'

'Good heavens! I must have a word with him.'

He affixed the ribbon, stepped back, and saluted. Hargreaves called, 'Three cheers for His Majesty!'

Caps were raised and the cheers rang out. The crowd applauded loudly and the band struck up.

The parade was dismissed and the crowd mingled. John immediately set off to find Jolinda, which was not difficult as she was staying close to her father who was escorting the King to where the Bayleys were waiting.

'Mark Bayley,' King George said. 'How good to see you. And surrounded by all these magnificent machines your people have made.'

Mark shook hands as he bowed. 'There are still not enough, sir.'

'I am sure there will be.' The King's gaze drifted to Joan.

'May I present my sister, Joan, sir.'

Joan curtsied.

'Of course. The resemblance is obvious. My pleasure, Miss Bayley.' He looked at Helen, who was shaking like a leaf.

'Mrs Stanton, a friend of the family,' Mark explained.

Helen endeavoured to curtsey and overbalanced, but Joan seized her arm to keep her from falling. The King kindly decided not to notice. 'A pleasure, Mrs Stanton.' He glanced at Hargreaves, who immediately indicated someone else he wished the monarch to meet.

'Whew!' Helen gasped. 'I feel such a chump. You said,' she accused Mark, 'that I wouldn't have to meet him.'

'But aren't you glad you did?'

'Here's Jim,' Joan announced.

Carling was panting. 'I got held up. Have I missed it?'

'By a mile,' Mark said.

'Ah, well, you can't win 'em all. But I must congratulate John.'

'I'll help you find him,' Joan offered. 'And then . . .'

'I have the rest of the afternoon off,' Carling said.

'Oh, right. You'll take Helen back, Mark?'

I suppose I'll have to, Mark thought. But he smiled and said, 'Of course, I shall be delighted.'

'So now you're one of us,' John said.

'Well, I told you I was going to join up,' Jolinda reminded him. 'And having an air-commodore for a father made it very easy.'

'You know, I can get the rest of the afternoon off as well.'

'To do what?' she asked.

'Well, we could go for a ride on my bike.'

'In this uniform? And I'm a private while you're a big wheel. I'd be run in.'

'Big wheels carry clout as well as air-commodores, you know.'

'But all your pals are waiting over there to buy you a drink. I think you should spend the afternoon with them. So, if you'll excuse me, sir . . .' She saluted and walked away, leaving him trying to decide whether he found her more attractive from the back or the front.

'How did it go?' Joan asked as she poured coffee the next morning.

'I think I am growing on him,' Helen said.

'Well of course you are. Did he . . . er . . .?'

'He never even touched my hand. We sat at opposite ends of the seat all the way home. But he did ask me in for a cup of tea.'

'Which I trust you accepted.'

'Yes, I did. But the conversation was absolutely formal.'

'You must understand that he's terribly shy.'

'Your brother? Shy?'

'About . . . well, it's his leg. He doesn't even like me to see it.'

'Is it that bad?'

'It's sort of . . . withered. That German bullet, although it missed the important arteries, cut through all the nerves, and, well, in those days they didn't know what to do about it. Their solution was to take the leg. When he refused they sort of shrugged and let him get on with it. If it hadn't been for Karo, I doubt he would have survived.'

'So *she* saw it.'

'Well of course she did. She never saw him without a gammy leg.'

'And he thinks I would be repelled by it?'

'You'll have to convince him that you wouldn't. He's still a young man, you know. He will want sex, when he marries again. *If* he marries again.'

'You're going a bit fast,' Helen said.

'But you'd be prepared to accept that?'

Helen considered, very briefly. 'He's a very attractive man. If you really think . . .'

'I'm thinking of what would be best for both of you. When did you say your nisi would be finished?'

'Not a sausage,' John said, taking off his helmet and shaking the raindrops on to the floor. 'Mind you, it would help if we had any vis.'

Yardley, the duty officer, looked at the window, against which raindrops were pounding. 'Just a shower,' he commented.

'Maybe. But they're coming along regularly enough to make life difficult. Jerry could sneak in under that lot.'

'Just be glad you're not up north. They've had solid rain all day. Anyway, there's been nothing on radar.'

'You really believe in that thing?' John asked.

'I do. It's the secret weapon that is going to win us the war. At least in the air. Don't *you* believe in it?'

'I want to, you can believe *that*. But it has given us a few bum steers. What about that Hurricane which was sent up to investigate a single suspicious aircraft and ran into twelve 109s?'

'That was not the fault of the radar,' Yardley argued. 'It was the fault of the operator, who misinterpreted the signal. Those boys are still learning their trade.'

'Well, let's hope they get it right before Jerry decides to make a move. Sir!'

Hawkins had emerged from his office. 'Thought I heard your voice, John. What a filthy evening. Come in a minute, will you.'

John followed him into the office, paused in consternation as he gazed at Jolinda just getting up from her chair, notebook in hand.

'Private Hargreaves,' Hawkins explained. 'My new secretary.'

'I have met Squadron-Leader Bayley, sir,' Jolinda said.

'Of course, you would have. Friend of the family, eh? Well, thank you, Hargreaves. That will be all for tonight.'

'Good evening, sir. Squadron-Leader.' She left the room, closing the door behind her.

'Intelligent girl.' Hawkins sat behind his desk. 'Pretty, too. Take a pew. I suppose you knew her as a child.'

'Yes, I did, sir, but I don't really remember her all that well. I only met her again the other night.'

'Of course. She pushed off to America with her mother when her parents split up. But she's a spunky kid to come back to stand with us now.' He lit a cigarette. 'I want to ask you how the new boys are settling in.'

'They're settling in very well.'

'But? There seems to be a but. You're not happy?'

'Turnbull is a natural. He flies as if he was born in a Spitfire. The other two . . . Higgins is a good pilot, but he's too tense. Martin, well, I can't really make him out. Half the time it's difficult to tell if he's awake.'

'In the air?'

'Don't get me wrong. He *is* awake. But he seems to live in some inner world, to which the rest of us don't belong. There's never any chatter. Actually, that's a bit of a relief. Most of them talk far too much in the air. But Martin doesn't say much on the ground, either. He simply doesn't integrate. He has a drink or two in the bar, but he never buys a round or accepts one. And he never goes into town with the others. It's those couple of pints, dinner, and bed. I believe he does a lot of reading.'

'Maybe he's studying for something.'

'I don't think so. They seem to be mainly detective novels – Agatha Christie and Dorothy Sayers. You know the sort of thing.'

'He sounds as if he could prove a spot of trouble. If the other lads get the idea he's not reliable . . . Would you like him replaced?'

'Can he be replaced?'

Hawkins pulled a face. 'Only with difficulty. We still haven't got enough pilots. And the real stuff hasn't started yet.'

'Well, we're into July. Maybe Jerry isn't coming this year.

I'm quite happy to hang on to Martin. Once we have some combat he may well prove a winner.'

'Let's hope you're right. Well, see you in the morning.'

'Going home?' Hawkins asked.

'That's the idea. If I can get there without being drowned.' John stood up, saluted, and left the office.

Jolinda was still in the outer office, watching the rain.

'Barracks far?' he asked.

'Not really, sir. But I have permission to go home, most nights.'

'Because that's not far either, is it?'

'Five miles. That's far, on a push bike, in the rain.'

'I could get you there in ten minutes.'

'On your motorbike?'

'It'll be wet and windy. But quick.'

'Ahem,' Yardley interjected.

'Something on your mind?' John asked.

'There was a telephone call for you, while you were inside.'

'Oh, yes? Who from?'

'A woman. She left a number for you to call back.' He sorted through various papers on his desk. 'Here it is.'

John took the slip, looked at it, recognized the number. How the hell had she found out where to reach him? 'Thanks, old man.' He put the slip in his pocket, looked at Jolinda. 'What about it?'

'Is it correct, sir, for an enlisted private to accept a ride from an officer?'

'If it is to stop her being drowned, it's a duty.'

'Oh. Right. Well then, sir, I accept.'

'Good girl. Do you have anything to wear?'

'I have a cape.'

'Right. Then you'll only get wet from the waist down.'

'Sounds exciting.' She dropped the cape over her head, adjusted her cap.

'I think you'll need either to tie that on or take it off.'

'But that would mean . . .'

'I know. You can always wash your hair.'

She tucked her cap under the cape. 'I hope I'm doing the right thing,' she muttered.

Yardley watched her with a quizzical expression, while John put on his raincoat. 'I tell you what,' he said. 'My cap has a strap. Why don't you use it?'

'But then your hair will get wet.'

'Ah, but there's less of it, so it'll dry quicker.'

'Well, if you're sure . . .' She took the cap, put it on, and promptly disappeared from the cheekbones up. 'I can't see a thing.'

John pulled the strap tight under her chin.

'Now I can't hear anything, either.'

'That's the best way to travel in the rain. I'll just take your arm.'

'And the best of British,' Yardley commented as John opened the door.

The rain was falling heavily and persistently, but at least there was no wind, although there would be on the back of the Harley-Davidson. John held Jolinda's arm to guide her to where the bike was parked, she giving little squeaks every time she stepped in a puddle.

'Here we are,' he told her. 'Now, I am going to get on first. Once I'm seated, swing your leg over and sit behind me.'

'I can't do that.'

'Why not?'

'This skirt is far too tight.'

'How did you suppose you were going to sit? Have you never ridden on a motorbike before?'

'Never. I thought I'd sit side on.'

'You'd come off at the first bump. You'll have to pull your skirt up to your thighs.' He seated himself. 'Come along now.'

He felt the slight thump behind him. 'Aaagh!'

'What is the matter now?'

'This seat is sopping.'

'I did warn you that it could be tricky from the waist down. If you clench your buttocks it'll keep the water out. Well, some of it.'

He felt her shifting about, but couldn't tell if she was following his suggestion or not. 'If an MP were to see me like this,' she remarked, 'I'd spend the rest of the war in the calaboose.'

John looked down at the long, slender, stocking-clad and already very wet leg being wedged against his own. 'If an MP were to see you like this,' he corrected, 'he'd say, "Cor, damn me, do WAAFs really have legs like that?"'

'Could we kindly get on with it? Sir?'

'Hang on tight.' Her arms went round his waist, he kick-started the engine, and they roared into the night. Immediately the rain started to drive into his face and splatter against his raincoat, while plumes of water spread to either side of the machine. He reckoned his body was mostly protecting Jolinda, but she gave little shrieks every time they hit a bump or went through a particularly large puddle, while she dug her chin into his shoulder as she tried to keep her head down. But it was only a short distance to the village in which Air-Commodore Hargreaves lived, and in fifteen minutes, as he had promised, he was swinging into the short drive before the modest two-storied house.

This was in total darkness. 'I see your dad believes in the blackout,' John remarked.

Jolinda released him, and slowly dismounted. 'I feel as if I've been through a wringer. I don't think Dad's home. I don't see his car.'

'But there's someone to let you in? Servants, I mean?'

'My father is an air-commodore, sir. Not a millionaire. He has a woman who comes in every day, but she doesn't sleep in. I have a key.' She went under the shelter of the porch, took off his cap, held it out. 'This is kind of wet.'

'So are you. Talk about drowned rats.'

'That was very kind of you, sir. I mean, the lift.'

'You mean I'm being dismissed? Without even the offer of a drink?'

'I have to get out of these clothes.'

'So have I. I'm wetter than you.'

Her tongue emerged and circled her lips. 'You have nothing to change into.'

'A dressing gown will do. Or even a towel. On a temporary basis.'

'I do not think this situation is covered by Regulations.' But she unlocked the door.

'Ah, but it is covered by the law of coincidences, which should never be disobeyed.' He followed her into the hall and closed the door.

She switched on the light. 'I do not understand what you are talking about.'

'Well, what about the coincidence of you being posted to

100

the same airfield as me? You could have knocked me over with a feather when I saw you sitting there.'

'Oh,' she said. 'Ah, well, actually, there are no such things as coin—' She peered at herself in the full-length mirror on the wall; despite having worn his cap, water was dripping from her hair, as it was from her skirt and beneath it. 'My God! Talk *about* drowned rats . . .'

'The most beautiful drowned rat I have ever seen.'

'Oh . . . pfft. Sir.' She went to the stairs. 'I have to get out of these clothes. I'll drop something down for you.'

'Make it something nice.'

She paused on the landing. 'I would like you to know that I am putting my trust in the fact that my father and your father were close friends before either of us was born, and that you are an officer and a gentleman.'

'Well, there goes the evening.'

'But you can pour us each a drink. There's a sideboard in the drawing room. Make mine scotch.'

He went into the drawing room, regarded the set but unlit fire in the grate. It was actually quite a warm evening, only feeling cold because of the rain – and because he was thoroughly chilled. But his clothes needed heat to dry. He struck a match and had a blaze going in seconds. Then he undressed down to his underpants, spread his wet clothes around the grate, went to the door at the slight sound, found that she had dropped both a towel and a dressing gown down the stair well. He used the towel, put on the dressing gown, which, as it almost fitted, he guessed belonged to her father.

He poured two scotches, added a splash of water, and faced the door as she came in. She had clearly rinsed her hair in hot water as it lay in smooth, if wet profusion down her back, and she was also wearing a dressing gown. He handed her a glass. 'If you are wearing nothing under that,' he pointed out, 'you are putting this officer and gentleman thing under a most severe strain.'

Jolinda drank, deeply and with great satisfaction. 'I needed that. I am wearing knickers, and I hope you are too.'

'Oh, I am. Because I am an officer and a gentleman. But they do get in the way of things, don't they?'

She held out her empty glass. 'I'd like a refill. Do you flirt like this with every woman you meet?'

He poured for them both. 'Only with the ones I intend to marry.'

She took the glass from his hand. 'Oh, really? You are a hoot, sir. What about the woman who is trying to get in touch with you?'

'She was my yesterday. You are my tomorrow.'

Jolinda sat on the settee, legs curled up beneath her. 'I don't believe you're an officer and a gentleman at all. I believe you're a cad.'

John sat beside her. 'I won't argue with that. But if you'll marry me I swear I'll turn over a new leaf.'

'I would need my head examined to believe a word you say.'

'Ah, but I can prove my sincerity.'

'Can you?' She sounded genuinely interested.

'The day I met you – was it only a couple of weeks ago? – when you insisted on peddling off on your bicycle, I said to my Aunt Joan, that is the girl I'm going to marry. You can ask her. Telephone her and ask her now.'

'But you'd only just met me.'

'If you were walking along the street, and you tripped over something, and bent to see what it was, and discovered that it was the Kohinoor diamond, wouldn't you know immediately that your life was irrevocably altered?'

'You should be a politician.'

'After the war.' He finished his drink, put the glass on the coffee table, knelt before her, pulled her legs down in front of her, parted her dressing gown, and then parted her knees as well.

'What are you doing?' she asked, but with no apparent alarm.

John inserted his chest between her thighs; her knees promptly closed to imprison him. 'I am doing the time-honoured thing,' he explained. 'Getting on my knees to ask you to marry me.'

'You're sure this isn't a ploy to get me to allow you upstairs?'

'I give you my word that I shall not attempt to have sex, I mean real sex, with you until after we are married.'

'Well, in that case . . . I think you had better get up.'

'You haven't said yes yet.'

'No, I haven't. But Daddy's home.'

'What?' He hadn't heard the front door. Now he turned on his knees as the drawing-room door opened.

'John?' Air-Commodore Hargreaves blinked at him. 'What on earth are you doing?'

'He's proposing marriage, Daddy.'

'In his underwear?'

'Well, we both got very wet coming home. On his bike.'

Hargreaves went to the bar and poured himself a drink; he clearly needed to think about the situation. John got to his feet. 'I really would like to marry your daughter, sir.'

Hargreaves drank, and turned to face him. 'Well, in the circumstances, I think you better had.'

'Now hold on just one minute,' Jolinda said. 'Don't I have a say in this?'

'You are also in your underwear. My God!' Jolinda was also getting up, and before she could retie her dressing gown she revealed that she was naked from the waist up. 'You're not even actually *wearing* your underwear.'

'I told you, we got wet. And nothing has happened. Nothing at all.' She gave a petrified John a condemnatory glance. 'He hasn't even kissed me.'

'I'm sure he was meaning to get around to it. Now look here, John, this is important. Hasn't your squadron got in touch with you?'

'Important?' Jolinda shouted. 'Just what is more important than this?'

'Do be quiet, Jolinda,' her father suggested.

'I've actually been out of touch for the past hour or so, sir. But Wing-Commander Hawkins knew I was taking the night off.'

'And he thought you had gone home to your father. Anyway, that's not important now I've found you. You, and all your pilots, are on duty at three o'clock tomorrow morning.'

'Sir?'

'Will someone please tell me what is going on?' Jolinda enquired, her voice a low rumble of distant thunder.

'We have information,' her father told her, 'that Jerry is about to start a full-scale aerial assault on England as a preliminary to an invasion.'

Five

The Channel

'Good God!' John said. 'You mean they're there, now? On radar?'

'Well, no, of course they're not on radar yet. This is an intelligence report,' Hargreaves said.

'From where, sir?'

'I have no idea. We have our agents all over Germany. You know the sort of thing. They lurk around bars, listen to conversations, get themselves invited to cocktail parties . . .'

'And one of these has reported that the invasion is about to start? Is there any confirmation?'

'Again, I have no idea. But we have to take it seriously. It could be right.'

'Yes, sir. Well, I'd better get on.'

'Where?' Jolinda enquired.

'Well . . .'

'It is half past eight,' she pointed out. 'You have not yet had dinner. And from the way your clothes are steaming it seems they are not yet dry. You are not going to do the RAF too much good if you're in hospital with pneumonia.'

'Well . . .'

'And you are on duty in under six hours' time, possibly flying into combat.'

'Well . . .'

'She's right, you know,' Hargreaves agreed. 'You need a square meal and some sleep. And you must give your uniform time to dry. You had better have dinner with us and stay the night.'

'Yes, sir. Thank you. Ah, perhaps if you would show me the spare room . . .'

'Ah,' Hargreaves said. 'We only have one spare room.'

'And I'm in it,' Jolinda pointed out.

'Now there's a problem,' her father said.

'Not in the least. John can sleep on this settee.'

'Brilliant. Right. If you'll get supper, Joly, I'll pour us all another drink.'

He went to the sideboard, and John caught Jolinda's wrist. 'Am I now also allowed to call you Joly?'

'No you are not. Daddy is privileged, because he is Daddy. You are not.'

'But you are going to marry me.'

'What gave you that idea?'

'Well, inviting me to spend the night . . .'

'I am doing my bit for the war effort. Sir.'

'You will be pleased to know that your clothes are absolutely dry,' Jolinda announced loudly.

John blinked at the ceiling light. 'Jesus! What time is it?'

'Two o'clock. I overslept. So you will have to rush.'

He blinked again. She was back in her dressing gown, her hair now dry and loose on her shoulders. 'Did I ever tell you . . .?'

'Yes, you have. Endlessly. Now you really have to rush.'

'Oh, right.' He sat up.

'And please take your blanket with you.'

'Eh?'

She held up his underpants, which had been lying beside the settee. 'Do you always sleep with nothing on?'

'Don't you?'

'I'll make breakfast,' she decided.

'Am I coming with you?' she asked her father as he munched toast.

'I don't think there's any necessity for you at this hour. Try to get in by six.'

'How?'

'Eh?'

'I left my bicycle at the station last night.'

'Oh, good God! All right. You'll have to get dressed. Hurry now.'

'That's not a problem, sir,' John suggested. 'I can take her in on my bike, whenever she's ready. I'll still be there by three.'

'Now wait just a minute,' Jolinda said.

'That's a brilliant idea,' the Air-Commodore agreed. 'I'll be away then. Mind you're there by three.' He hurried from the room.

'My father seems to have an absolute trust in your integrity,' Jolinda remarked.

'Well, he's known me all my life.'

'I'm not sure I follow your reasoning. But you and I need to have a serious chat.'

'About our wedding?'

'About who does what and to whom in this household. Now I'm going to dress. May I just remind you of one thing?'

'Such as?'

'If you venture up those stairs before I venture down, you won't be shooting down any Germans today, because you'll be in hospital.'

'I see. There are a couple of points outstanding.'

'Well, please be quick. We don't have too much time.'

'Point One: I haven't shaved yet.'

'You can use the bathroom as soon as I'm done. Five minutes. Point Two?'

'You still haven't said yes.'

'Yes to what?'

'Yes to marrying me.'

'That is something else we will have to discuss, when we have resolved the first matter. Sir.'

The eleven planes taxied to a halt, and the pilots climbed out into the drizzling rain and hurried across the tarmac into Dispersal.

'You look both wet and disappointed,' Yardley remarked.

'There is absolutely bugger all out there,' Newman said. 'I thought radar was going to tell us where Jerry is.'

'Well,' Yardley acknowledged, 'there has actually been nothing worthwhile on radar this morning.'

'But you sent us up anyway,' Rigg pointed out.

'There's a bit of a flap on. The information received, from an apparently very reliable source, definitely indicated that Jerry was starting something big today, and frankly, most of the brass has no more confidence in radar than you chaps.

I'm sorry. You can take the rest of the day off. Have you any idea when Turnbull will be coming in?'

'What?' John had taken no part in the somewhat animated conversation. He felt even more disgusted than his pilots. But for that entirely unnecessary flap, he could now be . . . It was difficult to pinpoint it, because Jolinda was so unlike any woman he had ever met before, not the least bit yielding to his male ego, or even his superior rank – presumably that came from being an air-commodore's daughter – but also suggesting that if she did ever decide to yield it might be to open the gates of paradise. Now . . . He did a quick head count. 'He's not here.'

'I would have said that was pretty obvious,' Yardley agreed, somewhat drily. 'We had a message from him twenty minutes ago to say that he was having a spot of bother and would have to put down.'

'We never heard that,' Rigg said.

'He was using the second frequency, probably to confuse Jerry if anyone happened to be listening. So . . .'

'Just one minute,' John said. 'Put down? He said he was putting down, twenty minutes ago? Twenty minutes ago we were over the French coast and the English Channel.'

'Ah,' Yardley said. 'Oh, shit! I beg your pardon, miss.' Hawkins had appeared in the inner doorway, Jolinda behind him.

'Do I gather we have lost a pilot?' the Wing-Commander enquired.

'Almost literally,' John confessed. 'We were in this –' he glanced at an impassive Jolinda – 'effing cloud until we were virtually over the field. Then we came in. As there had been nothing more than usual on the R/T it never occurred to me that we weren't all here.'

'And when he said he was putting down,' Yardley explained, 'I thought he meant somewhere in south-east England.'

'Well . . .'

The radio operator appeared in the other doorway. 'Excuse me, sir. I have Pilot Officer Turnbull on the blower.'

Hawkins led the stampede through the door, snatched the mike. 'Where are you?'

'Well, sir,' the voice was very faint. 'As far as I can make out, it's a place called Brueville.'

'Which county?'

'I don't know, sir. It's in Belgium.'

'What did you say? You are on the ground, in Belgium? And Jerry is letting you call out?'

'Jerry doesn't actually know I'm here, yet, sir.'

Hawkins looked at John who took the mike. 'What exactly happened, Ned?'

'My engine started to cough, and I knew I wasn't going to get home, and then I saw this nice-looking beach, and I thought, if I can put down there and maybe fix the fault, I might get up again.'

'So what went wrong?'

'It wasn't such a nice beach. I mean, it's a lovely beach, if you're into beaches. But where I came down the sand was softer than I thought, and she became bogged down.'

'And you can't get her out? Any chance of the locals giving a hand?'

'The locals are very supportive, sir. But . . . the tide is coming in at a rate of knots.'

'Oh, shit!' Yardley said again, and this time he didn't apologize.

'Then where are you calling from?'

'I'm in my cockpit, sir. I reckon I have about five minutes.'

'Right,' John said. 'We need some facts, and they have to be accurate. How much beach is left when the tide is full?'

'I would say, going by the seaweed line, not a lot.'

'Well, is there anywhere in your immediate vicinity that we could put a plane down? I mean, successfully enough to get it back up again.'

'There's a road just behind the beach . . .'

'That sounds perfect. What sort of road? Tarmac?'

'Why didn't the twit land on the road instead of the beach?' Newman inquired.

Turnbull might have been able to hear him. 'I think it was tarmacked once, but it needs repairing. But the road is only about three hundred yards in a straight line, then it takes a sharp right-hand bend. I have to go now, sir; water is coming into the cockpit.'

'Right. We'll see you on the road in forty-five minutes.' He handed the mike back to the operator.

'I hope you're not thinking what you appear to be thinking,' Hawkins remarked.

'We can't just let him be shot or carted off to a Jerry prison camp, sir.'

'Equally, John, we cannot possibly put a Spitfire down on what sounds like a very uncertain three-hundred-yard strip.'

'Well . . .'

'A Lysander would do it,' Martin said quietly.

Heads turned towards him. He was a relatively short, chunky young man with a mop of curly black hair.

'We don't happen to have a Lysander,' Hawkins pointed out.

'There are a couple at the next station, sir. I'm sure they'd let us borrow one.'

'Complete with pilot?'

'That's not a problem, sir. I flew Lysanders in France back in May, before transferring to train for Spits.'

Hawkins looked at John.

'He'll need cover,' John said.

'We seem to have definitely lost an aircraft, and maybe a pilot as well. I'm not risking the squadron to try to get him back.'

'Two planes, sir. One to escort the Lysander, one to stand guard above.'

Hawkins hesitated. Then he nodded. 'They must be volunteers.'

'I'll go escort,' John said.

'And I'll go guard.' Newman stepped forward.

'Very good, gentlemen. But I want it clearly understood that if there is any sign – any sign at all – that Jerry has got there first, or if you run into superior opposition in the air, you abort and come home.'

'Understood,' John agreed.

'There is just one thing, sir,' Martin said.

Again heads turned.

'The Lysander does not have an R/T system.'

'Dammit,' said Hawkins.

'That should not be a problem,' John said. 'Keep your eye on me at all times, except when landing or taking off, and if I signal to get out, get out.'

'Will do. Now it's just a matter of getting across to Lynechurch.'

'Can you ride a motorbike?'

'Yes, sir.'

'Then you can ride my Harley.'

'Yes, *sir*.'

'We'll rendezvous over Beachy Head in half an hour.'

Martin ran from the room.

'Well, gentlemen,' Hawkins said. 'Good luck to you two, and the rest of us will keep our fingers crossed.'

Jolinda stood next to John. 'Isn't this above and beyond the call of duty, sir?'

'Turnbull is one of my people. He's also a friend.'

'I meant, letting another guy ride your precious Harley. Suppose he smashes it up?'

'Then he'd better go with it.'

'And you seriously think you can rescue your friend?'

'Yes.'

'Well . . . do please come back, sir.'

'Is that a yes vote in the marriage stakes?'

'It is a request, sir. It would upset Daddy no end if you got yourself killed.'

The clouds had lifted, although it remained overcast, and the two Spitfires had only to circle a couple of times above the huge headland, no doubt totally confusing the radar operators below them, before the Lysander appeared.

'This low cloud base is a nuisance,' Newman remarked.

'But Jerry, if he's knocking about, will be above it,' John said. 'You'd better make it twenty thousand.'

'Understood.' The Spitfire roared away and vanished into the cloud.

John dropped down beside the Lysander and gave the thumbs-up sign. Martin responded, and they proceeded at the bottom of the cloud base, which was three thousand feet. There was a brisk wind, and below them the Channel was choppy. On top of that, the Spitfire did not handle well at half speed, which he had to maintain so as not to lose the Lysander. It seemed to take an eternity, as he did not wish to cross the coast and alert any German watchers until he reckoned he was close to their destination. But at last he calculated they

110

had to be about there and turned in, to find himself over Dunkirk with all its harrowing memories. But a few moments later the town was behind him, and he remembered that Brueville was only a few miles further north.

Unfortunately, there could be no doubt that they would have been spotted by people in the seaport but there was nothing he could do about that now, save get in and get out just as rapidly as possible. And then there was the village in front of him; he could see the beach and the half-submerged Spitfire and the road. He dropped down to five hundred feet to have a look, and discovered a small crowd of people looking up and waving. He couldn't identify Turnbull, but equally he could not see any evidence of Germans about.

Just to make sure he circled twice, by which time Martin had caught him up, and gave him the OK signal, then he climbed to two thousand feet and began to circle again. Martin himself circled twice at no more than a hundred feet, checking the road, then went down. He made a perfect landing, bringing up well short of the sudden right-hand bend. Instantly people surrounded the plane to turn it, and someone got in. Martin started his roll, and John heard a voice say, 'Bandits, one o'clock.'

'How many?' he asked.

'Nine at fifteen, but they're dropping into the cloud. They're looking for you and Martin. They haven't seen me.'

'Right. You've done your bit. Get out of there.'

'I can't abandon you, skipper.'

'You can and you must. Those are our orders. Nine to one are unacceptable odds.'

'If I go, you'll also be nine to one.'

'They have to find me first. See you at base.'

Martin was steadily if slowly climbing, blissfully unaware of his danger. John went down to him, waggling his wings and pointing upwards. Martin clearly got the message and signalled OK. If he could get into the cloud, he should be all right, John thought. But then the same thing applied to him.

'Did you hear that?' Gunther asked.

'I heard it,' Max said grimly.

'There is a Tommy above us. I did not see him. But I can find him. Shall I do that?'

111

'If he has obeyed his orders, which were to go home, you will never catch him. We must find the two others, the ones reported to be flying low over the coast. Those are the ones we want.'

Because one of them he wanted more than anything else in the world. His brother! But also the man who had killed Maartens. And he was there, somewhere beneath him.

The squadron was already sinking deeply into the cloud, at three thousand metres. 'Give me a base level,' he told Flight Control.

'You should be clear at one thousand metres, Herr Captain.'

Max checked his altimeter, and a moment later the information was proved correct as he broke into clear visibility, although the day remained grey.

'Where are the bastards?' someone asked.

'They've gone up into the clouds,' said someone else. 'We'll never find them.'

'They will also be trying to get home, so we split up,' Max commanded. 'Gunther, Flight A, return above the cloud; wait for them to come through. Sergeant Geisler, Flight B, sweep west by south. Flight C will follow me, west by north. One of them is reported to be a reconnaissance machine, and therefore cannot be very fast. We must catch it, at least.'

His pilots acknowledged his orders, and the remaining two planes of Flight C took up their positions to either side and just behind him. Flight A had already vanished back up into the cloud, and now Flight B disappeared as well. Max stared ahead. Which of the two enemy planes was John piloting? Almost certainly he would be the escort, but if he was the escort, he still had to remain in proximity to the slower machine.

The minutes ticked by, as the French coast rushed past below them, the choppy waters of the Channel churning whitecaps to his right. That was not something to come down in. Where *was* the bastard?

'Herr Captain,' a voice said, 'I am below half.'

Because they had scrambled so rapidly in response to the alarm, they had not waited to attach their reserve tanks.

'Fuck it,' Max muttered, glancing at his own gauge, which

112

was also showing dangerously low. 'It looks as if they have got away. Abort. Back to base.'

With an almost audible sigh of disappointment the three Messerschmitts turned to the north-east.

'Flight A, Flight B,' Max said. 'Abort. Return to base. Confirm.'

'But I have one,' Gunther said.

John, speaking fluent German as he did, had tuned in to the enemy wavelength and was well aware of what was going on, just as he was well aware that the opposing squadron-commander was his own brother. He actually felt more sorry for the poor blighter than any special enmity towards him, and he could never forget that Max had had him on toast over Dunkirk and had not completed the kill. Which was not to say that he would let their blood relationship come in front of his duty; he was only glad that they had not again encountered each other. Presumably, by the law of averages, as he was defending the line of the Channel and Max was engaged in probing that line, they had had to meet again at some time.

But, it seemed, now was not that time. He had no idea where Martin was, but then, apparently, neither did the Germans. And his own fuel gauge was showing low, although, unlike Max's lot, he was only fifteen minutes away from a friendly airfield. If they were turning back, he could gain altitude and shorten his return distance.

He pulled the stick back, soared out of the cloud into blue sky, looked left and right, saw nothing, and heard Gunther's voice.

'Where?' Max asked.

'Immediately below us,' Gunther said. 'He is a sitting duck.'

John twisted his neck, and made out the three aircraft, inescapably close. Shit! he thought.

'What is your fuel situation?' Max asked.

'I have five minutes in hand.'

'Five minutes,' Max said. 'Then go home.'

Gunther was already descending, very fast, his two comrades beside him. John knew he could not escape, and as he was still climbing, turned towards them. If he could avoid being hit for those five minutes . . . the four aircraft hurtled towards

113

each other, and all seemed to fire simultaneously. John aimed at the centre Messerschmitt, who he assumed was the flight-leader, and saw the tracer stream only just miss the cockpit canopy. Then he was past, and making a tight turn, blacking out as he did so, and listening to a tearing sound that indicated he had been hit.

But the aircraft was still functioning, and the tightness of his turn had given him the initiative. He was inside the third of the Messerschmitts and loosing a burst into the starboard wing at very close range. Instantly there was a spurt of flame followed by a cloud of smoke. One down, he thought. But then his plane shuddered again, and at the same time his engine coughed.

There was no smoke or flame or glycol – the liquid coolant – but the end result was going to be the same; a glance at his fuel gauge showed it now read Empty. But he did not necessarily have to bale out. He looked left and right. His propeller was now feathered and he had already dropped a thousand feet. The two remaining Germans were heading for home, but the third pilot was quite close, floating beneath his parachute, although John could see that his life jacket was stained with blood, which suggested that it was not going to be inflatable – supposing, in fact, if he had been hit in the back or chest, he was still alive.

And then he was gone, as the powerless Spitfire was falling faster. It was time to concentrate. He began using his flaps to try to control the aircraft and glide it down rather than allow it to go into a spin. It was hard work, and when he looked down from the cockpit he gulped, as he estimated the waves were several feet high. It was not going to be a soft landing!

He could see white cliffs ahead of him: the Seven Sisters. He thumbed his mike. 'Bayley going in,' he said. 'Four miles south of Newhaven.'

'We have you,' said a reassuring voice. 'Fifteen minutes.'

The decision whether to risk staying with the plane had to be taken now; his altimeter was showing six thousand feet. It was definitely safer to jump than to risk being thrown around the cockpit and perhaps trapped in it in those big seas. He reached up, pushed the canopy back, released his belts to heave himself upwards, and was suddenly aware of pain. One

114

of those jolts that his shocked system had not immediately recognized . . .

'Shit!' he muttered. When he had been shot down in France he had not been hit himself; the bullets that had killed his rear gunner had at the same time destroyed his aircraft. Now he had no idea how badly he was hurt; the wound was somewhere behind him. But he had to get out, now. He gritted his teeth, forced himself up, and felt the plane drop away beneath him. For a moment he was falling very nearly as fast as the metal, and then he pulled the cord.

Floating, for the first time he became truly aware of the strength of the wind; its buffeting accentuated the pain. How close those cliffs looked. He strained his eyes in an attempt to spot the Air-Sea Rescue launch, but could not. He looked back out to sea, and to his surprise saw the German parachute quite close, not more than a hundred yards away. But the pilot was showing even fewer signs of life than before.

He saw his aircraft go in with a huge splash, the surging water seeming to welcome it with open arms, and felt distinctly relieved that he had not been in it. But now the waves were reaching up for him with equal enthusiasm. When he was still some thirty feet up he began unbuckling his straps, at the same time inflating his life jacket, suddenly wondering whether it would respond. But it did as he fell from his harness.

He went into a trough, and was smothered by the next wave before he had properly caught his breath. But his Mae West stopped him from going under more than a couple of feet, and then he was gasping for air, but still lost in a foaming maelstrom. How would they ever find him in this mess?

Although it was July, the water was still extremely cold – but this, at least in the short term, had the effect of dulling the pain from his wound. He found himself on a crest, and saw the German pilot, only a few feet away. And he wasn't dead. If he had been unconscious during his descent, the water had clearly revived him, but he was handicapped by still being entangled in his parachute, and was beating the surface frantically.

'Hold on,' John shouted, and swam towards him. 'I will help you,' he said in German, as he slid down the trough.

The man stared at him. 'You are German?'

'No, no. But I speak the language. Listen! I will cut the chute away, right?'

'You help me?' The man seemed surprised. 'I am in such pain.'

'Help is coming.' John drew his regulation-issue sheath knife, intended for just such a situation as this, although perhaps not with an enemy airman in mind, and sliced through the straps.

The silk drifted away, but the man began sagging into the water again; John pulled the toggle to inflate the life jacket, but as he had feared there was no response. He got the German on to his back, put his hands into his armpits, and concentrated on keeping both their heads above water; his own Mae West stopped them both from sinking.

He looked at his watch: nine fifteen on a glorious summer morning as the clouds began to lift. But while the sun was reaching the surface of the sea it had not enough warmth to compete with the coldness of the water, and the constantly breaking seas were exhausting; he was beginning to feel sleepy, as all feeling left his arms and legs. Or was he actually dying?

He knew he had to keep awake. 'I say, old man,' he said into the German's ear. 'We haven't actually been introduced. I'm John Bayley. And you are . . .?'

The German preferred not to reply. John wondered if he had already fallen asleep, but his eyes were open. He was obviously not in the mood for chat.

Another hasty look at his watch: nine thirty. Presuming that he had gone in just after nine, the bloody ASR launch should be here by now. The two men rose on the next surge, and he saw it. It was a boat, certainly. But it seemed a very long way away.

He took one arm away from the German to wave, and shout, 'Hey! Over—' He got a mouthful of water as he was sucked down into the next trough. He spluttered and spat, and on the next crest saw the launch much closer, a man standing in the bow with a boathook.

'I see him,' the sailor shouted. 'Dead slow.'

The launch came closer, hardly seeming to move. The man with the hook went aft, where the topsides were lower, and now he was joined by two more. 'Easy, mate, easy,' the sailor said. 'Sorry we're a bit late, but you were hard to find.'

There was a roar as the engines were thrust astern. White water churned away from the propellers, and for a moment the launch lost way. In that moment the hook was lodged in John's lifejacket, and he was pulled against the hull. Then a wave broke on the stationary vessel and he began choking and spitting. But hands were soon reaching down for him. 'Take this fellow first,' he gasped. 'He's badly hurt.'

The German was pulled up and laid on the deck. Then the hands were back, reaching for John, and dragging him from the water. 'Shit!' commented one of the seamen. 'You ain't too good yourself.' He identified John's rank, and added, 'Sir.'

'What about him?'

'The Jerry is dead, sir. Has been for some time, I'd say.'

'You saw him go in?' Max asked.

'I saw him go down,' Gunther corrected. 'His engine had definitely failed, although there was no smoke. I think he may have run out of fuel. But then he sank into the cloud. Hans had already gone, and my fuel gauge was all but empty. So Fritz and I came home. We only just made it.'

'You did the right thing,' Max agreed.

'The point is,' Gunther pressed, 'am I entitled to claim a kill? I fired at him just before his engine conked out, and I know I hit him. I saw bits flying off his machine.'

'So did I,' Fritz added. 'I know Gunther hit him.'

'But you did not actually see him go in.'

'Well, no. But he was going down. As to whether he is dead, I cannot say. But his plane was definitely finished.'

'Well, then, I think you can claim a kill,' Max said.

'He was game, that Tommy,' Fritz put in. 'And a top pilot. The way he came at three of us, single-handed . . .'

'As you say,' Max said thoughtfully. 'He was game. And I can assure you that he was a top pilot.'

'You speak almost as if you know this Englander, Herr Captain.'

'Yes,' Max said. 'I know him. He is my brother.'

* * *

117

'What do you reckon?' John asked. He had no idea how long he had been in this bed; the hours since his rescue were a confused jumble of unconsciousness and moments of lucidity, of people moving about him and engines growling beneath him, of pain, and, above all, of cold. He had not supposed he was ever going to be warm again. But now he was just about warm, and the pain was dulled, and the transfusion he had been given had made him feel almost human again. He could even see his father's face clearly.

'There's a list,' Mark said. 'Shock, exposure, blood loss, the wound itself . . . But you'll recover, given time.'

'What about the wound? Straight up, please, Dad.'

'It cut through your left thigh. You were lucky there. It went through the outside of the thigh. Had it been on the inside, you could have had family problems. But it didn't even hit the main artery.'

'I'm not . . .' John bit his lip.

Mark grinned. 'Going to lose the leg? Or wind up a cripple like me? No, there's no prospect of anything like that. As I said, all you need is time to be back on you feet again.'

'How much time?'

'They think three weeks should do it.'

'Three *weeks*? That'll be August! Jerry will be here by then.'

'I think that's unlikely. Now look here, the quickest way back for you is complete rest and relaxation. Fretting is not going to do you any good at all. Everyone is very proud of you, both for rescuing Turnbull and for hanging on to that German pilot, both at the risk of your life.'

'The Jerry died,' John muttered. 'And it was Martin rescued Turnbull . . . You mean they got home safely?'

'Thanks to your covering, yes. Martin will get a medal.' The curtains were being drawn from round the bed, and Mark stood up, picking up his stick at the same time. 'Ah, yes, Sister, I'm just leaving. Now, here's some good news before I go. I've arranged for Avril to have special leave to come down and see you. She should be here tomorrow or the day after.'

'You've done *what*?' John almost shouted.

Sister bustled. 'Now, really, Squadron-Leader, you should not be exciting yourself.'

118

She glared across the bed at Mark, who ignored her. 'Don't you want to see her?'

Aunt Joan had clearly not confided the situation to her brother. 'Ah. Well, it's awfully good of you to arrange it, Dad, but the fact is, well, we quarrelled. As far as I know, the engagement is broken.'

'Happens all the time,' Mark said equably. 'Now is your chance to get it back on track. No woman can remain angry with her man when he's lying in bed with a bullet wound. I'm speaking from experience. I'll be in again in a day or two.'

He limped down the aisle between the beds. 'A forceful man, your father,' Sister remarked.

Hawkins came that afternoon. 'A bad business,' he remarked.

'I thought everyone was happy.'

'That is for public consumption. You are all heroes. Gallant British airman plucked from the hands of the enemy by even more gallant British airmen. But the truth of the matter, as you well know, is that we have managed to lose two aircraft and a pilot.'

'But we got a 109, and a pilot, in exchange. And I'm only out temporarily.'

'Two planes for one is not a rate of exchange we can sustain. As for you, you've been shot down and wounded. You're entitled to apply for a desk job.'

'I am not going to do that, sir.'

'Ah. Well, that's something. We'll be glad to have you back. Keep in touch.'

'Yes, sir. Ah . . . may I make a request?'

'Certainly.'

'Could you give a message to Private Hargreaves?'

Hawkins raised his eyebrows. 'What sort of message?'

'Could you tell her that if she can spare the time – and you can spare her, of course – I would very much like to see her.'

Hawkins frowned. 'There's nothing going on that I should know about, I hope. I don't think I could condone a relationship between one of my squadron-leaders and an enlisted private.'

'Our families are old friends, sir.'

'Oh. Yes. I'd forgotten.'

119

'Private Hargreaves is the nearest thing to a sister I possess.'

'Ah. Quite. I do apologize, John. I shall send her to see you.'

'Thank you, sir. However, to put your mind at rest, my "relationship" with Jolinda is known to, and approved by, the Air-Commodore.'

Hawkins gave him an old-fashioned look and left.

Jolinda came the next morning, wearing uniform and looking very proper, her hair all but invisible in its bun. 'There's a sight for sore eyes,' John commented.

'I am obeying orders,' she pointed out, sitting in the straight chair beside the bed.

'It's customary for visitors to remove their hats in the ward.'

'It is incorrect for a WAAF to remove her hat outside the office and when in uniform.'

'Is that a fact? One learns something every day. You mean you weren't planning to come and see your stricken fiancé at all?'

'I don't happen to have a fiancé, sir.'

'Your daddy thinks you do.'

'Daddy and I hold different opinions on a number of things. Actually, I did intend to visit you when I could spare the time. You're looking better than I expected.'

'I'm feeling better than I expected, after seeing you. Isn't it odd how things turn out? My father was shot down, just over twenty-two years ago. And in hospital he met the woman who was to change his life.'

'The famous Karolina.'

'You mean you knew of her?'

'I met her, at least once, before Mummy and Daddy split. I think she was the most beautiful woman I ever saw.'

'You haven't looked in the mirror recently.'

'Pfft. But . . .' She frowned. 'According to the records in the office, you were born in January 1918 . . .'

'You mean you've been looking me up?'

She flushed. 'I happened to be looking something else up, and came across your file, quite inadvertently.'

'I'll believe you because a man should always believe his wife. In answer to your next question, Karolina was not my mother.'

'Oh! Ah . . .'

'It's not something I like to talk about.'

'Of course. I apologize. It was unforgivable of me to raise the subject.' She stood up. 'I must be going.'

'You did not raise the subject. I did. And I don't want you to go right now. We have things to discuss.'

'I don't think now is exactly the time. You're obviously confused.' But she sat down again.

'I want you to listen very carefully to what I have to say. And please do not interrupt. Point number one: I love you. I fell in love with you the moment I first saw you. Uh-uh!' He raised his finger as she would have spoken. 'You're not going to interrupt. Point number two: I want to marry you. I intend to devote the rest of my life to you, either in, or out of wedlock. I would hope we'd get to the "in" stage before we're both too old to enjoy it, but I understand that you are an independently minded young woman, who is not to be coerced by either me or your dad. As I say, I am prepared to work on it for as long as it takes. However, there is something you need to know.'

She was gazing at him with unusual solemnity, which he thought might be a good sign. But he still needed to take a deep breath to continue.

'When I met you, at my dad's house, last month, I had just broken my engagement, as I think I told you.'

Now her mouth opened again, but she closed it of her own accord.

'This is a girl I met two years ago, when I was still training, and, well, we got together, and eventually I rather stupidly proposed marriage. I think as soon as I had done it I realized that I'd made a big mistake. But there it was. I had proposed, and she had accepted. And before anything else could devolve, the war had started and I was in France. I didn't come back for six months, and then it was on a stretcher . . .'

'You mean you've been shot down before?'

'And I survived then, too. The important thing is, she was in the Services as well, so we couldn't see each other very often – in fact, not at all. Then I was in Spits, and we had Dunkirk, and all that's happened since . . .'

'You mean you haven't seen this woman since the war started?'

121

'Well, not for a few months, anyway. We've spoken on the phone. And I have realized more and more that it simply wasn't on. So I broke it off. At least, I thought I had.'

Jolinda snapped her fingers. 'The woman who keeps ringing the station.'

'I imagine that was her, yes. I haven't taken any of the calls. So . . .'

'So you've done nothing more about it. The poor woman still thinks she's engaged to you.'

'What more am I supposed to do? I've indicated that I'm not going through with it. She can't send back her ring. She doesn't have one. The engagement, for various reasons I'd prefer not to discuss, was entirely private.'

'May I ask why you are telling me this?'

'Because there is a problem. As I said, our engagement was entirely private. But I felt obliged to tell Dad, and Aunt Joan. They gave their blessing, a little unwillingly, I suspect. They're very supportive. But I never actually got around to telling them it was over. So here I am, lying here wounded, and Dad decides I need a treat, and arranges for Avril to have leave to come and visit me.'

'How exciting for you. Did you get around to sorting things out?'

'She hasn't come yet. I think it's tomorrow.'

'And you thought I should know about it. Why?'

'I didn't want any kind of rumour getting back to you about how, while I'm proposing marriage to you, I'm actually seeing another woman.'

'That was very thoughtful of you,' Jolinda said, a trifle absently. 'Didn't you say just now that on the day you met me, you told Joan that I was the woman you intended to marry? You suggested I ask her if I doubted your feelings for me.'

'That's right. And you're welcome to do that.'

'But if you told her that, surely she understood that your engagement to this woman Avril was over?'

'Well, she must have done.'

'But she never told your dad?'

'Well, no. It appears that she didn't.'

'I see. May I ask what she said when you confided in her?'

'I think she said that I was an unmitigated cad.'

'I see. I think your Aunt Joan and I have a lot in common. I must be going.' She stood up. 'I will wish you a happy reunion tomorrow. Sir.'

'Well, gentlemen.' Reich-Marshal Goering beamed at the squadron-commanders and their superiors crowded into the room in front of him. 'I think there are chairs for all. Please be seated.'

Chair legs scraped as the assembly sat down.

'I am to congratulate you on carrying out the first part of our strategic plan so successfully. The English Channel traffic has virtually been eliminated, and from our reports as well as visual evidence, the RAF has suffered unsustainable casualties, and their morale is at rock bottom.'

The various captains and senior-lieutenants exchanged surreptitious glances. They had no means of judging the true overall picture; for that could only be obtained from the invariably optimistic circulars from Luftwaffe Headquarters, but they all knew the situation as regards their own squadrons, which was that the RAF were continuing to give at least as good as they got, and that they did not appear to be suffering any diminution in morale – quite the reverse. But there was no one prepared to argue with the Reich-Marshal.

'It is therefore now time,' Goering continued, 'to advance to the second stage of our campaign: the elimination of the RAF as a fighting force, at least in the south of England, by the destruction of their bases. You will each be given a list and location of these airfields. Our bomber crews are already in possession of them, and their targets allotted. Your business will be to escort the bombers and bring them back. The 109 squadrons will operate over the extreme south-east corner of the island, because even with your reserve fuel tanks your range is limited. The 110s will accompany the bombers further in. This will be your great opportunity to add to your kills, eh? The RAF must defend their airfields. So there will be more of them to shoot down.' Another beam. 'Are there any questions?'

There was a brief hesitation, while more glances were exchanged. But someone had to take the bull by the horns, and he was supposed to be this man's favourite pilot. Max took a deep breath and stood up. 'The RAF always seems to know exactly where we are going before we even get there. We are told this is because they possess the device known as radar. If this is correct, Herr Reich-Marshal, could it be explained to us just what this device consists of, and what steps we can take to offset this advantage.'

Goering looked at one of the officers seated at the table beside him. 'Colonel Olin will answer that question, Captain Bayley.'

Max sat down, and Olin stood up. 'Radar is, as its name suggests, simply a means of using radio beams to detect solid objects at a distance. It is strictly a defensive device, and so we have not paid a great deal of attention to it up till now. Now our scientists are working on developing a radar system of our own. The solution to the problem, at least as regards the coming battle, is the destruction of the radar stations the British have constructed around their coasts. This precision, and necessarily low-flying bombing, is to be carried out by our Ju-87s, as a dive bomber has much more accuracy than a high-level assault. However, as the Stukas are also relatively slow machines, they will need protection from the RAF interceptors. And this will be provided by the requisite 109 squadrons, as these will be very quick, hit-and-run raids. The relative targets' dispositions are listed in your control sheets.'

Olin looked at Goering, who nodded, and stood up again. 'There you have it. Nothing mysterious, or even sinister. In fact, this radar will work to our advantage. So the RAF may be able to see us at a distance, and before we see them. So they will come swarming up to intercept us. But that is what we want, is it not? The more of them that come up, the more of them we can shoot down, eh? And the quicker will be our victory. Now, it only remains for me to give the date that Stage Two will commence. It will be a week today, next Tuesday, thirteenth August. It will be an unlucky thirteenth for the RAF, eh? The code name is Adler Tag. Eagle Day. I have allowed four days for its completion. The destruction of the RAF. Thank you, gentlemen.'

'What do you think?' Gunther asked Max as they were driven to Ostend in the back seat of the command car. 'Does he really believe what he says?'

'I think probably our biggest problem,' Max said, 'is that he *does* believe it.'

'But four days to smash the RAF . . . that's a tall order.'

'I think, since it has to be done some time, the best time is now.' He wondered if John *had* survived that ditching into the Channel.

Six

Destruction

'You are a married man, Max,' Colonel Hartmann pointed out. 'You are entitled to leave in front of any of your men. And you are about to go into the greatest battle of your life. You owe it to your wife to spend a couple of days with her. It may be . . . Well, who can tell what might happen in a battle.'

You mean it may be the last time I ever see her again, Max thought. Did he want to see her again, at this moment? Because he was only too well aware that this promised to be the big one, just as he was equally aware that for him it could be bigger than for any of his comrades. Almost before Goering had finished speaking, his mind had been moving into gear, to fly, and fight, and kill – and perhaps to die. Not to even consider warm beds, soft bodies, and rampant sex.

But of course Hartmann was right. If his every instinct was to devote himself entirely to his duty to the Fatherland, his duty as a man and a husband was to say farewell to his wife before going into battle. As usual he flew his own 109 to Berlin, but did not actually land at Tempelhof until a quarter to nine. Taxis were scarce, and the evening traffic in the city heavy, so it was ten before he reached the Stumpff residence; he and Heidi had had neither the time nor the desire to look for a place of their own as yet, and although he had told her to go ahead and find one if she wished, he knew that, with him away so much of the time, she preferred the luxury of her father's home.

125

Reynald the butler opened the door, blinked at him. 'Herr Captain? We did not expect you.'

Max entered the hall, gave him his cap and belts and overnight bag. 'I reckoned I could get here as fast as any message. And besides, it will be a surprise. Herr Stumpff in?'

'No, sir. Herr Stumpff is out to dinner. We do not expect him back until midnight, at the earliest.'

'Then I will see him in the morning. But Frau Bayley is in, I assume?' Max went to the stairs.

'Ah . . . I'll just call her and tell her you are here.' Reynald reached for the house telephone.

'Don't do that,' Max commanded. 'I said it will be a surprise. She has gone to bed?'

Reynald gulped. 'Yes, sir.'

'Very good. You can bring the bag up later.' Max experienced a pleasant glow as he took the stairs three at a time. For all his monastic approach to life while actually on station, the thought of all that pale beauty waiting for him had sent adrenaline galloping through his arteries. The bedrooms were on the second floor of the mansion and, as there was another flight of stairs to be negotiated, he was slightly out of breath when he reached the wide, carpeted hallway. Here he paused for a moment to get himself under control, straightening his tie, when a door further along the hall opened and then closed again.

Max frowned; that had surely been Heidi's door. That blighter Reynald must have called her after all. But why, after obviously identifying him, had she closed the door again? He reached it, turned the handle, and found that it was locked.

'Heidi?' he called. 'What the devil is going on? Open up.'

'Max?' she cried from beyond the panel. 'Oh, Max, I am just coming.'

But it took several minutes before the door swung open. She had actually not turned the light on, but those in the hall illuminated her. She was wearing a dressing gown, and her hair was loose. She smelled of perfume, but also of woman. 'Oh, Max,' she said again, 'if only I had known you were coming.'

'What, would you have met me at Tempelhof?' He put his arms round her, lifted her from the floor, and carried her to the tousled bed. 'Now tell me what is going on.'

He laid her down and she fell back. 'I do not understand you. Going on?'

'The doors in this house are never locked, Heidi.'

'Oh . . . I did not wish to be interrupted.'

'And who was going to interrupt you, without knocking first? You did not know I was coming.'

'Well . . .' She rolled away from him, lay on her face. 'If you must know, I was tossing myself off. A woman does not like to be interrupted when she is masturbating. Do you like to be interrupted when you are masturbating?'

'I have neither the time nor the inclination to indulge myself.'

Another roll, and she was again on her back, looking up at him. The dressing gown had opened and she wore nothing underneath; even in the gloom, her body was, as always, breathtaking. 'Well,' she said, 'there you have it. I have all the time in the world. And I have the inclination, too. But I have no husband. I lie here, night after night, thinking of you, dreaming of you, wondering if you are alive or dead . . .'

'Well,' he said. 'I am here now.' He rolled her on her face to take off the dressing gown. It was only when he had also undressed and she was lying in his arms that he remembered he had not asked her why she had closed and locked the door when she had seen that it was him in the corridor. But that hardly mattered now.

'Well, here's a sight for sore eyes,' Yardley said. 'Welcome back. And on the thirteenth, too. There's another old wives' tale gone up the spout.'

John shook hands. 'It's good to be back. Have I still got a squadron?'

'Rusting away. I think Jerry must have known you were in hospital. There's been virtually no activity for the past week.'

'Johnnie!' Newman came hurrying in from the Mess. 'Am I glad to see you!'

'Yardley here says that everything is all right.'

'Well, it is. I think. But you can have the responsibility back. It's not my scene. Coming over to the mess? The boys will be tickled pink to see you.'

'In a minute. I'd better make my number, first!' He knocked on the WingCo's door.

127

'Come.'

John went in. 'Squadron-Leader Bayley, sir. Reporting for duty.'

'Johnnie!' Hawkins came round the desk to shake hands. 'Good to have you back. You remember Section-Officer Hargreaves?'

'How could I forget?' He gazed at Jolinda. 'Congratulations.'

'Thank you, sir. You're looking well.'

'I'm feeling well.'

'So sit down,' Hawkins invited. 'That will be all for the moment, Hargreaves.'

'Sir.' Jolinda left the room and closed the door; John noted that she no longer carried a notebook and pencil.

'She did visit you in hospital?' Hawkins inquired. 'I told her you wanted her to do that.'

'She came once, sir, yes.'

'Well, she's a busy girl. Now . . .' He picked up the sheet of paper on his desk. 'The medical report came in this morning. Says you're A-One.'

'I should bloody well think so, seeing the length of time they kept me in there.'

'Can't be too careful.'

'All I want to do now, sir, is get into my aircraft and fly.'

'That is a very sensible approach. However, I don't want you on patrol for a day or two.'

'Sir?'

'After a month, you cannot help being rusty, John. I can't risk you where there may be a chance of combat until I'm sure you're back on form. Don't look so alarmed. There has been almost no activity for the past week. Let Newman have the squadron for the next couple of days, and then when Jerry turns up again you'll be fighting fit.'

John pulled a face. But his boss was right. 'Any idea what he's up to? We're halfway through summer.'

'Well, as the man is widely supposed to be mad, maybe he's decided it would be better to invade us in the winter. Now . . . What in the name of God is that?'

A siren was wailing, and a moment later Yardley was shouting, 'Scramble, scramble!'

John leapt to his feet and ran to the window, to see his

128

pilots racing across the tarmac to their machines. 'I must get out there. Where the hell is my gear?'

'Now, John, simmer down,' Hawkins said. 'We agreed you'd take a couple of days to settle back in. Newman can handle an attack on a convoy. What exactly is the flap, Tom?'

Yardley had opened the office door. 'A radar report, sir. A very large group of bandits, a hundred plus, located just over Calais, and another one out of Ostend. They want every plane up.'

Hawkins joined John at the window. 833 Squadron had already taken off; 777 was just doing so. 'Well, they have it,' he said.

'And I'm missing it,' John grumbled.

'There'll be more later on. Maybe much more. You'll have your chance.'

'Yes, sir.' John left the office, stood in the doorway to watch the now virtually empty airfield; there were only half a dozen parked machines, amongst them his own. With the departure of the squadron there was an almost eerie quiet, which he had never known before – because before he had been in one of the departing planes – although groups of ground crew were still gathered, and both the fire engines and the fuel bowsers were waiting to go into action the moment the planes started to return.

He heard a sound and turned his head to look at Jolinda. 'Now you know how the women who have to stay behind feel,' she remarked.

'Only if they have a personal interest in one of the men going into battle, surely.'

'That is quite wrong, sir. I have a personal interest in the squadron. Every man and every machine.'

'Then that must include me.'

'Of course it does, sir.'

'Well, great. How about dinner tonight? Now you're an officer, no one can possibly carp.'

'Perhaps not. But aren't you engaged to be married?'

'My engagement is over.'

She raised one eyebrow disconcertingly. 'You mean you actually broke it off? Because . . .'

'Because of you, yes. So the least you can do is have dinner with me.'

Jolinda considered. 'I've never had an engagement broken,' she confessed. 'But that could be because I've never been engaged. Was she very upset?'

'I don't think I'm her favourite man. There was a bit of a scene. But fortunately Matron was there to sort it out.'

'And what was her take on the situation?'

'I don't think I'm her favourite man, either. But everyone is always sympathetic towards a wounded hero.'

'I suppose, once a cad, always a cad.'

'That was a quick trip,' Yardley said, joining them in the doorway. 'Must have been a false alarm.'

John looked up at the sky, which had suddenly become filled with aircraft, and frowned. Twenty-three planes had taken off half an hour before. The approaching cluster was still a good distance away, but he would have said there was something like forty of them. 'Shit!' he muttered suddenly. 'I beg your pardon, Section-Officer.'

'What?' Yardley asked.

'Binoculars!' John snapped.

Yardley hurried to the desk and handed them over. John focussed.

'Is there something wrong?' Jolinda asked.

'Those aren't ours. They're twin-engined, for a start. Tommy, signal air raid.'

'Here? On us? I say, old man . . .'

'Do it, God damn it!' John shouted.

Yardley gulped, and ran into the inner office. A moment later the siren again began its doleful wail.

Hawkins emerged from his office. 'What the devil . . .' He was interrupted by a distant crump. 'Jesus Christ!'

The ground crew outside had been alerted by both the siren and the noise of the first explosions, which were coming closer, and were scattering to the various shelters and slit trenches, hitherto only used in practice.

'Get into one of those,' John told Jolinda.

'Are you coming?'

'I have to get up there.' He went to the door.

Jolinda looked at Hawkins, as if expecting an order, but Hawkins was momentarily speechless. 'Gear!' she shouted. 'You have no gear. No Mae West.'

'I'm not planning on flying over the sea,' he said over his

130

shoulder, and ran outside, only to pause as he took in the extent of the catastrophe that was still happening around him. The bombers had reached the airfield now, coming in low, while above them hovered the protecting 110s. Plumes of smoke and stabs of flame were rising from the enlisted men's mess and barracks at the far end of the strip, and now he watched masses of earth and tarmac rising from the air strip itself, while shockwaves surrounded him and made him stagger, blowing off his cap.

He recovered and ran towards the parked aircraft, but knew he was not going to get there. A second wave of bombers was coming in, and he watched in horror as the fuel bowsers exploded, setting up a chain reaction that involved the fire tenders and then the parked Spitfires in a pyre of smoke and flame and exploding ammunition.

This time the force of the blast knocked him off his feet and stretched him on the ground, only just conscious, aware only of noise and heat, and then of someone tugging at his tunic.

He blinked at Jolinda. She had lost her cap, and her clothing was dishevelled and covered in dust and earth, indicating that she too had been knocked down at some stage. Now she was on her knees beside him, shouting at him. He couldn't hear what she was saying above the roaring in his ears, but she was obviously trying to get him up, and risking her life to do so, for now that the second wave of bombers had gone through, the Messerschmitts were coming down behind their chattering machine guns and exploding cannon.

He rolled over, carrying her with him – actually lay on top of her for a moment – then got to his knees and then his feet, lifting her with him. He watched earth being carved by bullets only a few feet away, and raced for the nearest slit trench, hurling himself into it, scattering three WAAF privates who were crouching there, and then landing on his back, Jolinda still clutched in his arms.

He gazed into her eyes from six inches away. 'Can you hear me?' he asked.

'Of course I can hear you, you great oaf.'

'And I can hear you. Thank God for that. I couldn't hear you earlier. I thought something might have happened to my ears.'

'Would you mind letting me go? I think you've broken every bone in my body.'

'I'll put them back, I promise. But right now . . .'

An anxious face was peering at them from beneath a steel helmet. 'Are you all right, sir? Ma'am?'

'I won't know until I can get up,' Jolinda said. 'If I can ever get up.'

John released her, and she knelt on him to push herself to her knees. 'I think you saved my life,' he said.

'I simply cannot imagine why, save that you saved mine back. How do I look?'

'Like something the cat would throw back out. But magnificent.'

She turned to the WAAFs, who exchanged glances. 'Well, ma'am . . .'

Jolinda looked down at herself. 'Shit!' Her skirt was torn, her stockings in tatters, one shoe had come off, and her tunic and blouse had been ripped open by the blast; all the buttons had disappeared.

'You're lucky,' John pointed out. 'I've heard of people who have been stripped naked by a blast like that. Still, I suppose you can't win 'em all.'

He realized that he was close to hysteria. But then, he guessed they all were, as they crouched together while the 110s ranged unchecked for the next ten minutes, until every building was blazing and every vehicle had been destroyed. None of the women had had any experience of actual warfare, of being under fire or watching people they knew die – however much they might have read about what had happened in Poland and France. They had worn their uniforms proudly, done their work efficiently, flirted and perhaps done more than that with various air crew or ground crew, looked forward to their next weekend pass . . . Now they stared at the destruction of what they had come to consider home, at dead bodies scattered about the place, some of them female comrades, as yet unable to understand that they, at least, were alive.

John felt that went for Jolinda as well, although, being an officer, better educated, with a more certain background, she was trying to absorb it. He felt only outrage and a seething anger, overladen with a sense of disbelief that this could have

132

happened. Unlike them, he was no stranger to death and destruction, or imminent physical danger, but he had never experienced it while in a totally defenceless position. Even when he had been required to fly Defiants against 109s, he had had the means of defending himself, though he had known he was outclassed. Since then, in the cockpit of a Spitfire, he had felt the equal of anyone in the air, even if he'd had it proved that he was not yet the equal of three 109s at the same time.

But this . . . He realized that the enemy aircraft had gone, and now scrambled out of the trench, the women following more slowly. He knew getting the station back functioning was the first priority, but where to begin? With Hawkins, obviously. He looked at the burned-out command office and scratched his head, only then realizing that he no longer had a cap.

Jolinda was standing beside him. 'What must we do, sir?'

He looked down at her. 'I don't suppose you have a change of uniform here?'

'Not right this minute. It was in the barracks.'

'Then you'll have to grin and bear it for the time being.' He listened to the wail of a siren and the clanging of a bell. Both an ambulance and a fire engine were gallantly coming out from Tunbridge Wells, which had apparently not been bombed at all, judging by the absence of smoke. 'Give the medics a hand with the wounded.'

'And the dead?'

'Yes, Section-Officer Hargreaves. They'll need help with the dead.'

She gulped. 'Yes, sir.'

He lowered his head. 'You'll have to keep those girls busy, otherwise we could have a problem.'

'You don't think we'll have a problem when they start messing about with corpses?'

'I'm relying on you, Jolinda. I have an idea that you and I are the only two officers left alive on this station.'

She looked at the still-burning command building. 'Oh, my God! Wing-Commander Hawkins!'

'I'm going to find out now. But for the moment, carry on.'

'Yes, *sir*.'

* * *

133

Air-Commodore Hargreaves arrived an hour after the raid, flying his own Hurricane, and being forced to land on the grass off the cratered runway. 'Bit of a mess, wouldn't you say, Johnnie?'

John had had all the survivors working hard for the hour. The fires had been put out, the dead had been laid out – amongst them being, as he had feared, both Hawkins and Yardley – and the wounded were receiving treatment. But the scale of the disaster was still evident. 'I'm afraid they took us by surprise, sir.'

'They took everyone by surprise,' Hargreaves said.

'You mean we weren't the only station hit?'

'Every goddam station in south-east England has been hit. We had ample warning they were coming in force, but we assumed that meant they were after Southampton, Portsmouth, Dover and places like that. But this . . . Maybe Goering has more brains than we've been allowing him.'

They walked slowly across the tarmac towards the shattered buildings. 'Is it very bad?' John asked.

'I suppose it could have been worse. All the damage, even this damage, can be repaired, and will be repaired, PDQ. And we brought down quite a few. On the other hand, they got quite a few of ours. So, when you consider the ground damage, I think we'll have to give the day to Jerry. Not that our propaganda boys will do that, of course.'

'And I wasn't there,' John growled. 'May I ask where my squadron is?'

'We brought them in at Lynechurch. That's not quite as badly damaged as here.'

'How many?'

'Ten.'

'We sent up eleven.'

'I know. I don't know who went in. Now tell me about your casualties here.' The question he had been dying to ask ever since landing.

'She's all right, sir. A bit shocked. We all are.'

Hargreaves released his breath in a long sigh. 'I never thought she'd be in any danger. Not here. Where is she?'

'Helping with the wounded. She's doing a magnificent job. Apart from saving my life.'

'Well, I suppose that's *de rigueur* for a future wife.'

'There seems to be some conflicting opinions about that, sir.'

'Oh, yes? Well, you'll have to knock some sense into her. It's being brought up in America, you know. Tell me about Hawkins?'

'I'm afraid neither he nor Yardley got out of the office before it was hit.'

'Damn! He was a good man. Well, then, you're in charge. Tell me what you want, and you will have it.'

'All I want, sir, is a new aircraft, and permission to join my pilots.'

'You didn't get my point, Johnnie. When I said you're in charge, I meant of the station, not the squadron. I'm promoting you to WingCo.'

'Thank you, sir. Am I allowed to decline?'

'What?'

'I would prefer to remain with the squadron, sir. At least until we've settled up with the bastards who did this.'

Hargreaves considered and then nodded. 'Point taken and understood. You have your squadron. But you'll have to hang on here until a new CO is appointed. It'll only be a day or two. Time to get used to your new aircraft, eh? It'll be here tomorrow morning. Now I really must have a word with Joly. Carry on.'

John started to salute, and then lowered his hand; he still didn't have a cap. 'Yes, sir.'

'Good man. Oh, by the way, if it'll make you feel better, we have every intention of paying Jerry back in kind.'

'Four o'clock,' Martin said. 'Minus four thousand.'

John looked in the required direction; he was using Martin as his wingman as, since the Belgian adventure, he regarded him as one of the most reliable pilots in the squadron, after himself and Newman. 'I have them. You know the drill,' he told his pilots. 'We deal with the escorts first. Go in fast, and hold your fire to a hundred yards. Break them up and we can do the bombers at our leisure.'

The squadron had only taken off a few minutes before, and their tanks were full, whereas the Germans, consisting as they did of Heinkels and 110s, had been up for over an hour, tracked all the way by radar; they would be watching their gauges. On the other hand, there were twenty of the bombers, escorted by ten fighters, and there could be no doubting the Messerschmitts' superior fire power – if they were allowed to use it. And that they were in turn aware of their inferiority as regards speed and manoeuvrability was immediately evidenced by their tactics as they saw the approaching interceptors. While the Heinkels held their course, the fighters, instead of coming to challenge the Spitfires, formed a circle round their charges.

Slightly out in front of his men, John aimed at the very centre of the enemy formation. He saw tracers emanating from the nearest 110, and did not doubt it had also used its cannon, but it had opened fire at too great a range, and where the shot went he had no idea. At a hundred yards he could see the crew, frantically swivelling his guns to bear, but he was too late. John used deflection fire, but did not waste too much time in calculating the correct distance: the enemy aircraft were so closely packed he was certain to hit something. In fact, the range was so close that the 110 flew straight into the prolonged burst, aimed only a few feet in front of it. The bullets smashed into the starboard engine, which immediately burst into flames, and continued into the cockpit to kill the pilot.

John pulled the stick back to soar over the stricken aircraft, and then down again to line up the bomber only a few yards beyond. The Heinkel was already past him, so he swung into line behind it, opening fire again as he did so, and again at almost point-blank range. This time it was the rear gunner's turn to receive the hail of shot, but it continued past him into the fuselage, and again there was an immediate issue of smoke.

Then John found himself in open space and could look around. At least three of the bombers had gone down, and two of the Messerschmitts; there were several parachutes floating earthwards. But the rest were continuing on their course with grim determination while the squadron was scattered. 'Close up,' he said. 'Once more.'

'I'm a little short of ammo, skip,' Higgins said.

'So use what you have left,' John told him. 'Once more.'

* * *

'Eight confirmed,' John told Yardley's replacement as despatcher, Flight-Lieutenant Coleman. 'Five Heinkels and three 110s.'

'And . . .?'

'Higgins and Rigg. But I think they both managed to bale out.'

'Still, that's as good a rate of exchange as anyone's.'

'If they got down all right,' John pointed out. 'Will you check it out?'

Coleman nodded. 'I'll chase up the relevant sectors.'

'John!' Wing-Commander Browne stood in his office doorway. 'Quite a success.'

'Our best so far, sir. Their tactics were faulty.'

'Still, it'll look good in the papers. And we need something to look good.'

'Bad news?'

'Come in.' He retired into the office, and John followed. 'It's bloody awful. They just keep coming. We shoot them down, but they shoot us down as well; not every squadron has had a plus score like yours today. And our airfields are being torn apart.' He brooded out of the window. The station had been patched up in a fortnight of intensive labour, but patched was the operative word. The runway was usable, but there were still craters everywhere, while the buildings, including this one, had been replaced with prefabricated Nissen huts; John reckoned one reason why they had not been strafed again was that the Germans knew they had been just about flattened the first time.

'Our people are exhausted,' Browne said, 'and our fields are in a mess. If they keep this up for too much longer, cracks are going to show. Ah, well . . . Look, you and your lads need a break. Stand down for forty-eight hours.'

'Sir? We're quite capable . . .'

'I know you are, John. Or you feel that way. But there is a limit to how long you can keep going on adrenaline. You haven't looked in the mirror recently. 833 has a forty-eight-hour pass, starting now. Go and get some solid sleep.'

'And when Jerry comes back tomorrow?'

'777 will cover for you. I'll see you on Monday.'

* * *

137

'Bloody hell,' Newman said. 'On the other hand . . . we're going down to the boozer, skip. Coming?'

'Ah . . . I may have something on,' John said.

'Interesting. Well, have fun. We intend to.'

John went in search of Jolinda. As she was now the senior WAAF officer on the station, she had her own office and general charge of all the women staff. They had seen very little of each other over the past fortnight since the raid, as she no longer operated out of the WingCo's office, and they had both been extraordinarily busy, he flying and she supervising getting the station back to rights. Now she stood up behind her desk, as did her secretary, as the Squadron-Leader entered. 'Sir!'

'At ease. What time do you knock off, Section-Officer?'

Jolinda looked at her watch. 'One hour.'

'Make it now, there's a good girl.'

'Sir?'

'I'm required to take you home, urgently.'

'Oh, my God! Daddy?'

'I'll explain on the way. Private, I wish you to telephone the Wing-Commander's office and inform them that Section-Officer Hargreaves has been called home on urgent family business and will be away for the night.'

The girl looked at Jolinda, who hesitated briefly, and then nodded and picked up her cap. 'Will he give me permission?' she asked.

'When one is the daughter of an air-commodore, all things are possible.' He led her outside.

'How do we get there?'

'On my bike.'

'Oh, shit!'

'One of the things I adore about you, and they are legion, is your colourful use of language. Do you know most English girls of your background do not even know what that word means?'

'Tell me what's happened to Daddy.'

'Let's get there.' He swung his leg over, started the engine, felt her behind him. 'Are you sitting comfortably?'

'No,' she said, putting her arms round his waist. 'Everyone's staring at me.'

'Everyone is staring at your legs,' he corrected. 'Lucky fellows.' He gunned the engine and roared out of the yard. 'There in fifteen minutes.'

138

'I know,' she said sadly, removing one of her arms to hang on to her cap.

'The car's not here!' Jolinda exclaimed as they drove into the yard. 'Where's Daddy's car?'

'You'll have to ask him.' John braked, waited for her to get off, then dismounted himself, watched her smooth her skirt and then clutch at her pocket.

'Shit! I've lost my keys!'

'You probably left them at the office.'

'Or they fell out on the road . . .'

'I am sure some kind person will pick them up and return them to you.'

'We'll have to ring the bell.'

'Move over Sherlock Holmes.'

'But if Daddy is unwell . . .'

'You worry too much.' He rang the bell and the door opened immediately; the middle-aged woman in the apron had clearly seen them arrive. 'Mrs . . .'

'Sutton, sir.'

'Of course. You'll see I have Miss Hargreaves with me.'

'Yes, sir. Miss Jolinda.'

'Tell me about Daddy, Mae.'

'Ah . . .' Mrs Sutton looked at John.

'I think I had better do that,' John said, holding Jolinda's hand to draw her into the hall. 'And you were just leaving, weren't you, Mrs Sutton?'

'Well, sir, if you think it's proper . . .'

'I'm just repeating what the Air-Commodore told me to tell you.'

'Yes, sir. I'll just get my hat. Good afternoon, miss.'

Jolinda freed herself. 'Just what the sh—'

'Please, darling, not in front of Mrs Sutton. You'd have to explain what it meant. Come along.'

He held her arm again to usher her into the drawing room, closing the door behind them. Again she freed herself and turned to face him, now beginning to get angry. 'I don't know what you're playing at, but this happens to be my house, and I will not be pushed around in it. So just step aside, sir. I am going upstairs to see Daddy.'

John stepped aside. 'I think going upstairs is a brilliant

idea. I'll come with you. But seeing Daddy may be a little difficult.'

Jolinda paused with her hand on the door knob, and listened to the front door closing. 'Oh, my God!' she said, and turned to face him. 'You're mad. You have to be mad. You should be locked up. You will be locked up.'

'I am perfectly willing to concede that I am bonkers. I suppose it's there all the time, but it only comes out when I have been in action. There's been a lot of action today.'

'So you're a hero,' she said. 'We all know that. But that does not allow you to . . . Well, you kidnapped me.'

'I am dealing with you as your father recommended.'

'What?'

'He actually recommended that I knock some sense into you. I think he had spanking in mind. So . . .'

'If you lay a finger on me . . . What are you doing?'

John had sunk to his knees on the carpet. 'I am asking you to marry me, again, in the time-honoured manner.'

'I have already refused you once.'

'Not in so many words. You felt obliged not to say yes, because you were under the mistaken impression that I was promised to somebody else. But as that no longer obtains, and it never did from the moment I first met you, you can now start to think positively.'

'Why should I want to do that?'

'Because I adore you, worship you, cannot contemplate living without you.'

'I've been told that shooting a line is occupational therapy for fighter pilots.'

'I have never shot a line in my life.'

'Oh, yes? How many kills are you currently claiming? How many times do you say you've been shot down?'

'Well, I know I've been shot down twice. Everybody else knows that too. Kills, well, it's difficult. You know, one reports, and claims, but other pilots may make the same claim, and it has to be confirmed. I've never really kept too close a tally. I'm pretty damn sure I got three today; that's why I'm on this high, I suppose. But again, that hasn't been confirmed.'

'Three? You are saying that you shot down three enemy aircraft today? In one morning?'

'It was actually around midday. And it was in ten minutes.'

'Pfft. All you really want to do is get your hands on my body.'

'I do not intend ever to lie to my wife, so I will admit I do wish to get my hands on your body. But I promise to treat it with the utmost tender, loving care. Unless, of course, you would prefer it otherwise.'

'You are impossible. I feel like a drink.' She turned to the sideboard, and checked. 'Daddy!'

She went into the hall and opened the door as tyres crunched on the gravel.

'Joly! Johnnie here?'

'Yes, he is. You and I need to have a chat.'

'About the wedding? Of course. You make all the arrangements, and I'll endorse them. Johnnie!' He entered the drawing room.

'Daddy!'

'I thought I might find you here, when I discovered you hadn't gone home. Congratulations, my dear boy.'

'She hasn't actually said yes, sir.'

'Eh? Of course she's going to say yes. I told you, knock some sense into her, if you have to.'

'Daddy!'

'But I'm not congratulating you about that. Those kills have been confirmed.' He threw his arm round his outraged daughter's shoulders. 'Would you believe it? This boy knocked down three German aircraft in fifteen minutes this afternoon.'

'What?'

'Even more important than that, this brings his kills up to ten. That makes you a genuine ace, Johnnie my lad.'

'Good lord!'

'You mean you honestly didn't know that?' Jolinda asked.

'Well . . . I had some idea. But . . .'

'Champagne,' the Air-Commodore announced. 'Open a bottle, Joly. No, make that two bottles, since we have two things to celebrate: Johnnie's new status, and your engagement.'

Jolinda gazed at John for several seconds, then went to the sideboard and the cold box.

'And you'll stay for dinner and the night. When are you due back at the station?'

'Not until Monday morning, sir. Unless there's a crisis.'

'Ah. Well, we'll have to sort something out as regards sleeping arrangements. Now for the really big news. Remember I told you a couple of weeks ago that we were considering every possible means of carrying the war into Germany, of making them realize that they *are* at war? Well, the idea has at last been passed as practicable. Risky, mind. Dangerous. We don't know how many are going to come back. But the crews are all volunteers.'

'Volunteers for what, sir?'

'To penetrate German air space and bomb Berlin.'

There was a moment's silence while Jolinda handed out glasses of champagne.

'Do you think they can bring it off, sir?' John asked.

'As I said, it's risky. But Bomber Command thinks they can. And if they can, well, what a propaganda coup. It'll show the Yanks that we're not about to lie on our backs with our legs in the air. With respect, Joly.'

'Accepted, Daddy. But is it legal? I mean, can Berlin be considered a military target?'

'Eh? What about Guernica? Warsaw? Rotterdam.'

'Yes, but those were crimes committed by the Nazis. Aren't we fighting the Nazis to stop that sort of thing happening again?'

Hargreaves stared at her with his mouth open.

'Well,' John put in, 'wouldn't you say Hitler's Chancellery is a legitimate target? Certainly if there's a chance that he may be in it?'

'I suppose that is a point of view.'

'That's brilliant,' the Air-Commodore said, holding out his glass for a refill. 'There you have it, Joly. You've been shot down by England's latest ace.'

'As you say, Daddy.' Jolinda drained her own glass and refilled them all.

'When is this to happen?' John asked. 'Or is that top secret?'

'Well, it is. But I think I can share it with you two. They're going in tonight.'

'Wow! And when will we know the result?'

'Not for a day or two, I imagine. We must keep our fingers crossed. Now, about this weekend. I don't really think we can ask our newest ace to spend two nights on the settee.'

'Of course we can't,' Jolinda agreed. 'Leave it with us, Daddy.' She brushed her glass against John's. 'We'll sort something out.'

'Gentlemen!' Reich-Marshal Goering projected his usual beam at his assembled flight-commanders. 'I congratulate you. Over the past three weeks you have just about won the war against England. The RAF is on its knees.'

Here we go again, Max thought, and it had taken three weeks rather than the original four days. He knew his perspective was necessarily limited to the small area of south-east England over which he and his men had been operating with the bombers they had been escorting. He knew they had inflicted considerable damage on the airfields they had attacked, and he also knew that they had shot down a large number of the enemy interceptors; he personally had had a highly successful time. But he also knew that the Luftwaffe, at least in his vicinity, had taken very considerable casualties – from his point of view the more serious because he had lost several of his veterans and was now having to operate with relatively inexperienced pilots. Obviously, not all those who had gone down had been killed; he had watched them parachuting to safety often enough. But to a German pilot, parachuting to safety also meant parachuting out of the war as a prisoner – unlike the British, who were simply picked up and returned to their squadrons.

Most important of all, he had discerned no diminution in the RAF's morale, the élan of its pilots. What he *had* noticed was steady improvement in their battle tactics, a readiness – indeed an eagerness – to mix it, in such strong contrast to the disastrously rigid methods of attack used over France in May. And why not, he wondered; they had the better planes, although he would not have admitted that to anyone.

But Goering was still speaking with the utmost confidence. 'Our aerial photography reveals that for all their efforts to patch up their airfields, they are nearly all still just a mass of rubble. Our agents report that morale is low and sinking. And when in addition we have casualty figures of the RAF suffering two or three losses to every one of ours, you understand what I mean.'

Max wondered from just where he obtained those casualty figures.

'I can now tell you,' Goering continued, 'that based upon this considerable victory in the air, the Fuehrer has named a date for the commencement of Operation Sea Lion, the invasion of England. It will be September fifteenth – that is, three weeks from today. As you may know, or have observed, the invasion fleet has been assembled, the barges are waiting, and forty of our veteran divisions are poised to make the crossing. For all their efforts, the British have no more than a dozen sufficiently well-equipped divisions with which to oppose us, and I may say that none of them can be described as veteran.' He grinned. 'At least in terms of winning battles.

'Now, that will be the decisive day of the war. And make no mistake, gentlemen, the British will fight like rats in a trap. We know that they retain considerable air forces in the north of the country. We intend to neutralize as many of these as possible by continuing our attacks from Norway, but some, perhaps most of them, will certainly be brought south to defend the coasts. So you see, you are not yet finished with shooting down Spitfires, eh? The last big battle lies ahead. All we need to do now is keep battering at their defences, keep destroying their airfields, keep shooting down their planes, keep their morale at rock bottom, for another three weeks, until we administer the coup de grâce.

'However, bearing all of the factors I have just outlined in mind, and most importantly, also bearing in mind that we need you to be fresh and ready to go on the fifteenth, I have decided that all squadrons will be given rest periods of two days, starting now. The date list for all pilots is being issued.'

He paused for another beam, and his officers broke into applause. Then he gave the Nazi salute, to which they responded, and led the way into the antechamber where champagne and canapés were being served by black-skirted waitresses. He immediately picked out his favourite airman. 'Well, Max,' he boomed. 'You will be going home to your so beautiful wife, eh? You must be looking forward to that.'

'I am, Herr Reich-Marshal.'

'Well, I am sorry that you're not on the first roster. But you will be home in a few days.'

'Of course, sir.'

'Meanwhile, see what you can do about your brother, eh?'

'Sir? My brother was shot down over the Channel, several weeks ago, by Senior-Lieutenant Langholm.'

'That is quite correct. But he wasn't killed. They apparently fished him out of the water and restored him to health. They are now calling him England's newest air ace. Do you know how many kills he has? Ten! That is what they call an ace, eh? What is your score, Max?'

'Thirty-two confirmed, Herr Reich-Marshal.'

'I think we will let them know this. Let them know the score of a *real* ace, eh?' He clapped Max on the shoulder, and went on to chat with other officers.

So John had survived his ditching. Max didn't know whether to be glad or sorry. But if a climactic battle was coming up, they might still meet again.

PART THREE

The Hour of Decision

'Never in the field of human conflict was so much owed by so many to so few.'

Winston Churchill.

Seven

Bombs

'My father certainly seems very fond of you,' Jolinda remarked. 'I think he regards you as the son he never had.'

She sat next to John on the settee, drinking port. The Air-Commodore had just gone up to bed.

'Well,' John said. 'I'm very fond of him. Everything about him. Particularly his relatives.'

'I don't think you'd be very fond of my mother, principally because I'm damn sure she wouldn't be very fond of you.'

'But you take after your dad, in everything. Every movement, every thought, every ambition, even in looks. Well, you're an improvement, of course.'

She regarded him from beneath arched eyebrows, and he put down his glass. 'There are some things about you, though, that I don't quite understand. Like how you became a section-officer after only a few weeks' service. I know it is probably rampant nepotism, but I don't see how even your dad could have pulled that one in so short a space of time.'

'Experience.'

'Say again?'

'I spent two years as a WAAC before becoming a WAAF.'

'I'm sorry, you will have to repeat that.'

She sighed. 'I belonged to the Women's Army Air Corps. That's American. I rose to the rank of lieutenant. Then with this thing over here getting serious I wrote Daddy and asked him if I could join the Women's Auxiliary Air Force. That, as you may know, is British. He said he'd love to have me, so I resigned my commission, and here I am. It was necessary to spend a brief time getting acquainted with your rules and regulations before I got my new commission.'

'But you always knew it was going to happen?'

'Yes. Or I wouldn't have come.'

'I see you only operate from the top. May I ask a very personal question?'

'I suspect you are going to.'

'How old are you?'

'I am twenty-two.'

'Brilliant! So am I. And I was born in January. So I must be older.'

'By nearly a year.'

'Right. Well that clears that up. I take it you have been kissed before?'

'Once or twice.'

'And . . . Aah?'

'Once or twice. Does that shock you?'

'That rather relieves me. But there's no, well, I mean, nothing permanent back there?'

'I'm not a mother as far as I know, and I think I'd pass a blood test.'

'Blood test for what?'

'Syphilis. But you don't have that law over here. I'm assuming you would also pass.'

As their faces were so close, he kissed her, and allowed his hand to drift up her thigh. She accepted the kiss, with some enthusiasm, but moved his hand. Then she took her mouth away. 'We still have some sorting out to do.'

He kissed her again. 'But if I'm to share your bed to-night . . .'

'I'm not sure it's a good idea to sleep with a man before you marry him. Sort of takes away the anticipation of the wedding night. Anyway, you promised not to screw me until we are married.'

'My idea was that you would screw me.'

'Eh?'

'That you would be on top.'

'You do seem to plan ahead. However, I'm not sure that's something one should do with a husband. It might give him an inferiority complex.'

'You mean if you weren't going to marry me, you would. Get on top, I mean?'

'If I liked you enough.'

'And you're not even sure of that,' he said sadly.

She regarded him for several seconds. Then she stood up, picked up both glasses, placed them on the sideboard, went to the door and turned back to look at him. 'What the hell. There's a war on, you're a hero, and we may all be dead tomorrow. In these circumstances, I really would like to be loved.'

As always Berlin glowed with light. And as before, Max did not touch down until just after dusk. He reached the Stumpff mansion at eleven, and was, as usual, greeted with some apprehension by Reynald.

But there were voices coming from the drawing room. 'Is Herr Stumpff entertaining?' Max asked, handing the butler his cap and overnight bag.

'Herr Stumpff and Frau Bayley are in the drawing room, Herr Captain. Shall I announce you?'

'Not this time, Reynald.'

The doors to the drawing room were actually open, and he crossed the hall and looked into the huge room where not only his wife and father-in-law were seated, but also Erika. She was the first to see him and sprang to her feet. 'Max! How lovely to see you!'

Heidi also stood up, rising rather like a startled rabbit. 'Max!' She hurried across the room to throw herself into his arms and shower him with kisses. 'How long have you got?'

'Two nights.'

'How wonderful!' But she turned to look at Erika, whose expression never changed, although she made a slight moue.

Stumpff also got up, more slowly – he was overweight. 'My dear fellow. You have come to make my daughter happy. Cognac?'

'That would be very nice, sir.' He accepted the drink, raised his glass. 'Heil Hitler! To victory.'

They joined him in the toast but Erika drained her glass and set it down. 'I must be off.'

'Oh! But . . .' Heidi looked from face to face.

'You two love birds will want to go to bed. Two nights isn't very much.' She kissed Stumpff, then Max, and went to the door.

'But you had a bag,' Stumpff said.

'Reynald will fetch it for me. Ta ta.' She disappeared into the hall.

'Actually, sir,' Max said, 'it would be nice to lie down.'

'Of course, my dear boy. I was young once myself, you know.'

Max held Heidi's hand and led her up the stairs. 'Were you two planning a night together?' he asked.

'Now, Max . . .'

'I'm not carping. I know I come second.'

'That's not true. But we've been friends for so long, shared so much, you know that.'

He opened their bedroom door. 'I do indeed. And as I said, I'm happy for you.'

'Oh, Max!' She put her arms around his neck to kiss him and move her body against his, then stepped away from him, and with her usual speed, unfastened her evening gown and let it slide down to her ankles. As always, she took his breath away.

He stepped towards her, and checked as the house became filled with a high wailing sound that was reverberating across the entire city. 'My God! What is that?' Heidi demanded.

'That's an air-raid siren!' Max ran to the window, watched the first searchlights beaming up into the night sky.

At that moment the first bomb fell.

'Aaagh!' Heidi screamed, and Max realized she would never have heard a bomb exploding before, and probably never a shot, at least one fired in anger. Now she screamed again, as there was another explosion.

He grabbed her shoulders and shook her. Her breasts trembled, her head bobbed up and down, and her hair flailed. 'Pull yourself together!'

Now the explosions were almost continuous, and very close: the house shook. 'What are we to do?' she wailed.

Max considered briefly. He knew there was a subway station nearby, which could be used as a shelter, but he was reluctant to take her there: she was too hysterical. 'I think your cellars would be our best bet.'

'Yes,' she said, and ran to the door.

'Not like that!' He picked up her dress and threw it at her.

'Oh!' She dropped it over her head, and the house shook again to a very loud explosion. She opened her mouth and he grabbed her arm.

152

'Screaming isn't going to help at all.'

By now there were shouts and screams from all around them. Herr Stumpff, who had followed them up to the second floor, was standing at the top of the stairs waving his arms and shouting. Reynald was standing at the foot of the stairs, waving his arms and shouting. Brushing past their employer, in their nightdresses, with plaited hair following them like comets' tails, three female domestics were on their way down from the attics, waving their arms and shouting.

'Heidi!' Stumpff bellowed. 'Hurry, girl, hurry!'

Heidi tripped over her dress and fell to her hands and knees. Max scooped her up and half carried her down the stairs. 'Get your people into the cellars,' he told the panic-stricken Reynald, who began ushering the women towards the doorway under the stairs. By now, Stumpff had come down, and Max handed him his daughter. 'You should be all right down there.'

'Where are you going?'

'To find out what's going on.'

He went to the front of the house, unlocked the doors, and stood at the top of the outside steps. The raid was already over, although the searchlights continued to scour the sky, and there were still bursts of anti-aircraft fire to be heard. But the Tommies had completed their daring venture, and were trying to get home. He wondered how many of them would make it.

The raid had been a success, at least in propaganda terms. He did not suppose an enormous amount of damage had been done, but there were several fires to be seen. As for morale, now that the All-Clear siren was going, the streets were filling with excited, frightened, and angry people. He wondered what Goering – and even more, Hitler – were going to make of this.

Erika staggered up the street towards him, and he went down the steps to hold her as she nearly fell on to the path. 'My God! Have you ever known anything like that?'

'I'm usually part of the force that drops the bombs,' he said. 'It's worth knowing how the other side feels. Are you all right?'

'I went into the subway. It was terrible. There were people everywhere, jostling me, grabbing me – some were even being sick. Ugh!'

'You need a drink.' As with Heidi, a few minutes before, he half carried her up the steps and into the drawing room, sat her in a chair, and poured brandy.

She held the balloon in both hands, and drank greedily. 'I was scared. God, I was scared. The thought of being blown up, or of having bits blown off me . . .' She seized his hand. 'Hold me, Max. Hold me.'

He sat on the arm of her chair and put his arm round her. 'It's something you may have to get used to.'

'But Goering always said it couldn't happen.'

'He does have a penchant for making mistakes.'

'Oh, Max!' She buried her face in his chest. 'Love me, Max. Love me!'

'Well, really,' Heidi remarked from the doorway.

'I'm glad you've done this sort of thing before,' Jolinda remarked, sitting on the edge of the bed and watching the dawn light filling the window. 'The most excruciating experience a woman can have is to be in bed with a man who doesn't know where to go, and what to do when he gets there. Do you still want to marry me?'

John supposed the quickest way to describe her was elegant. He had already known she had long, slender legs, but the rest of her matched exactly with small buttocks and delightfully shaped breasts. But all of that he had known, to differing degrees, in other women. The real conquest, which he knew he had not yet achieved, would be over that sophisticated, quick-fire and so stimulating brain of hers. 'I have never wanted to marry you more,' he said.

She stood up, fluffed out her hair and put on her dressing gown. 'Then we do need to make plans.' She left the room.

John lay back with a contented sigh. Had he any right to have, and be able to anticipate, such happiness, literally at his fingertips? He knew he had behaved very badly to Avril, but it was one of those decisions that had to be made. To marry in order to spend the rest of his life in guilty misery would have been to make her as miserable as himself. Now he could only hope that she would also find someone with whom she could be happy.

The door opened and he turned to look at her but instead came face to face with the Air-Commodore.

'Joly, can you tell me where John is?' He blinked in the half light. 'Ah!'

'You did say we could make our own arrangements,' Jolinda said from behind him. 'You also said, if I remember rightly, that he should knock some sense into me. Well, he's been doing that all night.'

'Ah!' Hargreaves said again. 'Yes. I have the most tremendous news. They brought it off.'

'Are you referring to us, or somebody else?' his daughter inquired.

'I'm talking about the raid, you silly girl.'

John felt it was safe to sit up. 'They've done it?'

'That's what I said. Harris is cock-a-hoop. Well, he should be.'

'Did they hit the Chancellery?' Jolinda asked.

'We have no details yet, but they certainly dropped their bombs. Over a hundred planes were used.'

'Casualties?' John asked.

'I'm afraid they were quite severe, but again, I don't have all the details. Now I think you two need to get dressed. I've had another phone call, and we are going to a wedding.'

'Already?' Jolinda demanded.

'This has actually been arranged for some time,' her father said.

'You old buzzard!' Jolinda exclaimed.

'Well, we didn't know if both of you, or either of you, would be able to attend,' Hargreaves explained, 'in view of what's been happening the last few days. But as you both have the day off, let's get to it.'

Joan Carling looked radiant; her husband was very proud. So was Mark, as he followed them out of the tiny church and escorted them to the waiting car. Then he showed Jolinda and John to the second Rolls.

'I'm not sure that we have actually met, sir,' Jolinda said as she settled herself on the cushions. 'At least since I was rather small.'

'Oh, I remember you,' Mark replied. 'Although I am bound to confess I'm a little confused about exactly what is going on. Delighted, mind, but still confused. Your father has attempted to explain it to me, but I'm not sure he actually understands it, either. It would be a help if someone could bring me up to date.' He looked at John.

'Ah, yes, well the fact is, Dad, that there has been so much going on that there simply hasn't been time to get home.'

'And when you have had time, you've been spending it at the Air-Commodore's home. I'm not criticizing . . .' He looked at Jolinda, trim in her uniform. 'I can see you had compelling reasons for doing so. But I would like to have known that you had sorted out the other matter in a decent fashion.'

'It really isn't possible to break an engagement in a decent fashion, Dad,' John said, 'but marriage to Avril would have been a disaster, and you know it.'

Mark looked at Jolinda again.

'Oh, I am undoubtedly the scarlet woman, but no one told me about that, either, until it was a *fait accompli* – in his mind, anyway.'

'But it's what you want?' Mark asked.

'Oh, yes.'

'Well then, am I allowed to kiss the bride to be?' He did so. 'Which will be when, do you think?'

'As soon as Jerry allows us more than a weekend off,' John said.

'Yes,' Mark agreed, a trifle grimly. 'Anyway, for today we have two couples' happiness to celebrate.'

There were only half a dozen guests, comprising, apart from John and the Hargreaves, Mark and Joan's younger sister, Millie, and her husband, who was a bank manager, and their two children. These all seemed to regard Mark and Joan with some apprehension, and they also seemed overwhelmed by the presence of an air-commodore, resplendent in full dress uniform. There was also Helen Stanton, who had driven over in her horse and trap, as she lacked the petrol allowance of the service officers. She was Joan's matron of honour, and was mostly obscured beneath an enormous hat.

Joan took Jolinda to one side after the toasts had been drunk. 'Mark has just told me your good news. I'm delighted.'

'No reservations?'

Joan raised her eyebrows.

'Did you know my predecessor?'

156

'I never met her.'

'But you knew about her?'

'John told us, yes. And we went along with it. I can't pretend we were over the moon, but John has a lot of his father in him and is difficult to deflect from his chosen course.'

'You can say that again!'

Joan kissed her. 'But I think if anyone can control that course, that's you.'

Jolinda hugged her in turn. 'Are you going to be living around here? It'd be so nice to have a chat from time to time.'

'Unfortunately, Jimmy has a place in London and I'm moving up there this afternoon. But I will be down as often as I can.'

Her place was taken by Helen, peering out from under her brim. 'A little bird has been whispering to me that you're the next Mrs Bayley.'

'It's beginning to look that way,' Jolinda said. 'I don't think we've met . . .'

'Helen Stanton.' They shook hands. 'I hope to see a lot of you.'

'Now what did she mean by that?' Jolinda muttered to John, as Helen moved away. 'She's not a relative, is she?'

'No,' John said, watching Helen holding Mark's arm. 'But I've an idea she would like to be. Well, it'd be a bit rough for Dad to be left all alone in this pile. But of course,' he added brightly, 'this'll be your home, too, soon enough.'

Helen stood beside Mark to watch the last of the guests departing. 'They make a lovely couple,' she remarked.

'I think Joan is an inch or so taller,' Mark objected.

'I was talking about John and Jolinda Hargreaves. She's such an attractive girl. Are they really going to get married?'

'I fervently hope so, even if I wonder if the girl really knows what she is taking on.'

Helen went back into the hall and picked up the hat she earlier discarded. 'Did Karolina?'

He grinned as he closed the door. 'I think she had some idea. I was an invalid and virtually at her mercy during the beginning of our relationship.'

'What a romantic life you've led.' She peered at herself in the mirror as she adjusted the hat.

'These things only appear romantic on reflection. When they are actually happening you are too busy having them happen, if you follow me. You don't have to rush off, you know. Why not stay to supper?'

She gave him a quizzical look. She had not yet attempted to follow up the advice given her by Joan, nor had she been encouraged to do so before this minute.

'That is, if you're prepared to risk it.'

'Even if I have no idea what I'd be taking on,' she commented. 'Tell you what, if you'll help me feed Willow and settle him, I'll say yes.'

'Settle him for how long?' Mark asked.

Helen took off her hat again. 'As you said, when it happens you're too busy having it happen to worry about time.'

This morning there was no beaming smile. Reich-Marshal Goering stamped into the room and surveyed his assembled officers with a scowl.

'Three days ago,' he announced, without his usual preamble, his voice harsh, 'the Royal Air Force bombed Berlin.' His angry gaze swept their faces. Max sat up straight. 'It appears you gentlemen were not aware of this.'

There was a moment's silence. Then Colonel Hartmann ventured, 'We were told one or two isolated planes got through into the interior.'

'There were over a hundred planes, Herr Colonel. But there were no interceptors to check them.'

'We had spent the entire day over England,' another colonel protested. 'Our people were exhausted, and we were not given sufficient information.'

'Was a great deal of damage done?' asked someone else.

'In purely physical terms,' Goering said, 'very little. And our anti-aircraft defences did shoot down a number of the enemy planes.'

'And my squadrons got quite a few on their way back,' declared another colonel.

'That may be, but as you say, that was after they had dropped their bombs. The people were shocked. I am shocked.' He drew a deep breath. 'The Fuehrer is furious. Fortunately, he was not in Berlin on that day, but I have never seen him so angry. That none of you gentlemen has been cashiered is because I defended you. However, he has now grown entirely tired of these wearisome people. He told me if they want war to the knife they will have war to the knife. His orders are specific. London is to be razed to the ground.'

There was an enormous rustle as the officers looked at each other. Again, Hartmann was the first to speak. 'When you say "razed to the ground", Herr Reich-Marshal . . .'

'I mean, razed to the ground, Herr Colonel. Every plane we possess is to be launched against the city. We will use a mixture of high explosive and incendiary bombs. They talk of the Great Fire of London nearly three hundred years ago. This will be the Greater Fire of London, eh? It will be the duty of you gentlemen to escort and protect the bombers. I know there will be problems with fuel, so the 109s will take them to London, return to base, fuel up and go back to escort them home again. The 110s will afford protection over the city itself.'

Another silence. 'What of the RAF?' someone asked.

'They will undoubtedly come up to meet you and you will shoot them down. Have you not been doing this successfully for the past month?'

Another rustle. 'The job of depriving them of their airfields is not yet completed, Herr Reich-Marshal,' Max ventured.

'Bah! Enough has been done to severely limit their ability to continue. The assault will commence one week from today, September seventh, by which time all of your machines must be fully serviced and ready for sustained action.' At last the glimmer of a smile. 'That goes for you also, gentlemen.'

'And for that week, Herr Reich-Marshal?'

'You will maintain limited operations over south-east England, just to keep them occupied. Thank you, gentlemen. You have your orders. I wish to see them carried out.'

Hartmann accompanied Max and Gunther into the antechamber. 'Would you agree this is an overreaction to a few bombs?'

'I would say it is a strategic error of the greatest magnitude,' Max replied. 'It is not possible to destroy a city the size of London by bombing. It is actually not possible to destroy a city the size of London at all, certainly with any weapon presently known to man. This is going to give the RAF the breathing space they must have been praying for. And I cannot see that the diversion of our air strength to one limited objective is going to assist our armies to cross the Channel.'

Hartmann nodded. 'The Fuehrer is allowing prestige to get in the way of military sense. Still, gentlemen, as we have tied our futures to his star we must, and we will, carry out our orders to the very best of our ability.'

'You were in Berlin at the time of the raid, were you not, Max?' Gunther asked as they got into the car to be driven back to Ostend.

'Yes,' Max said. 'When you think of what we did to Warsaw and Rotterdam it really was meaningless.'

'But your wife is in Berlin. Was she all right?'

'My wife,' Max said, 'is never all right.'

'Seems a bit quiet,' Browne remarked.

'Has been all week,' John agreed.

'Do you think he's packed it in? I mean, we're into September. He can't expect the weather to last much longer.'

'Who's complaining? Do you realize, sir, that both 777 and 833 are at maximum strength for the first time in a month?'

'That's splendid.'

'So I, ah, was wondering if I could have a couple of days' leave?'

'Don't you see enough of her here?'

'Actually, no, as we are mostly situated at opposite ends of the runway. What I would like is to marry her, while we have this opportunity.'

'Good God! I had no idea things were that serious. She doesn't wear a ring.'

'She feels it would be incorrect in uniform, sir. As a matter of fact I haven't actually bought a ring yet.'

'But she's in on this marriage idea? Does the Air-Commodore know?'

'We have his blessing, sir.'

'Well then, you'd better get on with it. You can have three nights, starting today. But I must know where you are honeymooning, so that I can call you back if needs be.'

'Thank you, sir. I take it this leave also applies to Section-Officer Hargreaves?'

'It would be a bit tricky going on honeymoon all by yourself. Congratulations, John. Have a nice wedding.'

John left the office and hurried across the apron, past his pilots who were lounging either in deck chairs or lying on the grass, chatting or reading newspapers. His rapid movement aroused their interest, but as he didn't approach them, they subsided again. He reached the WAAF office and opened the door. The girl at the typewriter hastily stood to attention. 'At ease,' he said. 'The boss around?'

'She's in her office, sir.'

John opened the inner door, and Jolinda looked up from the papers she had been studying, then, like her secretary, she rose and stood to attention. 'At ease,' John repeated.

'Trouble?' she asked. 'You look agitated.'

'I am agitated. We've just been given permission to get married. Collect your gear and we'll nip up to town, get a special licence, be married tomorrow morning, and have a two-day honeymoon. We'll go to the Savoy. Dad can foot the bill.'

Jolinda sat down again, somewhat heavily. 'Phew!'

'Don't you want to?'

'Well of course I want to. It's just a bit sudden. You mean, I have leave as well?'

'Darling,' John said, 'as the man has just pointed out, this is not something I can do on my own. I'll pick you up in ten minutes.' He leaned across the desk, kissed her on the forehead and went to the door.

As he opened it the secretary said, 'Wow! Look at that.'

John stood at the window and watched the Verey pistol cartridge exploding above the field in an arc of light. 'Oh, Jesus Christ!' Jolinda had also come to the door. He squeezed her hand. 'Looks like we'll have to hold.'

He ran back across the tarmac. His pilots were already getting to their planes. Coleman had come out of Dispersal. 'What in God's name is happening?' John shouted as he reached his machine.

Coleman panted up to him. 'London! The bastards are making for London. And in strength, apparently several hundred. They want every machine over there.'

Max looked down at the waters of the English Channel, and then left and right at the planes to either side and below him. The squadron was maintaining six thousand metres, the bombers three. There were a great number of them, Dorniers, Heinkels, and Junkers 88s – the much slower Stukas had suffered such heavy losses in their attacks on the radar stations that they had been withdrawn by Goering – all surrounded by 110s. At the higher level there were four squadrons of 109s: forty-eight planes.

When he looked further to his right he could make out another large formation a few kilometres away. This was certainly the biggest air offensive in which he had ever taken part.

Ahead of him he could now see the white cliffs of Dover and a few minutes later they were over land. He cast a quick glance at his fuel gauge, but he was still over half full.

Gunther was, as always, highest of all with A Flight, acting as watchdog. Now he said, in his usual quiet voice, 'I have babies, ten o'clock, five thousand. There are a lot of them.'

'Squadron will engage,' Max said, swinging his machine to the left. The sun was still rising behind them and shining into the eyes of the enemy. That, with their height advantage, gave the Messerschmitts the better position at least until battle was drawn. For a few moments, indeed, it seemed the British squadrons had not noticed them. Then there was violent reaction as they climbed as quickly as they could, but the 109s were on them before they had gained a parity in height.

A furious mêlée ensued. Max picked up target after target as the planes circled round him, and kept firing in short, sharp bursts. He was sure he hit at least three times, but it was impossible to spare the time to make sure.

The air was filled with excited chatter, not all of it in either English or German: he thought he recognized some words in both Czech and Polish. So, he thought, the English are scraping the bottom of the barrel in their search for pilots. Not that there was any indication of a diminution in either skill or determination – or élan, as the RAF planes hurled themselves at their enemies without the slightest hesitation.

The fight lasted about ten minutes. Then a voice said in German, 'I have no ammo.'

'Break off and go home,' Max ordered, and checked his own. He still had about 500 rounds left. But that was only a couple of bursts, and he had used most of his cannon shells, while, owing to the revving and maximum speed required of his engine, the gauge had now dipped well below half. 'Squadrons will return to base,' he ordered.

They had done their job. Their assailants deflected, the bombers had continued serenely on their way. Presumably they would meet more resistance, but he could do nothing about that, and at least those interceptors also needed to break off to rearm and refuel.

He looked down and saw the usual parachutes floating earthwards, whether English or German he could not tell. As his planes hurried away for the Channel and home, he discovered he had only nine left. The other 109 squadrons had also taken heavy losses, but then, so had the RAF. They might claim a small tactical victory, but the strategic win, to this point at any rate, was with the Luftwaffe: the bombers had got through.

Joan opened the door of her new flat. It was, of course, Jim's flat, but he had given her carte blanche to reorganize it as she thought fit. She had not yet done so in the two weeks she had lived here.

She carried the bag of groceries across the small sitting room and into the surprisingly large kitchen, placed them on the table and looked at her watch. It was just after ten. She put the kettle on and prepared a cup of coffee.

Then she took a turn around the flat, standing in the bedroom doorway for several seconds. She was still uncertain of her mood. Although during their brief courtship Jim had been unfailingly gentle and polite, it was with some apprehension that she had approached the matter of actually sharing a bed with him. She had had a somewhat wild youth, frowned upon by her parents – and also, she knew, by Mark. Her friends had been the other factory girls, and although she did not suppose that her background, as the daughter of a postmaster, was vastly better than many of theirs, she had known, because of her parents' interest in books, that she had been better educated. Yet she had thrown herself into the utterly hedonistic world of a society at war when, although they as women had been in no physical danger themselves, it had seemed entirely appropriate to equal their men folk in the idea of living for today, because tomorrow may never come.

The arrival of Karolina had changed all that, and not only

by their sudden elevation to wealth. Karolina had willingly given herself to Mark before their marriage, because she had determined that he was the man she wanted to marry, but she had been a most moral and upright character. She had made Joan feel ashamed, even though she had never, ever, criticized her sister-in-law or offered her anything but the warmest friendship and affection.

And so Joan had turned her back entirely upon her old life and had been happy to do so. Her new life had been built around Mark and Karo and the two boys. When that had disintegrated following Karo's death, and then Max's subsequent defection, she had felt every bit as adrift as Mark, and as a result had built a cocoon around her emotions.

Luttmann and his Gestapo thugs had shattered that cocoon, and her rescue by Klaus, followed so tragically by his death, had left it in ruins. Of one thing she had been certain: it had to be rebuilt as rapidly as possible. She had felt she was making progress, when along had come this man asking her to relive much of that trauma. She now knew that relating the events to a comparative stranger had done her a world of good, just as she knew that replacing the cocoon was impossible. That had resulted in a desperate desire to stay close to this man who had, no doubt unwittingly, entirely changed the direction of her life.

Jim was a very easy man to love. He had no apparent vices, and if he undoubtedly held strong opinions, he was too much of a gentleman to impose them on his wife. Yet he was a man. He had fallen in love with her body as much as with the idea of her: she did not suppose he understood, or ever could understand, the tortured workings of her brain, although he had made it very plain that he wanted, and intended, to be her support for the rest of her life.

But the body had been part of the deal, and she had not known how she would react to the yielding of it. On the first night they had spent together she had trembled with a mixture of fear and exhilaration. Yet he had been as gentle as always, and she had discovered he had a considerable appetite. In all her forty-three years she had never had anything like regular sex; Jim had wanted it twice a day on their honeymoon, and once a day since their return to London.

She could not complain about that, nor did she want to;

she continued to enjoy it. But it did rather seem to have taken over her life. Jim was, of course, very busy; he never got home before six and left early in the morning. Equally he did not feel able to discuss his work, as much of it was top secret. She had no friends as yet, although the other women in the building had all seemed friendly enough, and so her life had become very much a matter of preparing meals and waiting for Jim to come home when, so far at least, he would be randy as hell. As he knew her background he had not expected her to be caught up in any household drudgery, and so a woman came in every morning to clean and dust. She was, in fact, due in about ten minutes. But although it was pleasant to have company, they really had nothing to talk about. Beryl only knew that her employer's work was ''ush-'ush', and she knew absolutely nothing of her mistress's background.

Still, she was better than nothing. And there she was, using her own key to let herself into the flat. Joan returned to the sitting room.

'Good morning Beryl.'

'Good morning, ma'am. Nice day.'

'I know. I've been out in it, collecting the groceries. Today, I think . . .' She frowned. 'What's that noise? Sounds like an ambulance.'

'Ooh, ma'am, that's an air-raid siren.'

'In London?'

'Oh, yes, ma'am. They had it on a couple of weeks ago. Bombs and things. They said it was only two planes, which had got lost or something. But, ooh, it was startlin'.'

'Good lord. I suppose we had better close all the windows.'

Beryl, who was a short, thin woman, with greying mousey-brown hair and pinched features, looked sceptical. 'They do say, ma'am, that when the siren sounds, everyone should go to the nearest shelter.'

'Oh, really, Beryl. We aren't a military target.'

'No, ma'am,' Beryl said. 'Ooh!'

There were several sudden large explosions, none very close at hand, but not the less alarming for that. The two women ran to the window. Looking east towards the Thames they saw a column of smoke rising into the clear September sky. Above their heads there was a forest of barrage balloons, but beyond these they could now see the aircraft, at only a few thousand feet, clearly identifiable as bombers. Amongst them there now appeared little puffs of black and in fact they could hear the distant pop-pop of anti-aircraft batteries, but this did not appear to be making any impression upon the almost stately procession of the planes.

'Where is the RAF then?' Beryl demanded. 'They're supposed to be defendin' us.'

'I'm sure they're up there,' Joan snapped.

'Yes, but . . . Ooh!' she shrieked, as there was a huge crash from somewhere very close at hand, and the entire block of flats shook. 'We 'ave to get out of 'ere, ma'am. We're six floors up!'

Joan bit her lip. It was incredible to suppose that here, in this flat, where she was coming to feel so secure and protected by Jim's strength, she could be in any danger. But the glass in the window was cracked, and several ornaments had fallen off the occasional table by the settee, while the framed, faded photograph of her mother and father was hanging at a crazy angle. 'Yes,' she agreed. 'You'd better go down, Beryl. Where did you say the shelter was?'

'Just round the corner, ma'am. But ain't you comin'?'

'I'll be down in a minute.'

Beryl hesitated for a few seconds, then grabbed the hat she had just discarded and hurried through the door. Joan went into the bedroom. A hat, she thought vaguely. And a coat? It was a warm day, but would she be coming back before night-fall? She opened her wardrobe, pulled out a light summer jacket and a wide-brimmed summer hat, put them on, looked at herself in the mirror, and pulled a face.

Then she surveyed the room. Suppose she wasn't coming back? Suppose there was nothing to come back to? All of the things with which she was surrounded had a special meaning to her. The thought that she might never see any of them again was paralysing.

But she couldn't take *any* of them with her, much less all. She picked up her handbag, made sure the front-door key was in it, and went out into the lobby. She summoned the lift and was joined by another woman, who she had met briefly; she had the other flat on this floor.

'Oh, Mrs Carling, isn't it terrible? Huns, they are. Just Huns.'

'I suppose they don't think too much of us, either,' Joan said.

The lift arrived and the doors opened.

'You're not going in that?' Mrs Easton protested. 'That'll be dangerous, that will.'

Joan hesitated. Presumably this woman, having lived here since the war began, knew more about these flats than she did.

'The stairs,' Mrs Easton said. 'Harry always said if there's a fire, use the stairs. Never the lift.'

'But we're not on fire,' Joan countered.

'It could happen,' Mrs Easton insisted. 'Come along, dear.'

She led the way to the top of the stairs as the roof fell in.

Eight

The Battle

M ark heard the clip-clop of hooves and got up. But he had not reached the door when Clements appeared. 'Mrs Stanton is here, Mr Bayley.'

'Helen,' Mark said, and went into the hall. As it was a Saturday morning and he had not gone into the office, he had hoped she might drop by. Just as with Karolina, he was in her hands as regards their meetings: she was still a married woman, even if her nisi period was nearly completed.

'I'm not interrupting something?' she asked from the doorway behind the butler.

'You're interrupting only my lonely boredom.' He was still unsure how to regard her. She was the first woman he had slept with since Karo's death, and he was pretty sure he was the first man, apart from her husband, she had ever slept with. His withered leg, almost as much as Karo's memory, had put him off risking sex with any woman for those long six years. But she had coped, and indeed behaved, as if they had been two twenty-year-olds on the threshold of life.

Helen came closer, and, Clements having withdrawn, he took her in his arms and kissed her, then escorted her into the study.

'Heard from Joan?' she asked.

He grinned. 'I imagine she's still honeymooning. Drink?' He went to the bar.

Helen looked at her watch. 'It's past eleven. I could stand a pinkers.'

Mark splashed Angostura Bitters into a glass and added two fingers of gin. 'Water?'

'Don't let's spoil it.'

He gave her the glass, poured a scotch for himself and sat beside her, put his arm round her shoulders. 'How much time have you got?'

'I can stay to lunch. Did you see all those Jerry planes a couple of hours ago? There must have been hundreds of them.'

'They were a long way away from here,' Mark said. 'And I didn't hear any explosions.'

'They seemed quite close to me,' Helen said. 'But, as you say, they didn't drop anything in my vicinity, just kept on heading north. Most of them. Our lads were up and at them. The sky was a mass of vapour trails and quite a few came down. Some of ours did as well, of course.'

'You're making me green.'

'Do you think Johnnie was up there?'

'I imagine so.'

'Does it worry you, to know . . . well . . .?'

'It's not something one can really worry about. One waits for the phone to ring and hopes it will be him. I'd rather talk about you and me.'

She flushed, and finished her drink. 'What's there to talk about?'

Mark got up, took her glass and refilled it. 'When does your divorce become final?'

'A fortnight.'

'And no . . . er . . . repercussions?'

'I have not seen or heard of him for six months, if that's what you mean. For God's sake, he abandoned me, and I know he's living with another woman.'

'So how would you feel about trying it all again?'

'I think I'd like that.' She giggled and finished her second drink. 'But I am a little nervous.'

'So am I. I think this calls for champers.' He opened the cold box. 'And then, we'd better eat.' He rang the bell and

Clements hurried in. 'Mrs Stanton will be staying to lunch, Clements. Will you tell Mrs Steele? And would you air a bottle of claret?'

'Of course, sir.' The butler hurried off.

'That sounds most awfully civilized, although we're going to be pissed as newts,' Helen said.

'Why not? We're celebrating, and there's absolutely no reason for you to leave in a hurry.' He poured champagne. 'Would you mind if I switch on the radio? It would be interesting to know where that Jerry formation was actually going, if he wasn't after our airfields as usual.' He switched on the set. The bulletin was just beginning.

'. . . large formations appeared over London at ten o'clock this morning. Anti-aircraft fire, and our interceptor squadrons, have inflicted heavy casualties upon the enemy, but early reports indicate that there has been considerable damage. Several oil installations on the river are on fire, and residential areas such as Chelsea have been severely hit . . .'

Mark switched off the set. 'Shit!' he said. 'I do beg your pardon, Helen.'

'Well, I suppose it had to happen. I don't imagine Joan will be in any danger. I mean, there are six million people in London, aren't there?'

'Joan lives in Chelsea,' Mark said.

Pain. Nothing but pain. And confusion. Joan was surrounded by swirling dust, which made breathing difficult, and rendered thought impossible. Yet, as she was conscious, she had to be alive. And she was no longer falling, therefore she was on the ground.

I have fallen six storeys, she thought. And I'm alive? Then memory started to drift back. It had not been a direct fall, but a series of jolts as she had gone through a succession of disintegrating floors and stairwells, accompanied always by falling timbers and debris.

That she was alive had to be a miracle. Something must have broken the final impact. And she could feel it, a sort of cushion beneath her. Biting her lip, she put her hand down, and felt liquid. Hastily she pulled it back, then put it down again, and felt cloth encasing . . . a human leg!

169

Mrs Easton had been immediately in front of her on the staircase, and they must have come down together. The dust was settling and she could actually breathe now. 'Mrs Easton,' she said, not recognizing her own voice. 'Mrs Easton!'

She made herself fumble about beneath her, and felt a considerable amount of flesh but absolutely no response. Now the pain seemed to be growing; she had no idea where it was coming from – she could herself be dying.

She was also suddenly aware that she could not see. At eleven o'clock on a bright summer morning? She put her hand up, and encountered a very solid slab of timber about six inches above her head. That *was* a miracle. The beam, or whatever it was, must also have come down with them and prevented the rest of the building from falling on to her and crushing her to death. Which meant she was far from safe, and not necessarily going to survive.

She could hear nothing for several minutes, but she realized that was probably because of the ringing in her ears. Think, she told herself. I must not panic. What would Mark do? He would know people would be looking for survivors, and would eventually find her. Eventually!

The waves of pain were making her feel quite sick, and were emphasized by the absolute dryness of her throat. And then, suddenly, she thought she could smell smoke. Jesus! To lie here, unable to move, and be burned to death . . .

But the smoke seemed to fade, unlike the pain. And, as more and more awareness returned to her, she was increasingly conscious of Mrs Easton. Unlike her men folk, her acquaintance with death was limited. Daddy, Mummy, and Karolina, each stretched out in their coffin wearing good clothes and looking almost peaceful. She did not suppose that Mrs Easton was looking peaceful, and decided she was probably fortunate in being unable to see her.

Noise! Joan had no idea how long she had lain there. She had actually determined that she was going to die, and had found it a curiously relaxing thought, as it would mean the end of the pain. But now she wanted to live. There were people somewhere above her, pulling at timbers and shouting at each other. She drew a deep breath. 'Help!' she shouted. 'Help me!' Her voice was so thin she did not suppose anyone could possibly have heard her, but . . . had the noise stopped for a moment?

Then it resumed, a steady tapping and picking at the rubble above her. And suddenly there was a shaft of light creeping through the timbers. 'I am down here!' she shouted.

'Take it easy,' someone said. 'And you be careful,' the man said to people beside him. 'That stuff could come down.'

Joan blinked, time and again, and saw a fireman's helmet.

The pain was still there, but it was distant now, and the light was bright. She shut her eyes, opened them again and gazed at an anxious face beneath a starched, white cap.

'Doctor Hooley,' the face shouted, 'she's awake!'

Another face, this one split in two by a moustache. 'Hm! Can you speak?'

'Am I going to die?' Joan asked.

'Oh no, Mrs . . .' He looked at his clipboard. 'Carling, is it?'

'Then can I have something to drink?'

He snapped his fingers and the nurse held a glass of water to her lips while raising her head with her other hand. Immediately the pain tried to break through the sedative barrier, but nothing had ever tasted so good. 'Mrs Easton?' she asked.

'The lady they dragged out with you?' Dr Hooley asked. 'Was she a close friend?'

'Just an acquaintance.'

'Hm. I'm afraid she did not survive.'

'She saved my life.'

'How did she do that? She had been dead for two hours when they found you; that is, from almost the moment the building was hit.'

'She was underneath,' Joan explained. It seemed very important to get the facts exactly right, as if she were giving evidence to a policeman.

'I see what you mean.'

'So tell me why I'm alive?'

'The short answer is that you were lucky. But you have broken both legs and a couple of ribs. You're going to be all right, but it will take time. And . . .' He sighed. 'You've lost the baby.'

* * *

171

Joan awoke to find Jim sitting at her bedside. 'Sorry,' she said. 'I must have dozed off. They keep pumping me full of pills and injections.'

He kissed her on the forehead. 'You were fast asleep. Best thing for you, the doctor says.'

'I'm not going to be much use to anyone for a week or two, I'm afraid.'

'I think it may be more like a month or two. But as long as you get well . . .'

'Some marriage.'

'We've time.'

'What will you do? I mean, where will you live?'

'I'll take a room somewhere. We'll start house hunting when you are up and about.'

She caught his hand. 'Jim, I didn't know . . . I mean, did Dr Hooley tell you anything?'

He squeezed her fingers. 'Yes, he did. I'm most terribly sorry.'

'I didn't know. The embryo was only three weeks old. Must have come along on our honeymoon.'

'Well, when you're able, we'll have another honeymoon, right? Just don't worry about it. Don't worry about anything.'

'Mark . . .?'

'I telephoned him, and told him you are going to be all right. He's coming up tomorrow morning. I haven't been able to get hold of John, who's spending most of his time in the air shooting those bastards down.'

'Is it very bad?'

'It's difficult to inflict mortal damage on a city the size of London. And, as I said, we seem to be shooting them down in droves. But they keep coming in droves, hundreds of them at a time. They seem to have only one idea in mind and that is to do a Warsaw here. Again, as I said, they won't succeed, and it's difficult to see how this can possibly assist their invasion, supposing they do actually intend to invade. But, they are inflicting a lot of damage and too many casualties. The worst of it is, they are using incendiaries on a large scale. This is exacerbated by the destruction of so many water mains by the high explosives. They say on the news you can see the smoke for miles. But they are not winning. Now, you had better get back to sleep. You'll want to be on top form when Mark gets here.'

* * *

172

The pilots chattered excitedly as they left their machines and headed for Dispersal.

'Did you see that chap go in? It was a ball of fire.'

'Mine just went straight down.'

'Which one was that?'

'That big fat Heinkel.'

'Oh! I got him. I saw his wing breaking up.'

'But I hit him first. I saw the rear gunner die. I'll swear I was only fifty feet away from him.'

John and Newman followed more slowly, exchanging glances. There were only five of the original squadron left. The others were excitable tyros, most with less than twenty hours on Spitfires. They were eager and had the immortality complex of youth and lack of experience. It was incredible to recall that he had shared that emotion only four months ago. Now he no longer had any illusions about either himself or the situation he was in. When he got into his machine all doubts, all fears and all distractions disappeared as if he had turned a switch. His business was shooting down enemy aircraft, and he knew he was good at it, one of the best.

But he also knew that, by the law of averages, he had to run out of time and luck eventually. Sooner rather than later if this attritional conflict were to last much longer. He did not fear this prospect. He would go down where he most liked to be, in the cockpit of a Spitfire, and doing what he most liked to do, flying it.

Only the thought of the as yet unfulfilled joy of sharing his life with Jolinda caused him regret. He had slept with her on that single occasion; there had simply not been the opportunity since. It was not an experience he would ever forget. He could still feel the silky sheen of her skin, still hear her soft grunts of pleasure, still mentally enjoy the rapture of the mutual climax they had reached – after some considerable foreplay, to be sure. He was human enough even to feel a spark of anticipatory jealousy at the thought that after his death she would share that supreme experience with another man, because, however much and however long she might mourn him, there was no possibility of a girl like Jolinda not eventually finding a husband. But, as he would know nothing about it, he could only wish her well.

Dispersal continued to be filled with agitated chatter and

argument as to whose kills were genuine. This ceased momentarily as John sat before Coleman's desk. At twenty-two he was hardly older than any of his men, but to them he was the chief, a man with fifteen kills and superlative skills in combat. Now Coleman waited, pencil poised.

'Bowring went in,' John said. 'And Halliwell. I saw Halliwell bale out, but you'd better check that he got down safely. Bowring didn't make it. He just burst into flames. Can you fish me out his family's address?'

'Will do,' Coleman said. 'And you?'

'I think one for certain,' John said. 'And I'm pretty sure I hit three more, but I can't swear they went down. It was a bit hectic.'

'I'll check for confirmation,' Coleman agreed and looked up as the inner door opened.

'Nice going,' Browne said. 'We're claiming sixty kills for twenty-four of ours. That's a winning margin.' The pilots exchanged glances. Statistics were all very well, and good news for the BBC bulletins, but they brushed over the personal losses, as of their own two.

'A word, John.' Browne retired into his office. John followed, closed the door. 'Sit.' He waited while John settled himself. 'There's been a phone call.'

John's head jerked. A sequence of possibilities flashed through his mind. Dad? Jolinda? Or Max, shot down and taken prisoner? If he had every intention of bringing down his brother should he ever have the opportunity, he wanted him dead, not forced to stand trial for treason.

'It's your aunt, I'm afraid,' Browne said. 'Did you know she was living in London?'

'Yes. She moved up there when she married, to be with her husband.'

'Damn bad luck,' Browne said. 'The block of flats in which she was living apparently took a direct hit.'

'She's not dead?'

'No. But she's fairly badly hurt. I'd like to give you leave, John, but we simply can't spare anyone right now. Especially you.'

'Of course, sir.' John stood up. 'I must call Dad.'

'It was your father who called here,' Browne said. 'He was informed by Mrs Carling's husband, and said he was going up to town this morning. This all happened yesterday, apparently. As I said, damn bad luck.'

'Yes, sir. Then I'll call him later. Does Jolinda know?'

'I thought you should know first.'

'Thank you, sir. I'll just go over there now.'

The WAAF secretary stood to attention, as always.

'At ease.' John crossed the office, opened the door.

Jolinda stood up. 'I saw you come in. But . . .'

'Only ten. Yes. Bowring and Halliwell bought it, although I think Halliwell may be all right.'

She came round the desk and into his arms. 'Every time the flight comes back,' she said when she had got her breath back, 'and you're not all there, I think I lose a year of my life. But . . . there's something, right?'

He hugged her again. 'A bomb got Aunt Joan.'

'Oh, shit!'

'She's alive, but pretty badly hurt.'

'Can you . . .?'

'Not right now. Dad is representing the family. I thought you'd want to know.'

'I'm so sorry, Johnnie. She is going to be all right?'

'Given time. Well, I must go and have a shower and a lie down before the next call.'

She watched him leave the office, her eyes sombre.

Beerman stopped the Rolls in the house forecourt. He had been Mark's mechanic in the Great War and his chauffeur ever since demobilization. He had been present on the dreadful day Patricia Pope had arrived at Hillside with baby John, and had narrowly escaped death himself as he had tried to save his friend and employer's life. They had no secrets from each other, and he knew Mark's moods very well. Thus they had hardly spoken on the drive down from London. Now he said, 'She'll pull through, Mr Mark. She's as tough as they come.' He also knew, of course, that Joan had once been a prisoner of the Gestapo, even if he did not know the details.

'I know she will,' Mark agreed. 'But I'll be happier when they're certain there are no permanent injuries.' Beerman was already out of the car to hand him his stick; he knew exactly what was going through Mark's mind. 'And happier yet when we've got the bastards who did this.'

He limped towards the house, pausing to look at the horse which had been turned out to graze. Knowing that she was still there was an oddly satisfying feeling. He *was* lonely. For twenty years there had been a woman always in this house, providing both company and support. Now he was taking on another. He wondered, however fond he had become of Helen, if there was any woman alive who could possibly replace Karolina.

But perhaps this was essential. There could not be a stronger contrast between the tall, sophisticated, cool and yet totally erotic – when she wanted to be – Karolina, and the shorter, plumper, perhaps more vivacious, Helen, who was also capable of being erotic. He was in the mood to be selfish, and simply wait for events to unfold.

'Mark!' She was at the door before Clements, who hovered behind her, looking embarrassed at having his prerogatives pinched. 'Is she . . .?'

'She's going to be fine. It may take a little while.'

'Oh, Mark!' she stood in front of him. He took her in his arms and kissed her mouth.

Clements silently withdrew.

'I have called you here today,' Colonel Hartmann said, facing his flight-commanders, 'because the Reich-Marshal is not satisfied. Oh, we are winning the battle. There can be no doubt about that. Our pilots report that London is burning from one end to the other. However, we are suffering heavy and virtually unsustainable casualties. What I am telling you is, of course, confidential. But the fact that the 110 is proving no match for the Spitfire, which means not only that they are themselves suffering heavy losses, but that the bombers are, to a large extent, being left defenceless. The Reich-Marshal therefore requires that our attacks should be protected by 109s.'

There was a murmur of unease.

'I know it does not seem a practical proposition. However, it must be done. The intention is to fit a second extra fuel tank.'

He paused, and this time the murmur was more evident. 'With respect, Herr Colonel, this extra weight will reduce our speed to an untenable level,' Gunther said.

'In combat, yes,' Hartmann agreed. 'But you do not engage

in combat until you meet the enemy, eh? At that time you will immediately jettison both tanks whether they are empty or not. It will be an aid to the attack if you drop a half-full fuel tank on an already burning target. This procedure should allow you to reach the London area with full orthodox tanks and therefore allow you to remain over the target area for perhaps half an hour, depending on the amount of combat you're engaged in.' He looked over their faces. 'The new tactics come into force tomorrow, September fifteenth. There will be six squadrons in the first wave. Three of these squadrons will provide cover over south-east England. If they are engaged they will fight off the enemy, and if they consider their fuel situation to be doubtful, they will return to base. If not, they will continue behind the main body. The other three squadrons must not be deflected from their task of protecting the bombers and assisting the 110s until the raid has been completed. JGs 41, 43 and 62 will form the wing unit. JGs 36, 37 and 48 will remain with the main body. I will wish you good hunting.'

'What do you think?' Gunther asked Max as they went out to their car.

'It should be interesting,' Max said. 'But we will stick to our usual tactics. You will maintain station two thousand metres above us with A Flight.'

Dawn broke soon after they took off. This was an even more impressive and spectacular event than the first London raid. The air fleets rendezvoused over the Channel at first light and droned to the north at four thousand metres – several hundred of them in all. The coast of England was clearly visible, and the skies above were clear, although there was heavy cloud building over the North Sea to the east. They were there in a few minutes, even flying at virtually half speed so as not to outpace the bombers. This made the 109 a very difficult aircraft to control and the concentration necessary precluded any consideration of what might lie ahead. But it did occur to Max, with some amusement, that this would be only the second time in his life that he had actually seen London. His father had taken both boys up for a weekend in 1935.

They had only just crossed the coast when a voice said,

'Babies, ten o'clock, several squadrons, five thousand metres.'

Immediately the designated three squadrons peeled off to meet the oncoming foe. It was a strange sensation to be ignoring the battle and continuing on his way. Nor was it entirely successful, as the RAF smashed through the outer defences to reach the bombers. Max made an instant decision. 'Engage,' he commanded, 'but rejoin as quickly as possible.' He turned his own plane, climbing as he did so, and found a Spitfire on his tail travelling much faster than he could. Another instant decision. He jettisoned both reserve fuel tanks. The plane responded as though let off a leash. He dived under the next Spitfire, losing the man on his tail who had apparently been distracted by the sight of what appeared to be a large part of the 109's fuselage breaking away, and came up on the tail of another. He loosed a burst of cannon fire into it at almost point-blank range, saw bits of fabric breaking away, and was then past it, seeking to regain his station.

He looked around, saw that eight of his nine planes were coming behind him, looked up and saw Gunther also hurriedly regaining his position, but he too had lost one.

From then on, for the next fifteen minutes, the battle was non-stop, as time and again the Spitfires regrouped and attempted to break through. Many of them did, and bombers kept spiralling downwards.

But now the pall of smoke that hung over London was clearly visible, dotted with shafts of flame. Above them the barrage balloons hovered majestically, but he was not required to become involved with them. He was, however, very aware of the clusters of exploding anti-aircraft shells.

Now the bombers were delivering their deadly cargoes, and there were more eruptions of flame and smoke below him. He looked at his fuel gauge and gulped. He was down to half full. 'Gunther,' he said, 'I have lost my reserve tanks.'

'So have I,' Gunther said.

'So have I,' said somebody else.

'JG 36 will break off combat and return to base.'

'Message understood, JG 36,' said the commanding colonel.

Max swung away, out over the Thames Estuary and the North Sea. He checked his instruments and swallowed. His compass was shattered. He had not been aware of being hit but now he realized that the side of the cockpit had been ripped open. Miraculously the bullets had missed him, but he was hurtling through space at more than 500 kilometres an hour, in which direction he did not know. Desperately he checked the sun, which gave him east, as it was still very early in the morning. But he needed to be more accurate than just east. He looked around in search of the squadron and could not see them. 'Gunther,' he called. 'Do you read?'

'Where are you?' Gunther asked.

'About fifty kilometres east of England. I've lost my compass. Where are you?'

'We have the Belgian coast in sight. Come into the sun and we will find you.'

At that moment Max found himself in the thick cloud coming up from the east, obliterating the sun and dislocating his sense of direction.

'Max?' Gunther called.

'I can't see a damn thing. What is your fuel situation?'

'We have enough to get down.'

'But not to search for me. Go home. That is an order.'

'But Max . . .'

'An order. I'll be along.'

But as he spoke his engine coughed. 'Correction,' he said. 'I may be a little late. Take command and go home. Flight-Commander down.'

'You saw him go in?' Hartmann asked.

'No, Herr Colonel,' Gunther said. 'He was in thick cloud. But I heard him.'

'Explain.'

'He had got separated from the rest of us. He said he had lost his compass. He could see the sun and must have turned towards it, but I think by then he was too far out into the North Sea, and then he entered the cloud. We were all low on fuel and he ordered us to get home if we could. He said he would follow, but then he said he was dry and going down.'

'And you have no idea exactly where he went in?'

'I can give you fifty kilometres either way,' Gunther said.

'In the middle of the North Sea,' Hartmann observed grimly. 'That does look fairly conclusive. Thank you, Herr Lieutenant.

You will take command of the squadron pending confirmation.'

'Heil Hitler!' Gunther left the office and Hartmann picked up his telephone.

Reynald opened the front door to the jangling bell, and peered at the officer wearing the uniform of the Luftwaffe. 'Is this the residence of Frau Heidi Bayley?' the officer asked.

'Frau Bayley lives here, yes, Herr Lieutenant.'

'May I have a word with her, please?'

Reynald considered. 'Frau Bayley is entertaining a friend to tea,' he pointed out.

'This is an urgent matter,' the lieutenant insisted.

A further brief hesitation, then the butler stepped back, pulling the door wide. 'If you will wait here, sir.'

The officer entered the hall, taking off his cap. Reynald hurried to the double doors of the drawing room. 'There is a . . . ah . . . gentleman here to see you, Frau Heidi.'

'Oh yes,' Heidi remarked. 'What sort of gentleman?'

'A Luftwaffe officer,' Reynald explained.

'Oh!'

'It's about Max,' Erika said.

'Whatever . . .?'

'You'd better see him,' Erika insisted.

Heidi went to the door, and the officer clicked his heels. 'Lieutenant Jurgen, Frau Bayley. At your service.'

'You have a message from my husband?'

Jurgen looked embarrassed, and glanced at Reynald, and then was even more embarrassed as he looked past Heidi at Erika, who had appeared behind her. 'Would you prefer to see me in private, Frau Bayley?'

'Why should she want to do that?' Erika inquired.

'Frau Haussmann is my oldest friend,' Heidi snapped.

'Yes, Frau. And . . .' Another glance at Reynald.

'Reynald is my butler. Come on, man, come on. Say what you have to say.'

Jurgen stood to attention and drew a deep breath. 'Captain Bayley is reported missing in action, believed killed.'

All three people stared at him for a moment, then Heidi's knees appeared to give way. Erika caught her round the waist before she could fall. 'Is this confirmed?' she asked.

'It is confirmed that he went down in the middle of the North Sea early this morning, Frau. We do not know if he was shot down or if he ran out of fuel. There had been a prolonged air battle immediately before. However, nothing has been heard of him since, and there is no word from the British of his being picked up. So we must assume the worst. Reich-Marshal Goering wishes me to express his deepest sympathies. His sentiment is shared by us all. Captain Bayley's feats will be long remembered.'

Erika half carried Heidi back into the drawing room and sat her on the settee. Heidi was by no means a dead weight, and Erika knew that her apparent faint had been largely theatrical. 'Reynald!' she called. 'Brandy for Frau Bayley.'

Reynald hurried to the sideboard, while Jurgen stood uncertainly in the doorway. 'Is there anything I can do, Frau?'

'I think you had better have a brandy, also. And pour one for me, too, Reynald.'

Reynald obliged, and Erika raised her glass. 'Is this what you do, inform wives that they are now widows?'

Jurgen sipped. 'It is something that has to be done, Frau, from time to time.' He looked at Heidi, who was now sitting up, knees pressed together, holding her balloon in both hands but not actually drinking. 'Is the Frau all right?'

'Well, of course she is not all right. Would you be all right if you had just been told that your wife was dead?'

'I am not married, Frau.'

'Is that so? You are an unfortunate boy –' he was quite a good looking fellow – 'never to have known the comforts of the marriage bed. My husband is at the other end of Germany,' she added meaningfully.

Jurgen hastily drained his glass. 'I must be leaving. There is work to be done. Again, my profound condolences, Frau Bayley.'

Reynald escorted him from the room, closing the doors behind him. Heidi also drained her glass and held it up. 'I need another.'

Erika poured. 'You did that very well. One would almost suppose you *were* shocked.'

'I am shocked.' Heidi sipped her second drink. 'I mean, I knew he was bound to get killed . . .'

'And you were anticipating being a famous widow,' Erika

reminded her. 'Now you are, or you will be once this news spreads.'

'Yes, but I didn't anticipate it just happening like this. So sudden. It took my breath away.'

'Death in war should always be sudden. This is far better than if he had been brought back here all torn to pieces by bullets, so you could watch him die. This way, you don't even have to look at his face.'

Heidi shivered, then looked up. 'What happens now?'

'Well,' Erika sat beside her. 'As they don't have a body, there can't be a hero's funeral. But, as he is a hero – how many kills did he have, thirty-five?'

'I think that was it. But he may have got another one or two today.'

'Well then, there will certainly be a memorial service. All the bigwigs will be there, perhaps even the Fuehrer. As Max's widow, you will be the centre of attention. You must look very beautiful, but also very tearful, even if it means using an onion.'

'But until then . . .?'

'You wear black, and a veil, and you go out as little as possible.'

'Damn! Pieter is coming to see me tonight.'

'Don't tell me you're still seeing that piece of shit?'

'He is very good in bed,' Heidi said sulkily. 'And so attentive. And polite.'

'Well, you will have to put him off.'

Heidi pouted.

'You have to do it,' Erika insisted. 'You have to be the grieving Frau.'

'But you'll be here?'

'Later. I have to go back to the hotel.'

'Why?'

'To telephone Father.'

'We have a telephone.'

'I'd rather do it . . . well . . . in private, if you don't mind. I have an idea he will be very upset. He was actually very fond of Max.'

Coleman put his head out of Dispersal window. 'Telephone call for you, John,' he said.

John, sitting on the grass playing chess with Newman, scrambled to his feet and hurried inside.

'It's your old man,' Coleman told him.

'Oh God!' John picked up the phone. 'Dad! Has something happened to Aunt Joan?'

'No.' Mark's voice was strange. 'It came through on the early news. The Germans have announced the death in combat of Flight-Commander Max Bayley.'

'When?'

'Apparently yesterday morning, in that monumental scrap over London. Were you there?'

'Yes I was. I had no idea . . .'

'How could you? Anyway, brace yourself. The Germans are making a big thing of it – Englishman joins the Luftwaffe and becomes an ace. They are saying he had thirty-seven kills. Do you believe that?'

'Actually, I would say that is entirely possible. He seems to have been an outstanding combat pilot and leader of men. A chap who came down a week ago, who I spoke with before he went off to prison camp, told me his men worshipped him.'

'Hm. Well, as I said, the papers will be full of it by tomorrow so . . .'

'Aren't you the least bit proud, Dad?'

'I wish it could have been different, but Max made his choice and has paid the penalty. Oh, there's something else you should know. I am getting married again. To Helen Stanton. I hope you approve?'

John was taken completely by surprise, and it was a second or two before he could reply. 'Well, of course I approve, Dad, if it's what you wish.'

Jolinda listened to what he had to say with obvious sympathy. 'Were you very close?' she asked.

'As little boys, I think we were,' John said. 'But you know how it is, or perhaps you don't. In the English public school system, although we went to the same school, as I was nearly two years older than him we didn't really see a lot of each other, except in holidays, when Karolina used to take us all off to Germany. But then I went to Cranwell. He was supposed to as well, but the summer before he was due to come up – that was two years ago – he became embroiled with Erika and I never saw him again.'

'Do you hate him now?'

'Not now he's dead. I don't think I ever hated him, although I never had any doubts that if I ever got him in my sights I would shoot him down. It was that bitch Erika I hated, and still do.'

'What about your new stepmother to be? I don't mean do you hate her,' she hastily added, 'but how do you feel about it?'

'I don't actually know her very well. I always thought she was more a friend of Aunt Joan's than of Dad's. Nor would I have said that she was the ideal wife for him. But if he thinks she can make him happy, well, he's entitled to a bit of that. He's had a pretty lonely and somewhat disappointing life since Karolina died, mainly because of Max, and . . .' He checked himself before he involved her in any of the family skeletons: they weren't married yet. 'There have been other problems.'

'You mean apart from his lame leg?' Jolinda suggested.

'Oh, I imagine he's used to that by now. But of course it has hampered his social activities; I mean, Karolina was virtually there when he was shot down. She never knew him as anything else but a cripple. I can see that getting too close to another woman must have been a daunting thought. I mean to say, it would be a bit traumatic to get into bed with someone and have her say, "Ugh!"'

'And you reckon this Helen person can handle that?'

'She's been a friend of Aunt Joan's for quite a few years and Dad has been closer to Aunt Joan than to anyone. I imagine Mrs Stanton knows what she is taking on.'

They were in her office and the door was open, so she could only squeeze his hand. 'I want to be part of it, Johnnie. I want to do my damnedest to make both you and your dad happy. Just stay alive, will you.' She turned away, picked up the sheet of paper on her desk. 'Have you seen these figures?'

'Yes, I have.'

'You sound sceptical.'

'A hundred and eighty-plus enemy aircraft shot down in one day? It would be great if it were true, but somehow . . .'

'What figure would you think is accurate?'

'Maybe half. And we suffered quite a bit, too.'

'I know. But . . . isn't it strange that they haven't come today?'

'Yet. They'll be along.'

* * *

Heidi walked along the pavement, heels clicking on the concrete. She felt totally irritated. Although she had not expected Max to die so soon, before she was really ready for it, she had anticipated the aftermath of the event with pleasurable excitement. But now she had been thrust into some kind of social limbo, apparently for the foreseeable future. Field-Marshal Milch had come to see both Papa and herself and explained that while there was going to be a memorial service, it would have to be delayed for a little while. The air battles were still raging over England so that no member of Max's squadron could be spared to come to Berlin at this time, and, as the invasion was still imminent, few high-ranking officers were available either, the Fuehrer least of all.

That had been last night, not long after Jurgen's visit. And she had had to put Pieter Leitzen off and there was no hope of getting together with him again for some time to come. What a mess!

She reached the gate to her father's front garden, opened it, and a car drew up behind her. She turned her head, hoping it might be Erika, but this was a black Mercedes, not a taxi. Two men got out. They wore belted coats and slouch hats.

'Frau Bayley?' one asked politely.

'I am she.'

'Would you come with us, please?'

'Come where? This is my father's house. My house, at the moment. My father is Helmuth Stumpff. You know this?'

'We know who your father is, Frau Bayley. But you must come with us.' From his pocket he took a wallet and flicked it open.

Heidi stared at it. 'Gestapo? You are from the Gestapo? What have I got to do with the Gestapo?'

The man's smile was cold. 'It is what the Gestapo has to do with you that matters, Frau Bayley.'

Heidi had an urgent desire to scream, combined with an even more urgent desire to run up the path, up the steps, and slam the front door behind her.

The man might have been able to read her mind. 'Please do not make a scene, Frau Bayley. It will be embarrassing for you. We only wish to ask you a few questions, and then we will, I am sure, be able to bring you home again.'

185

The car door was open. Heidi got in and was pushed, gently enough, to the centre of the back seat. One of the men sat on each side of her. They did not touch her with their hands, although their thighs were pressed against hers, and she began to regain a little confidence. Even if she had no idea what this could possibly be about, the very word 'Gestapo' carried such connotations that it was terrifying even to think about it. No one ever knew what the Gestapo knew, or what line of inquiry they might be following. It could be something to do with Erika. Erika kept some very shady company from time to time, and she had accompanied her to some of the less salubrious bars in the city. But now that she was in the hands of these thugs, she could only be patient, and concentrate so as not to say or admit anything that could be harmful to her friend.

No one paid much attention to the black car as it was driven through the streets: it was not a good idea for anyone to reveal interest in any Gestapo activity. Then they were through the gates of the imposing building above which a huge Swastika flag fluttered in the breeze.

The car stopped in the courtyard before one of the several doorways surrounding them. There was an armed, uniformed guard waiting for her as she got out, and the man who had arrested her accompanied her into the building, along a corridor between offices, to a flight of stairs. To her great relief, although most of the office doors were open to reveal clerks of both sexes, no one seemed the least interested. She climbed the stairs and was shown into a spacious office, dominated by a huge, full-length portrait of Hitler looking noble.

A man sat behind the desk beneath the portrait and stood up as Heidi was shown in. He wore a lounge suit, and although his features were harsh, he did not look very hostile. 'Frau Bayley! It is good of you to come in.'

Heidi, gaining in confidence, sniffed. 'I was not given much choice, Herr . . .?'

'I am Colonel Luttmann. Do sit down.'

Heidi sank into the chair before the desk and crossed her knees. The door closed, but she knew that at least one of the men had remained.

'Cigarette?' Luttmann invited.

186

'Thank you.'

Luttmann offered her a gold case, and a man appeared at her elbow with a lighter. Heidi drew smoke into her lungs and felt more confident yet. 'Now will you tell me what this is all about? I am sure you know that I am the widow of Squadron-Commander Max Bayley.'

'I do indeed, Frau Bayley. And my condolences are extended. Now, tell me about Pieter Leitzen.'

Heidi's head jerked, and ash fell on to her dress. She hastily brushed it away. 'Who?'

'We know you are acquainted with the gentleman, Frau Bayley. For instance, you telephoned him last night.'

Heidi stared at him. 'How can you know that?'

'We have been tapping his telephone for several weeks now. Would you like me to play you the tape of your voice?'

Heidi continued to stare at him. She wished she could get her brain working, but it seemed to be frozen.

'Well, it is there if you wish to hear it. I can tell you what it says. "You cannot come tonight. I have to be very careful until this Max business blows over." And he replies, "It is urgent that I see you." And you say, "I will call you as soon as it is possible." We would like you to tell us what this urgent business was.'

'Oh,' Heidi waved her hand, 'he is one of those men to whom everything is urgent.'

'He was your lover.'

'Well . . .' Heidi stubbed out the cigarette.

'You,' Luttmann said, his voice suddenly harsh, 'the wife of one of Germany's leading aces, have been carrying on with this unspeakable shit bag?'

Heidi fell back in her seat. Both his words and his demeanour seemed like a physical assault.

'You deserve to be punished for that,' Luttmann said, 'and you will be. But there is the far more serious matter of your treason to the Reich.'

Heidi sat up again. 'What are you saying?'

'Are you trying to deny that you have been giving Leitzen information on aircraft movements and dispositions?'

'He has told you that?'

'And a great many other things. He has told us every detail of your relationship, beginning with the night when he picked

187

you up in the bar at the Albert and you confided in him the plans for the initial air assault on England.'

Heidi felt as if her legs were turning to water – and other parts of her as well. 'I don't believe you. Pieter wouldn't . . . Well, why should he say something like that?'

'Because we, shall I say, persuaded him to do so.'

'You have arrested him? On what grounds?'

'He is an English agent. We have had him under surveillance for some time. But you knew this.'

'Of course I did not. Whatever he has told you is a pack of lies. I wish to see him.'

'I don't think you would enjoy that, Frau Bayley. At this moment he is a rather unhappy sight. I am sure you would not like to become an unhappy sight as well.'

Heidi gasped. 'Listen, I will tell you everything.'

'Thank you. That is most co-operative of you.'

'We met in the bar, as you say. He bought me a drink and, well, I found him attractive.'

'And so you immediately went to bed with him, although you are a married woman? Is this a habit of yours, to go to bed with any man who picks you up in a bar?'

'Well, I was distraught. My husband had just gone off to war, after only two days of marriage, and I . . . well, I needed comforting.'

Luttmann gazed at her for several seconds. 'You are a whore.'

Heidi bit her lip.

'But not content with being a whore, you are also a traitor to the Reich.'

'Look,' Heidi said desperately, 'he was nice to me. He was interested in me. When he asked me what Max was doing, or going to do, I thought he was just being nice. Showing interest. I didn't know he was a spy.'

'A whore, a traitor, and also a very stupid woman. However, stupidity does not excuse a crime. Take her downstairs, Braun. Prepare her. I will be down in a few moments.'

A hand closed on Heidi's shoulder. 'Listen!' she shouted. 'You cannot do this. My father is Helmuth Stumpff.'

'Herr Stumpff will be informed,' Luttmann assured her. 'But I hope he will have more sense than to attempt to interfere. The father of a traitor is often considered to be as guilty as the child. Take her away, Braun.'

The fingers closed more tightly now on Heidi's arm and she felt herself being lifted from the chair. She burst into tears.

Nine

The Sea

Max wished he could see the surface of the sea. He wished he could see anything. He was surrounded by swirling grey, and also by pouring rain which splattered on the cockpit canopy with a noise like machine-gun fire, the louder because there was no engine.

His altimeter had also been shattered by the bullets and he had no idea how high he was, but he knew he was descending quite fast. He had never in his life been forced to bale out, nor did he care for the idea now. Not knowing how high he was he might be about to fall thirty or more metres without any support. So it was a matter of going down with his machine.

The cloud broke and he discovered that he was indeed only sixty-odd metres above the surface. At least there were no white caps. The sea was an oily calm, kept that way by the rain which dotted the surface. Even down here visibility was hardly more than a few hundred metres; he could be anywhere.

First things first. He released the canopy, pushed it back. He was still trying to control the machine by using the stick and flaps, and in fact he made a passable belly-flop landing, the sea seething about him. The impact was not as severe as he had feared it might be; his belts prevented him from being thrown about the cockpit. But the plane immediately began to settle. He released the belts, unclipped his parachute and pushed himself upwards. As he did so the cockpit filled. He attempted to leave and his foot caught. For a moment he was sucked down, but he kicked desperately, and at the same time inflated his life jacket. Immediately he was carried back to the surface and could take long breaths of air. He looked around himself, but there was nothing to see. Even the disturbance caused by the plane going in was already settling. He was utterly alone, and even his most optimistic calculation told him he had to be at least eighty kilometres from the nearest land. And that land was England, and a hangman's noose.

So I am going to die, he thought. He would not drown, because of his life jacket, but he would die of exposure, and fairly soon, he estimated: the September water was probably warmer than at any time during the rest of the year, but it was penetrating his flying suit, and he was already feeling chilled. So do I kick my legs and work my arms and try to keep my circulation going for as long as possible, or do I just lie back and wait to go to sleep as rapidly as possible?

John had been shot down in the Channel and survived. But that had been within a few kilometres of the English coast, and he would have had an ASR launch out looking for him within minutes. Lucky John! Perhaps he was being punished for abandoning England in favour of the regime he had always distrusted but which had been so bewitchingly glamorous. But he did not believe in divine retribution any more than he believed in divine reward. A man did what he considered honourable and best and took the inevitable pitfalls in his stride.

He would have preferred to have gone down in combat, killed in action. But at least he had commanded his men to the best of his ability to the very end. He hoped that would be his epitaph. And Heidi? Heidi would survive and continue her delightfully banal course. He did not expect her to indulge in any prolonged or extravagant bout of mourning. Erika, now, he thought might feel his demise the more. He had gained the impression over the past few months that she was regretting not having married him herself. But she, too, would get over it. And Dad? Or John? The news of his death would certainly be released in England. Would they say good riddance? Or merely that he got what he deserved?

He awoke with a start. He had no idea how long he had been floating, but he had lost all feeling in his arms, legs and face. But there was a sound. For almost the first time in his life he had a spasm of fear: one thing he had never anticipated was

190

being eaten alive by a fish. But then he remembered that, even in summer, sharks were rarely found in the North Sea. With difficulty, he twisted his head to and fro. The rain had stopped, but the clouds were still very low and there was no sign of the sun. Yet visibility had certainly improved, and he could make out a shadowy shape some distance away. The noise was an engine.

'Help!' he shouted. But he knew his voice was so thin he would not be heard. Yet it was a chance at life . . .

Frantically he worked his fingers, trying to restore feeling, and scrabbled at the holster on his hip. He got it open, and closed his hand tightly on the butt of the Luger, desperate not to drop it. He thumbed the safety catch, got his arm above the water, and squeezed the trigger. The report was disappointingly quiet, but he realized that could be because his helmet flaps were still over his ears. And whether the shot had been heard or not, the boat was definitely approaching; he could make out that it was a small drifter.

This time he levelled the gun as best he was able, and fired again. The drifter altered course towards him, and a few minutes later was looming above him.

He looked up at two men standing at the rail and peering down. 'God damn!' one said. 'How long have you been there, mate?'

'Too long,' Max said, his teeth chattering.

'And you were shooting at us?' asked the other man.

'I was afraid you would go away without seeing me.'

The drifter had now lost way altogether and was rolling lazily in the swell. Two more people appeared on deck. One, Max estimated, was the skipper; he wore a battered blue peaked cap and was definitely older than the first two. The other, although wearing a woolly hat and a heavy, roll-necked sweater, was clearly a woman. Or girl, he thought would be more accurate. She had pert features and a mass of red hair.

'He looks done in,' the skipper said. 'Let's get him up.'

They were about ten metres away, and Max tried to swim towards them, but no longer had the strength.

'Coming at you,' the skipper called, and the two crew members put down a small boat. They rowed towards him, and with a great effort hauled him over the side to lie panting in the bilge. 'Shitting arseholes,' one of them said. 'He's a bleeding Jerry.'

'Are you going to throw me back?' Max inquired.

'And he has a gun!' the other man said.

Max looked down his arm; he was still holding the Luger, his frozen fingers clamped round it. He doubted he'd be able to squeeze the trigger again.

'Grab it,' snapped the first man.

The Luger was torn from Max's grasp. 'Bloody Jerry bastard.'

'Hey, Bill!' the other man shouted. 'He's a Nazi. With a gun!'

'Well, bring him in,' Bill said.

They rowed back to the drifter, and Max tried to get up the topsides, but lacked the strength. It took the combined efforts of the two crew, the skipper, and the girl to get him over the gunwale and on to the deck.

'Is he going to die?' the girl asked.

'Probably, if we don't get some warmth into him pretty quickly.' Bill knelt beside Max and used his knife to cut away the life jacket.

'Gosh!' the girl said. 'He's got a cross thing.'

'He's a bleeding Jerry hero. What did you get that for, mate? Shooting down British pilots?'

'As a matter of fact, yes,' Max said faintly.

'Well, you won't be doing that again. Let's have that pistol.'

The sailor who had taken the gun handed it up. 'Do you think it's still loaded?'

Bill tucked it into his belt. 'It'd hardly have held only two bullets. Come along.' Between them, he and the girl got Max up and half carried, half pushed him to the wheelhouse door, while the crew brought the dinghy aboard and secured it. The wheelhouse was blessedly warm and the cabin behind it even more so. Max half fell down a short ladder and landed on his hands and knees before a table. There were bunks to either side.

'We'll have to get this wet clobber off. You go up, Molly, and send Alf down.'

'Give over, Bill. I know what a man looks like. I've brothers, remember? And I've always wanted to see what a Jerry looked like.'

'All right, then.' Bill put his sea-booted foot on Max's shoulder and pushed him on to his back, then knelt beside him and began undoing buttons with great speed and expertise. One of the crew joined them and pulled off his boots.

Max made no effort to resist them; he was too weak and he was still shivering.

'He's blue,' Molly remarked, removing his sodden underwear.

'Get him on that bunk,' Bill commanded. 'And wrap him in a blanket. No point having him die on us after all this trouble.'

Max was lifted and laid on the mattress and a blanket wrapped round him. He didn't suppose he would ever be warm again, but this was a step in the right direction.

'Brew up some tea,' Bill told Molly.

Max relaxed and closed his eyes. He was actually alive. He wondered for how long. But for the moment it didn't matter.

A cup of steaming liquid was held to his lips. It nearly scalded his mouth, but the pain took some moments to get through the cold barrier.

'Now, the best thing is to let him sleep,' Bill said.

'We going straight back?' Alf asked.

'Hell, no. We didn't come out here to go straight home. We've a catch to net. Tuck him up, Molly, and keep an eye on him.'

'Me?' Molly demanded. 'Suppose he gets up? You'd better give me the gun.'

'You'd not know what to do with it,' Bill pointed out. 'He's not getting up right now, and I'll be in the wheelhouse.'

The men left the cabin and the engine, which had been growling in neutral, now became louder as the boat began to move. Waves of utter exhaustion roamed through Max's brain. He felt he needed to think, to understand the exact situation, to try to work out if there was anything he could do about it. But it was no use.

He awoke as the men came into the cabin, which was filled with a deliciously appealing smell.

'His nostrils twitched,' Molly said.

Bill stood above the bunk. 'Has he moved?'

'Not till now.'

Max's nostrils twitched again as, overcoming the smell of frying fish, the cabin was now filled with the stronger smell of the fresh variety. He understood that while he had been out they had made a haul. He wondered how big a catch it had been. Presumably the moment their hold was filled they would be heading home. There had been no mention of a radio, but surely a boat going perhaps a hundred kilometres offshore would have a wireless.

He opened his eyes, and Molly grinned at him. He wondered what she would look like after a visit to a good hairdresser, and wearing make-up and a smart frock instead of the sweater. 'Hey,' she said. 'He's awake!'

The three men all stood above him, and he realized that the engine was again in neutral, the drifter rolling gently, the cabin light on. So, if he had gone in around nine o'clock this morning, it had to be more than nine hours ago. Presumably the news of his apparent death would have been broadcast by now. But these people did not seem to know just who they had picked up.

'Then you'd better feed him,' Bill recommended. 'After you've fed us.'

They sat around the table and there was much rattling of steel cutlery, enamel plates and mugs of tea. Max started to realize just how hungry he was, but he still didn't feel strong enough to attempt to move. So he lay there, his eyes shut, until someone sat on the bunk beside him. He opened his eyes again, saw it was Molly, holding a bowl and a spoon, and also that the men had left the cabin, although from the mutter of their voices he estimated they were gathered in the wheel-house.

'Wake up and take some food,' Molly told him.

He didn't know what the fish was, but it tasted very good, and his salivary glands became quite painful.

'Chew it,' she admonished, 'or you'll get a pain.'

'Would that bother you?'

'Who's a cheeky chappie then? I'm to look after you until we get you back to the police.'

'And when will that be?' In between words he masticated slowly.

'When we've made our catch. I reckon we'll be heading home tomorrow night.' The meal was finished so she moved the bowl and again held a mug of tea to his lips. 'That feel better?' He looked at her. 'When I first saw you I thought you were a goner.'

Max lay back with a sigh. 'When I first saw you, I thought here's an angel come down from heaven to take me back up.'

'You *are* a cheeky chappie!'

She took the plate and mug away and he heard her pumping water to wash them. 'Are you a regular member of this crew?'

'I'm the cook. They have to have a cook.'

'But a good-looking girl like you, alone at sea with three men?'

'I've known them all my life. Anyway, I'm bespoke.'

He hadn't noticed the rather cheap little diamond on her finger. 'Well, congratulations.'

'How come you speak English so well?'

'I learned it at school.'

'But you've no foreign accent. We had a Frenchman living in the village for a spell, and he spoke English very well, but anyone could tell he wasn't. English, I mean.'

'I had a good teacher.'

Alf appeared. 'How long is he going to stay in my bunk?' he inquired.

'Well, he's in no shape to move,' Molly pointed out. 'And he's in the nud. You want a naked man running around the cabin? That wouldn't be decent. You can share Ned's bunk. One of you will be on watch anyway.'

Alf pulled a face, then went round the table, sat on the other bunk, pulled off his boots, rolled under the blanket and appeared to be asleep in less than a minute.

'Doesn't he take anything off?' Max asked.

'He took off his boots.'

'But . . . how long do you spend at sea?'

'Three or four days. Depends on the catch.'

'And in all that time none of you take anything off?'

'Where's the point? We'd just have to put it back on again. Now, you've prattled enough. You need to sleep.'

The cabin was darkened, but throughout the night there was constant movement as the three men came and went from their watches. Max slept fitfully and was wide awake well before dawn as the hitherto gentle movement of the drifter became more animated and he could hear the whistle of the wind. No one seemed particularly concerned about this, however, and at first light Molly was serving him breakfast and all the men were out on deck, having pulled on yellow oilskins with waterproof hats.

'Is the weather bad?' Max asked. He was feeling almost human again, although he still did not know how much strength he had regained.

'Just a bit of wind,' Molly said.

The engine was growling again and the drifter was moving forward easily enough although there was the occasional thump and the boat seemed to stop before regaining way.

'And they can fish in this?'

'As long as they can bring the net in. They'll be wet, mind. Nobody ever said fishing was an easy way to make a living. You want to be out here in January. How are you feeling?'

'A whole lot better than yesterday. I need to use the toilet.' This was a necessary exercise, not only for bodily reasons, but to discover just how strong he actually was.

Molly helped him out of the bunk. 'Keep that blanket wrapped around you,' she ordered.

'Or you'd get ideas?'

'Or I might have to clobber you. And I'd say you've been clobbered enough.'

He found that he could move quite comfortably, although as he was not used to the motion of the ship he staggered from one side to the other. When he came back from the compartment, which was situated at the rear of the cabin – and after some delay as he had had to work out how the pumping system was used – Molly had laid his clothes on the table.

'These are almost dry. Are you strong enough to put them on?'

'I'd like to do that.'

'Then I'll turn around.' She faced the ladder to the wheelhouse while he dressed himself. 'That looks better.'

'It feels better, too.'

All trace of the cramp that had afflicted his fingers and feet had gone, and he felt almost as strong as at any time in his life. He wondered where his pistol was; the magazine would still be holding seven bullets. What was he thinking of? These people had saved his life. But they would be taking him to his death, however inadvertently. They had to be considered enemies. And the girl? He supposed that if he could dispose of the men, she would be at his mercy, but she would hate him the more for that.

But it had to be done. And then what? He had no experience of navigating a small boat, especially when he did not know where he would be starting from. The amazing thing was that none of them, least of all Molly, seemed to have the slightest apprehension that he might be dangerous. They had concluded, and he had admitted, that he might have shot down some English pilots, but they seemed to feel that out of his aircraft he had suddenly become a non-combatant, like them.

On the other hand . . . 'Do you have a wireless?' he asked.

'We have a receiving set,' she said.

'But not a transmitter?'

'There is a VHF set, but it doesn't have sufficient range to call land from out here.'

'But your wireless is always on?'

'Of course.'

'Then you get the news?'

'We don't listen to the news. We work on 2182, that's the Shipping Channel. That's what matters to us.'

'I see.' Another temporary relief. This was a private world, into which he had fallen like an alien from outer space. And if the girl was correct, they would not even be able to call for help – unless there was another ship close by. 'Do you think I could go up top? It's awfully stuffy down here. I'm beginning to feel quite queasy.' The motion was actually much easier than that of a dogfight in his 109.

'Well, we don't want you puking all over the cabin. But I wouldn't go on deck in those leather boots. She's moving a bit, and if you start going you'll find it hard to stop.'

'Point taken.' He held the grab rail and cautiously went up the steps, his shoulders touching the bulkheads as the ship rolled.

Bill was on the helm, not straining in any way, but being forced constantly to adjust the course while he peered out of the spray-coated windscreen. He turned his head at the sound behind him. 'Something on your mind?' he asked.

'It's on his stomach,' Molly said from behind Max.

Max leaned against the door. It was a brighter morning than

197

the day before. The freshening breeze had broken up the overcast, and although there was still a lot of cloud, it was possible to see patches of blue, and even the sun shone through from time to time. The breeze was easterly, and seemed to be coming straight out of the glow. The sea was choppy, with quite a few whitecaps, and Bill was steering into it, which was why there were flurries of spray coming over the bows; this course made it easier for the two men working the net aft.

'It's building,' Bill remarked. 'They're forecasting eight by this evening. I've a mind to pack it in as soon as we haul this one.' He turned his head to look at Max. 'We'll have you on dry land by lunchtime tomorrow.'

Max looked around the wheelhouse. The two radios were mounted on the aft bulkhead above the companion ladder; the wireless was crackling feebly, and from time to time someone spoke, but Max could not make out anything that was said, nor did it seem to interest either Molly or the skipper. Beside the helm there was a broad sloping shelf on which there was spread a chart. In front of the helm was a large compass. There was no other furniture or obvious equipment. Nor was there any sign of his Luger. But under the shelf there was a drawer, firmly closed. He supposed that was his best bet, but he knew that to make his play on that assumption and be mistaken could be disastrous: all three seamen were at least as big as himself, and probably stronger, while Molly, however young, was not exactly a babe in arms. Yet, if they were turning for home as soon as this catch was brought in, he had to go for it now, while his opponents were separated.

Molly returned down the ladder into the cabin. Bill continued to ignore him. He looked through the aft window, over the cabin roof, into the well and saw the crew hauling the net on board: it was filled with struggling fish, and they were totally preoccupied as they emptied the catch into the hold. But in another ten minutes they would be coming inside, looking for a hot drink.

Max had, as part of his training, been taught unarmed combat. He stepped behind Bill, clasped his hands together and brought them down on the base of his neck. Bill gasped and his knees gave way. As he slid down the wheel Max hit him again, and when he struck the deck he did not move.

Max grasped the handle of the drawer, depressed the catch and it slid open. At that moment the uncontrolled ship swung away from the next wave and went right over. Max fell across the wheelhouse. Below, Molly had obviously fallen across the cabin, judging by the howl of anguish. Other shouts came from aft as the crew nearly went overboard. But the drawer had flown right out, and in the midst of pencils, a ruler, a logbook and several folded charts, the Luger clattered to the deck.

Max dropped to his knees and grabbed the gun as the drifter rolled the other way, just as violently. This time he brought up against the exterior door, while green water surged over the deck.

'What the hell . . .?' Molly came up the companionway, hanging on to the grab rail, and uttered a shriek as she saw Bill. 'Bill!' She dropped to her knees beside him, and then turned her head and saw Max, who was pushing himself slowly to his feet, bracing himself against the next roll. She also saw the gun. 'You bastard!' she shouted.

'Just stay there,' Max said, 'and you won't get hurt.'

He opened the leeward door and was greeted by a blast of air. He went outside, hanging on to the rail, and water swirled around his boots as the drifter rolled again. He looked aft, to where the deck was covered in slithering fish, in the midst of which Alf and Ned were trying to regain their feet.

'Get into the hold!' Max ordered.

'What the . . .?' Alf shouted.

Max levelled the gun. 'Just do it.'

They stared at him and then rose together and started to make their way forward. Max fired into the deck immediately in front of them and splinters of wood shot upwards. 'Next time it's you,' he warned. 'Get into the hold and live. Come any closer and die.'

They hesitated, looking at each other, and then retreated and dropped out of sight. He reckoned it would take them a few minutes to regain sufficient courage to venture out again. In that time he had to sew this up.

He opened the wheelhouse door and was thrown back against the rail by another violent lurch. He threw himself forward, entered the house in a stagger, and was struck by Molly in a shoulder charge.

Thrown sideways, he fell down the companionway with the girl on top of him. The pistol flew out of his hand and skidded across the deck. Molly rose above him and tried to get off him to reach the gun. But he caught her arms and threw her to one side. She almost snarled, and struck at him with her nails. Again he caught her wrist, but there was no time to continue wrestling with her; he could hear movement from the wheelhouse.

He closed his fist and struck her on the chin with all the force he could manage. Her eyes glazed, and she again fell against the bunk, sliding down the lockers to hit the deck. Max reached his knees and crawled across the deck to regain the pistol, just in time as Bill appeared at the top of the companionway.

Max levelled the gun. 'I will kill you if you make me,' he said.

Bill was holding on to the grab rail as the drifter continued to roll violently. 'You Nazi bastard!' he snapped. 'We saved your fucking life.'

'And for that reason I will try to keep you all alive,' Max said. 'Move back against the console.'

Bill hesitated; he was much the bigger man. Then he retreated to the wheel.

Max went up the companionway, keeping the gun levelled at him. 'On deck,' he commanded.

'Just what the hell do you think you're doing?' Bill demanded. 'This is piracy. You'll likely hang.'

'It's on the cards,' Max agreed. 'Move.'

Bill opened the leeward door, stepped on deck.

'Aft,' Max instructed, and followed him into the open. Just in time, for Alf and Ned were cautiously crawling out of the hold. Max fired, again aiming at the deck immediately in front of them, and they hastily fell back. 'Go down with them,' he told Bill.

Another hesitation. 'You know how to handle this thing?'

'I'm going to learn. Get on with it.'

Slowly Bill made his way aft. 'You can't keep us down there,' he protested.

'You won't starve. Most dieticians say that raw fish is about the best thing for you.'

Bill dropped through the hatch, and Max darted forward,

releasing the handrail, losing his footing, and sliding the last ten feet in a flurry of water. He tucked the Luger into his holster, grasped the hatch cover and pulled it across. There were shouts of protest from below him. The hatch had a padlock hanging from the bracket, and this he snapped shut. Then he made his way forward to the wheelhouse and got inside to find Molly at the top of the companionway, using the VHF.

'Mayday, Mayday, Mayday!' she shouted. '*Silver Fish, Silver Fish, Silver Fish*! We are being attacked by a German pirate!'

Max plucked the mike from her hand and replaced it. She turned to face him, eyes blazing. Her chin was swollen and red. 'Why don't you hit me again, you bastard?'

'I will if I have to,' Max warned. 'Get back against the bulkhead and stay there.'

'*Silver Fish, Silver Fish*,' said the radio. 'Position please.' The voice was disconcertingly close; Max reckoned not more than fifteen kilometres distant.

He grabbed the binoculars from their pouch, opened the door, and swept the horizon. With the freshening wind, he gauged that visibility had lifted to about ten kilometres. But studying the limited horizon was very difficult with the drifter rolling scuppers under, and the constant showers of spray. Yet he could not see anything, or any puff of smoke.

He went back inside. Molly had not moved, although she looked as though she was considering it. 'Stay put,' he recommended. He stood at the wheel and turned the bows into the swell; the motion continued to be violent, but now it was controlled. To his enormous relief, the compass showed east, which was where he intended to go. Now the engine was growling happily and the drifter was surging up the backs of the waves, crashing into the troughs beyond, to send cascades of spray high into the air, but always coming up the other side. It was actually exhilarating stuff.

'You won't get away with this,' Molly said. 'They'll have the navy out.'

'After a stray drifter? But you can tell me something. Do you know our position?'

'No.'

But her eyes had moved towards the chart. Hanging on to

the wheel with one hand, Max pulled the stiff paper towards him, and saw that there were a series of small, pencilled crosses joined by ruled lines. It seemed reasonable to assume that the last cross was their most recent position; how this had been attained he had no idea. But he could see that they were a hundred kilometres due east of the Suffolk coast. Unfortunately the chart only just showed a glimpse of the French – or was it the Belgian – coast.

He calculated by looking at the measurement scale that he might have about 120 kilometres to go – roughly eighty nautical miles. 'What sort of endurance do we have?' he asked.

'Maybe another twenty-four hours.'

'And do you have any idea what speed we're making? There doesn't seem to be any indicator.'

'Ships don't have speedometers,' she said contemptuously. 'A skipper knows how fast he's going by his engine revs. If he's in any doubt he can stream the log.'

'I have no idea what you're talking about. But you claim to have sailed on the boat for two years. How fast are we going?'

'Maybe six knots.'

Another hasty calculation. Twelve to fifteen hours. 'Then we should just about make it,' Max said.

'Are you out of your mind?' Molly shouted. 'You think you can take this ship to Holland?'

'It's there,' Max pointed out.

'But that coast is covered in mines. And German guns. If the one doesn't get us, the other will.'

'I guarantee that whichever one it is, you won't feel a thing,' Max assured her.

'God, God, God! You're mad. And what happens to us if you do get us there?'

'I'll sort something out. I'm grateful to you. Now off you go and prepare some lunch. And, Molly, please do not get any bright ideas about things like frying pans. If you make me I will hurt you.'

'What about Bill and them?'

'I imagine they'll be eating the same as us, only theirs will be raw.'

'But they have to have something to drink.'

'No one ever died of thirst after a few hours. Now get on with it.'

She glared at him, then staggered across the heaving wheelhouse and down the ladder. Max peered ahead. The wind was now howling, and there were whitecaps everywhere, but the waves were not as big as he had expected. The continuing showers of spray limited visibility, but the clouds were clearing all the time.

Behind him the radio continued to crackle but the noise of the wind and the sea made it difficult to pick up more than the occasional word. He did not think any of the other drifters in the neighbourhood would be able to catch him up. The real danger was if there was a warship in the vicinity to be called in to aid the search – or worse, if the skies cleared sufficiently for an aircraft to be sent out.

He looked at his watch, which had survived immersion. It was just coming up to noon. That meant, if Molly's figures were correct, it would be nearly dawn when he approached the coast; he had no idea whether it would be Belgium or Holland. He did know, from his long stay in Ostend, that those coasts were fringed by massive sandbanks over which, at low tide, there was only a few feet of water. There were passages through the banks to allow steamers in and out of the various ports; these were buoyed during peacetime, but all the markers had been removed.

There was also the threat of mines. But it was a case of just going ahead and hoping for the best. Suddenly he felt very tired. For all the considerable hours he had spent in the bunk, he knew he was still suffering from exposure, as well as the delayed psychological reaction of having to come down for the first time in his life. He had to empty his mind of everything save steering this boat straight ahead and due east.

Molly served him lunch, her eyes smouldering as she watched him eat. He knew she was trying to think of some way of reversing the situation, of getting on deck to open the hold. But the only way out of the cabin was through the wheelhouse. On the other hand, he had at least another twelve hours standing here and he was already exhausted.

'Do you wish coffee?' she asked.

203

'Yes.'

She went below and returned a few minutes later with a steaming mug.

'I'd like you to drink the first third of that,' Max said.

She stared at him.

'I have no idea what poisons you have down there,' he pointed out.

She sipped the coffee, gave a little gasp as it scalded her lip. 'It's too hot to drink.'

'It'll cool.'

She eventually did drink the required amount, and he finished it off; he did not suppose she was into suicide, and for both of them to die would not help the three men in the hold.

She returned below with the empty cup and stayed there. He knew she was still considering possibilities, and had to steer half turned towards the companionway; beyond which he could see her legs as she stretched on a bunk. The afternoon passed slowly, while the drifter prodded into the waves. There was nothing else to be seen, and the voices on the radio were now too faint to be made out at all. But the skies were gradually clearing; the gale was travelling west and he was travelling east. From inside the wheelhouse he could only look ahead or to either side, he could not see overhead.

Movement. He swung round as Molly emerged. 'Tea?' she asked.

He was surprised to realize he had already spent four hours on the helm. The heaviness of the wheel, and the effort of keeping the drifter straight – such strong contrast to the lightness of the controls of a 109 – was immense. In any event a Messerschmitt patrol had never lasted more than a couple of hours at most; his arms and shoulders were aching. 'Tea would be very nice,' he agreed. 'What are you going to put in it?'

'Bugger off,' she said, and made the tea, this time drinking part of it before handing it to him.

'Do you think the wind is dropping?' Max asked. 'I think the seas are smaller.'

'The wind generally drops for an hour or two around dusk,' she replied. 'But it often gets up again afterwards.'

He nodded and resumed watching the waves. He was getting

204

used to both the ship and the motion, and but for the aching muscles and the feeling of exhaustion that kept threatening his brain, he felt he could have enjoyed himself. But he was also beginning to realize that he was not going to last the distance. 'What are the tides around here?' he asked. 'I mean on the French coast.'

'They run up and down.'

'But not westerly?'

'Only if the coast runs westerly. And when it turns it runs easterly again.'

'So if we drifted for six hours up and then down, we should wind up roughly where we started?'

She scratched her head. 'It's possible, if we didn't hit something.'

'I think we'll have to chance that. If I stop this engine, how do I start it again?'

'You turn the key.'

'It's a diesel.'

'So you have to wait for the heat start.'

'You'll have to show me. And your batteries are high?'

'They should be.'

'Then let's have an early supper.'

He kept going for another three hours, by which time the wind had dropped to a breeze and the seas had definitely moderated. Again, if Molly's calculations were right, they must have done some thirty kilometres and thus be within some ninety of the coast. He reckoned that would be closer to German-controlled territory than any of the other drifters would care to find themselves. He took a deep breath and turned the ignition key off. The engine died, the drifter turned broadside to the waves and began to roll, but by no means as violently as earlier. It was now all but dark. He opened the door, stepped outside with the binoculars. He swept the entire horizon, but could see nothing; obviously in these dangerous waters no ship would risk carrying lights, and he was too far offshore for anything to reach him from the land.

He then swept the sky. Nearly all the clouds had gone, and he could make out the stars. If there was an aircraft up there he couldn't hear it. He went back inside, and turned up the volume on the wireless, but all the noise was indistinguishable. He did not see what more he could do. He went below.

The cabin light was on, and Molly was washing the dishes. 'I need to sleep for a few hours,' he said.

She shrugged. 'There are four bunks, take your pick.'

'You have to sleep as well,' he pointed out.

'I'll be all right.'

'I'm afraid I must insist. Show me some rope.'

'You mean to tie me up?'

'It will only be for a few hours. Then we will be on our way again. The rope.'

She opened a locker under one of the bunks, where there were several coils of rope. He selected one. 'Lie on the bunk.'

'You are a Nazi bastard. Are you going to rape me as well?'

'I'm sure that would be most enjoyable. But I'm simply too tired. Now lie down, make yourself comfortable and be quiet.' He tied her wrists and ankles, and then secured her wrists to the grab rail immediately above the bunk, leaving the line sufficiently slack to permit her to rest her arms. 'Sleep well,' he recommended. 'Tomorrow we will be home.'

He was asleep in seconds, and awoke to noise.

Molly was also awake. 'They've got us – got you!' she said triumphantly.

Max rolled out of bed; he was fully dressed save for his boots. He stumbled across the cabin and up the companion ladder to be blinded as the wheelhouse was suddenly illuminated by a searchlight from very close range. For a moment he was unsure what to do, but the light had picked out his movement, and a voice shouted, in English but with a considerable accent, 'Come outside with your hands up or we shall sink you.'

Max opened the door and stepped out on deck. The sea had gone right down. He raised his hands leaning against the bulkhead, and shouted in German, 'I am a Luftwaffe officer.'

The other ship had hitherto been only a grey shape in the darkness, but now it came virtually alongside, the crew hastily putting out large fenders; others leapt aboard with warps, and the two ships rolled gently against each other.

An officer stood on the deck opposite Max. 'This is an English ship,' he said, now also speaking in German. 'Where is the crew?'

'Under restraint,' Max told him.

The officer swung his leg over the rail and came on board the drifter. He had been carrying a pistol, but this he now holstered as he gazed at Max's uniform. 'What is your name?'

'Captain Max Bayley, Commanding-Officer Fighter Squadron 36.'

The officer peered at him. 'Bayley?' he asked. 'Max Bayley? The air ace? But you are dead. It was reported that you had crashed into the North Sea.'

'Well,' Max said, 'as this is the North Sea, you can see that the report was at least half accurate. Can you take me in?'

'But of course, Herr Captain! This is wonderful news. Well . . .' He hesitated. 'Yes, wonderful news! You must come aboard. We will take control of the vessel.'

'Thank you,' Max said. 'I do not wish the crew to be harmed. They saved my life.'

'And agreed to bring you to Germany?'

'Well, no. They had to be persuaded, and are now, as I said, my prisoners.'

'Then they are now prisoners of the Reich. We will take care of it. Where are they?'

'Three are in the fish hold and one in the cabin.'

'Very good, sir. My captain awaits you.'

Max boarded the motorboat and climbed the brief ladder to the bridge. The lieutenant in command had been listening to the conversation. Now he shook hands.

'Herr Captain, this is a great honour. Your death has been mourned. I am only sorry of the circumstances.'

'That I came down? That is an occupational hazard of flying. But I am very pleased to see you.'

'And we shall get you home just as rapidly as possible. Tell me what you would like.'

'A glass of brandy, and . . . is it possible to have a bath on this boat?'

'There is a shower stall, sir.'

'But not a change of clothing?'

'Not a new Luftwaffe uniform. But we can fix you up with some clean gear.'

'And a bunk?'

'Certainly, sir.'

'You are making this ship sound like a pleasure yacht. There is just one more thing; you say I have been reported dead?'

'Well, yes, sir. It was known you had gone in, and that was two days ago. We could hold out no hopes for your survival.'

A sailor, having been alerted, was at Max's elbow with the drink. 'That is good.' Max sipped. 'What I would like you to do, Herr Lieutenant, is to wireless my headquarters in Ostend, to inform them that I am coming back, and ask them to inform my wife. She will have been very upset.'

The lieutenant gulped. 'I will inform Ostend, Herr Captain.' He looked at his watch. 'It will take us about three hours to get back; they will probably have a car waiting for you.'

'But I would like my wife to know as soon as possible.'

Another gulp. 'Yes, Herr Captain. I will inform Ostend.'

Max frowned. He had just said that. 'Is there something wrong?'

'Well, sir, Ostend will—'

'Something has happened,' Max snapped. 'Tell me, man, what has happened to my wife?'

'Well, sir . . .' The lieutenant licked his lips. 'It was on the wireless today.'

'What?' Max shouted.

'That Frau Heidi Bayley has been arrested on a charge of treason.'

Ten

Decision

Max slowly put down his glass. 'What did you say?'

The lieutenant was looking terrified. 'It was a wireless report, Herr Captain. There were no details. I am sure it is all a mistake.'

'A mistake,' Max muttered. Of course it had to be a mistake. Who would dare arrest the daughter of Helmuth Stumpff, who was also the wife of Captain Max Bayley? But they had thought she was the widow; the fact that Heidi had been arrested the moment he had been proclaimed dead was too great for it to have been a coincidence.

'Herr Captain?'

Max looked up. 'Get me to Ostend just as fast as you can, Herr Lieutenant.'

'Of course, sir. Do you wish me to scuttle the English boat?'

'Good God, no. I told you, they saved my life.'

'To escort it in will take time. It is not a fast boat.'

'Then turn it loose.'

'Sir?'

'I would like you to top up their fuel tank and then turn it loose,' Max repeated. He got up and went to the rail, looked down at *Silver Fish*. The three crew had been released from the hold, and were on deck, where they had been joined by Molly, and were being watched by three sailors, rifles levelled. 'We are sending you home,' Max told them in English. 'And thank you.'

'They have a wireless,' the lieutenant protested.

'And do you seriously suppose they can summon assistance here before you get back to Ostend? It has a limited range. Just make sure they have enough fuel to reach an English port.' He reverted to English again. 'Go home, and good luck.'

He saluted, and German sailors began passing a fuel hose from their own tanks to that of the drifter. The task completed, the German sailors returned on board, the engines were gunned and the little warship roared away, leaving the drifter bobbing in its wake. In front of them the sky was just beginning to lighten.

'Max?' Gunther said. 'My God! It is a miracle.'

'What happened?' Max demanded.

'Nobody knows.' Gunther was totally embarrassed. 'It just came over on the news last night.'

'So do you have a warrant for my arrest also?'

'Well, of course not. You are our premier ace. All Germany will rejoice at your survival.'

'And my wife is in a Gestapo cell, being . . . God Almighty!'

'Now you know those are only rumours – I mean about Gestapo methods. I am sure everything will be sorted out. Colonel Hartmann is most anxious to see you.'

'All I want from Colonel Hartmann is permission to go to Berlin,' Max said.

*   *   *

209

Reynald opened the door. 'Herr Captain! It is so good to have you back. We all thought . . .'

'So did the Gestapo, apparently,' Max said grimly.

Reynald's shoulders humped. 'We did not know what had happened. She just did not come home. And when Herr Stumpff called the police, he was just told she had been arrested.'

'Where is Herr Stumpff?'

'He is in his room, Herr Captain. He has had a breakdown, and the doctor has put him to bed.'

Max realized there was nothing to be gained there. 'Call me a taxi.'

'Immediately sir. Will you be in to dinner?'

'I have absolutely no idea,' Max said.

'Colonel Luttmann will see you now, Herr Captain,' the secretary said.

Already agitated, Max was in a fury at having been kept waiting. Now he stamped into the office. He was wearing a fresh uniform and had his cap tucked under his arm; his Iron Cross was prominent against his tie.

'Heil Hitler!'

Luttmann was on his feet. 'Heil Hitler! I am pleased to meet you again, Herr Captain. I wish it could have been on a happier occasion.'

'We have met before?'

'Indeed. I met you at your mother's funeral.'

Max frowned as a vague memory came back to him.

'And since then you have come a long way. Sit down, Herr Captain.' Luttmann also sat. 'And two years ago I had the great pleasure of renewing my acquaintance with your aunt.'

'You mean when she was here in Germany, looking for me?'

'Why, yes. I entertained her for a while. Not long enough, but it was enjoyable while it lasted.'

Max stared at him. 'You . . . you bastard!'

Luttmann held up a finger. 'I think you need to apologize, Herr Captain. You may be a famous pilot, miraculously restored from the dead, but I hold the rank of colonel.'

'So are you going to lock me up and torture me?' Max inquired. 'I have come here to see my wife and to take her home.'

210

'I am afraid that will not be possible. Your wife –' he looked at his watch – 'was executed an hour ago.'

Max seemed frozen as he continued to stare at him.

'It was a very straightforward business,' Luttmann explained. 'When confronted with the evidence, and with her accomplice, she confessed everything. It is unbelievable that she should so carelessly have sent you and so many of your comrades to their probable deaths. She actually seemed quite proud of it.'

'You expect me to believe that?' Max said. 'My wife, who you have just murdered.'

'My dear captain, you do need to watch your tongue. Even you. Your wife was tried and convicted in a People's Court. On the evidence presented, along with her confession, the judge had no hesitation in pronouncing the death sentence. It was all very quick, but then we try to expedite these unhappy matters.'

'And you claim my wife confessed? She had nothing *to* confess.'

'You'd be surprised.' Luttmann smiled. 'It was necessary to persuade her, of course. But do you know, Herr Captain, I have an idea that she actually enjoyed what was being done to her. I know we enjoyed doing it.'

Max launched himself across the desk.

'It really is a serious matter,' Field-Marshal Milch pointed out. 'The Reich-Marshal is very upset. I mean to say, Colonel Luttmann is a senior officer in the Gestapo, and the Reich-Marshal is the man who virtually created the Gestapo, and was its commander for several years. God knows what would have happened had you killed Luttmann.'

'I intended to kill him,' Max said, 'but he managed to call for help.'

'And now he is in hospital with a broken jaw, a dislocated shoulder, and breathing difficulties.' Milch grinned. 'You did a magnificent job on a thoroughly nasty human being. Just as you did an unbelievably magnificent job in returning from the dead, having taken over an entire British ship.'

'It was a very small ship, Herr Field-Marshal.'

'That is not how the newspapers are presenting it. It could have been the *Queen Mary*. You are now a national hero rather

211

than merely a Luftwaffe hero. So there is no way you can be punished, or even disciplined. Colonel Luttmann's unfortunate accident will remain an unfortunate accident.'

'And my wife's murder?'

'Nothing more will be said about that. It was an unfortunate leak to the press that she had been arrested. Nothing more will be said.'

'But I know what happened,' Max said. 'And Stumpff, I assume.'

'Herr Stumpff has been informed that his daughter died of a heart attack. I do beseech you, Max, not to pursue this matter. You will get nowhere, you will ruin a glittering career – and you still have a war to fight. And win. We took a beating the day you were shot down. The RAF are claiming more than a hundred and eighty kills. That is propaganda rubbish, of course. The actual number of our planes lost was fifty-nine. But still, those are unsupportable figures. The Reich-Marshal has decided that there will be no more large daylight raids on London. We are going to concentrate on night raids.'

'You mean we have lost that battle,' Max said bitterly.

'Let us say that we did not win it as decisively as we had hoped.'

'And the invasion?'

'In all the circumstances, as we have not yet achieved the necessary air supremacy, I can tell you, in the strictest confidence, that the Fuehrer has determined to postpone the invasion until the spring of next year. However, we do not intend that the British should know this, and we do intend to keep up the pressure on the RAF.'

'You told me once, Herr Field-Marshal, that we had lost the war by not invading England in June. Is it not more definitely lost now?'

'That opinion was given to you in confidence, Max. I hope you have never repeated it.'

'I have not, sir. But . . .'

'Yes,' Milch agreed. 'We must hope that the position is not irretrievable. We still hold the continent and, well, there may be some important events coming along. There are already important events concerning you in the Luftwaffe. We have a new machine waiting for you and your pilots. It is a 109, but the design has been refined. It is an F model. It incorporates all the refinements to the problems we encountered this last summer. It has long-range fuel tanks, but this is compensated for by an improved engine which will give greater speed. You will operate as fighter bombers, carrying out low-level strafing and bombing raids on selected targets in the south of England. You will be challenged – and therefore, hopefully, you will be able to go on shooting down the enemy. So I will wish you every success. I am recommending you for promotion to major. At the age of twenty-one, that is a remarkable achievement. I am also recommending you for another Cross, this one First Class.' He stood up and held out his hand. 'I hope you understand how terribly sorry I am that this has happened. But we are at war, a war in which the very survival of the Reich and all it stands for is at stake. We can consider only victory. Anyone, man or woman, who stands in the way of that victory, or who impedes it in any way, is an enemy of the State and must be so treated.'

'Can I get you anything, Herr Captain?' Reynald asked solicitously.

'Brandy,' Max said, and went towards the drawing room. 'Is Herr Stumpff up?'

'I'm afraid not sir. Dr Keller has placed him under sedation. The doctor is rather worried. But he said you could see Herr Stumpff if you wished.'

'Not tonight, Reynald. I'll see him tomorrow morning, before I leave.'

'Then you will be staying the night, sir?'

'And dining in, Reynald.' Max went into the drawing room and sat down. Suddenly he felt surrounded by Heidi; he had only ever been in this room in the company of Heidi. Reynald placed the balloon glass on the table beside the settee. 'I think you should put the decanter there as well,' Max said.

Reynald obeyed, hesitated, and then left the room, closing the doors behind him.

I have been bribed, Max thought, sipping his drink, by a piece of iron, an extra stripe, and the promise of a glorious future in the services of an utterly inglorious regime. So, was he contemplating following Heidi just as quickly as he could? Actually, he was. But not by blowing out his own brains. He would rejoin his squadron, he would lead it into battle, he would kill, and kill, and kill, until inevitably he would be killed himself. It was a curiously satisfying thought.

The front doorbell rang. He hardly heard it, but a few minutes later the drawing-room doors were opened. Reynald made no announcement; no doubt he had been warned not to. Max did not look up. 'I do not wish to be disturbed.'

He smelled that so familiar scent as Erika sat beside him. 'I came as soon as I heard. I feel so guilty.'

He turned his head to look at her. 'Guilty of what?'

'Well . . . I knew she was seeing some fairly risqué characters.'

He frowned. 'What exactly do you mean by "seeing"?'

'Well, you know Heidi. She is, well . . .'

'A free spirit, even when married.'

'Well, yes. That is a very sophisticated attitude.' She got up, went to the sideboard to select a glass, returned and filled it before sitting down. 'Max, you must not be hard on her. After a few days in a Gestapo cell she will be a changed woman, believe me.'

'A few days,' Max muttered.

'I know. It sounds dreadful, if all the rumours are true. But they must release her. I am sure she really did nothing wrong. All sorts of people are working on it, including Papa, and Bitterman Manufacturing is terribly important, particularly right now.'

Max put down his glass and turned to her. 'Erika, Heidi was executed this morning.'

She stared at him with her mouth open, then it closed like a steel trap. 'I think that kind of joke is in extremely bad taste.'

Max felt in his inside breast pocket, took out the heavy envelope and laid it on the coffee table. 'They were generous enough to give me a copy of their file. She was tried in a People's Court yesterday afternoon, condemned and executed at dawn. She was hanged on piano wire.'

Erika was still staring at him, and now both hands were clasped to her neck.

'I arrived in Berlin about six hours too late.'

'And they told you? What did you do?'

'I appear to have broken Luttmann's jaw. Disappointing really. I had actually meant to break his neck.'

Erika caught his hand. 'You are not under arrest? I mean, striking a Gestapo officer . . .'

'My dear Erika, I am a war hero. I am inviolate. But my wife was not,' he added savagely.

'Oh, my dear, dear Max. But Heidi!' Tears suddenly poured down her cheeks as if the fact of her lover's death had only just penetrated her consciousness.

'Did you know a man called Leitzen?'

'Oh . . .' Erika took a long drink of brandy. 'I did not know him. I was present when they first met. When he picked her up.'

'Do you mean when she allowed herself to be picked up?'

'Well . . . You were just going off to fight and she was in an upset state. I never saw him again after that night. I could see they wanted to be alone, so I left.'

'But you know he became her lover?'

Erika sighed. 'She told me . . . well, he was good company.'

'You mean he was good in bed.'

Another sigh. 'She couldn't help herself, really. Even a touch on the hand had her going.'

'And she liked to be spanked,' Max said. 'I think I disappointed her because I did not ever really wish to hurt her.'

'Oh, Max!' They gazed at each other, and then she was in his arms, kissing him savagely, her hands searching his clothing. But then, he was doing the same to her.

'You'd better stay to dinner.'

'I'll stay with you as long as you wish.'

'I'm leaving at dawn.'

'To go and get killed?'

'Undoubtedly. But I would like a night to see me on my way.'

'You shall have it,' she promised.

She lay naked in his arms, her head resting on his shoulder. 'I loved her, you know,' she said.

'I do know.'

'But I wonder if she ever loved me.'

'I wonder if Heidi ever loved anyone, except herself, of course.'

'Did you love her?'

'I don't know. She was a supremely beautiful object who came into my possession by accident, you could say. If you

215

and she had not been dining at the Albert on that night in June, and if I had not been ordered by Goering to go to Berlin and find myself a woman, all of this would never have happened.'

'You can't possibly blame yourself.'

'I suppose not. But wouldn't you say that we are all damned, Erika?'

She kissed him.

'Have you seen the newspaper?' Mark asked.

John grinned. 'I'm afraid I've had other things on my mind. And so should you, Dad.'

The two men sat in the back of the Rolls on its way to the village church. John wore uniform; Mark was in a morning suit. John wondered if his father was as nervous as himself.

'I have a copy here.' Mark gave him *The Times*. 'Page three.'

John opened the broadsheet, studied the page.

REMARKABLE TALE COMING FROM GERMANY.
AIR ACE HAS MIRACULOUS ESCAPE FROM DEATH.

It seems that Flight-Commander Max Bayley, reported missing over the North Sea and presumed dead on 15th September, has reappeared. Captain Bayley was rescued from drowning by the crew of the Lowestoft drifter *Silver Fish*, and in an act of daring piracy took over the vessel, imprisoned the crew, and sailed it virtually to Ostend before being met by a German patrol boat.

'He was a right terror,' says Molly Smith, the drifter's cook. 'But, oh, he was a gentleman. And so good looking.'

'He was all right,' says Bill Morris, the drifter's skipper. 'Bit of a bastard, but he was fighting a war, and he made the Jerries turn us loose when he was rescued and give us enough fuel to get home.'

Max Bayley will be known to our readers as the son of Mark Bayley, a leading executive with the Fairey Marine Company, and an English fighter ace in the Great War. He is also the brother of Squadron-Leader John Bayley, DFC, presently serving with the RAF. Max Bayley, who had a German mother, has preferred to fight for the Nazis instead of the country where he grew up and was educated.

216

'Nothing like publicity,' John remarked. 'I must say, Dad, he's a hard blighter to kill.'

'Yes. Sometimes I can't help feeling proud of him.'

The Rolls was pulling in to the churchyard. 'Do you think the girls will have seen this?' John asked.

It was Mark's turn to grin. 'I suspect that, like you, women on their wedding day tend to concentrate on the matter in hand.'

'So do we show them this?'

'After the ceremony.'

They gathered at Hillside for the wedding breakfast. The vicar was still a little bemused, never before having married two couples at the same time – and certainly had never contemplated marrying a father and son in the same ceremony. The brides were in the strongest contrast. Helen wore a flowered silk dress, high heels, gloves, and an enormous picture hat; Jolinda was in uniform, very spick and span, with a neatly knotted tie, and regulation low-heeled lace-up shoes.

Joan leaned on a crutch and her husband's arm. Air-Commodore Hargreaves, who had gallantly agreed to give away both brides, beamed. Millie and her husband and their children looked embarrassed as always, as did the smattering of Helen's relations who had been able to attend. Bob Newman was John's best man; Mark had chosen his oldest living friend, Jim Beerman. Clements presided over the drinks and catering with complete assurance. Rufus, looking apprehensive with a blue ribbon tied to his collar, sought stray canapés.

The speeches and toasts were completed before Mark stood up again. 'I would like to offer one last toast,' he announced, 'to someone who, in happier circumstances, would have been here. I give you Flight-Commander Max Bayley of the Luftwaffe.'

'I wonder if I shall ever meet him?' Jolinda asked.

As they both had only a forty-eight hour pass, they had elected to forego London, and honeymoon instead at Hillside, which Jolinda was now to consider her home, at least for the duration of the war.

Now she sat at the dressing table brushing her hair while John lay on the bed to admire her. He still found it a strange delight to realize that so much beauty was all his, although he was also very aware that the decision – and probably most future decisions as to how much she gave – would always be hers. He did not in the slightest regret or resent this: once he was off the station and away from the responsibilities of leading his squadron, it was the greatest of pleasures to hand himself entirely over to such a strong and yet loving personality.

'I don't think there is much chance of that until this show is over,' he said.

She turned to face him. 'But when it is over, do you suppose you could ever be friends again?'

'We have to get there first,' John said, and held out his arms for her.

The officers of JG 36 and the adjacent squadrons gathered to cheer Max as he got out of his aircraft. The new 'Gustav' had been made ready for him in Berlin and he had to be pleased with its performance. It had a faster rate of climb than the older 109E, and he felt it was also more manoeuvrable than the earlier version. Now he was totally embarrassed as they gave him three cheers.

Hartmann escorted him into the inner office. 'Welcome home, Herr Major.'

'I am not yet confirmed, Herr Colonel.'

'But you will be, as will your new medal. Sit down, Max. You are . . . perfectly fit?'

Max considered. 'Yes.'

Hartmann stroked his chin, clearly uncertain as to what he could, or should, say.

'My private life can have no bearing on my fighting ability,' Max said. 'Nor do I intend that it should ever have.'

Hartmann nodded. 'Then the matter will not be mentioned on this station. But as you are in the process of receiving promotion, you do not have to fly in combat unless you wish to do so. Senior-Lieutenant Langholm has proved himself a capable flight-commander. In fact I have recommended him for a captaincy.'

'I wish to fly in combat,' Max said.

'Then you will take command of both 36 and 47 for the time being. Are you up to date with affairs?'

'I had a meeting with Field-Marshal Milch before returning to duty.'

'Then you will know that our strategic plan has been altered. I'm afraid we took very heavy casualties last week, so daylight bombing of London has been suspended. I understand the night raids are proving successful, but the 110s are taking care of those. You have flown the Gustav; what do you think?'

'That it is a match for the Spitfire, certainly.'

Hartmann nodded. 'That has yet to be proved but I believe you could be right. Now, our new operations will begin the day after tomorrow. This will give you a day to get to know your pilots.'

Max raised his eyebrows. 'I have flown with these fellows for three months.'

'As I said, we took very heavy casualties during the past week. But I believe they will prove a good bunch. Your orders are to sweep south-east England, bombing and strafing as disruptively as possible.'

'That is not exactly prime strategy, is it?'

Hartmann shrugged. 'Someone must have a plan. I suppose disrupting road and rail transport – and hopefully destroying morale – will be an aid to the invasion.' He paused and waited for Max to comment, but Max said nothing; the Luftwaffe would be informed of the postponement of the invasion when the High Command was ready. 'So there it is. Are you happy with that?'

'No,' Max said. 'But if those are our orders I will carry them out. I really don't see that we can be very effective.'

'Well, with your new tanks you should have an endurance of at least half an hour over England.'

'Dropping small bombs and firing twenty millimetre cannon.'

'Tactics that were very effective over France,' Hartmann reminded him.

'Over a beaten and demoralized people,' Max countered as he stood up. 'I must go and meet my men.'

Gunther embraced him. 'When I heard you had survived it was the happiest day of my life. But then . . .'

'That is not for discussion. We have a war to win. You will be pleased to know that you are confirmed as Flight-

Commander of 36; your promotion to major is on its way. Now let me meet these fellows.'

A glance at the assembled pilots confirmed what Hartmann had said; of the original squadron that had fought in the battle of France, only four of the eighteen were left, and that included Gunther and himself. These were fresh-faced and enthusiastic, but very young boys – a ridiculous thought, he supposed, for a twenty-one-year-old, but he felt old enough to be their father. And if they were obviously lacking in combat experience, he knew that owing to the meticulous and lengthy German training programmes, they would all be capable airmen.

He shook hands with each of them in turn. 'I look forward to flying with you,' he told them. 'We take off at first light for battle tactics.' He gestured at the bar. 'The drinks are on me.'

'Captain, sir!' Heinrich looked ready to burst into tears.

Max embraced him. 'You are always just out of date, old friend. I am a major.'

Heinrich squeezed his hand. 'I am so proud, sir. For you and for me. Is there anything . . .?'

'There is nothing to be said or done outside of squadron business. I wish to be called at oh three hundred hours, and breakfast, as usual, at oh eight hundred.'

He sat on his bed with a sigh. This was the only true home he had – or would ever have.

'So how is the marriage business?' Browne asked.

'When I find out I'll let you know,' John replied. 'Still quiet?'

'Down here. I believe there is still some night activity over London. Do you think the man has called it off?'

'If he doesn't come in the next fortnight it will be called off for him, by the weather. When you think what a magnificent summer we've had, he really has squandered his time.'

'I'm sure we had something to do with it,' Browne suggested, and looked out of the window at the Verey cartridge arcing through the sky. 'Hello, we may have been optimistic.'

John ran outside to join his pilots, who were already running towards their machines. Jolinda was standing in the doorway of her office to watch him go.

The squadron was airborne in under two minutes. 'Map reference G8,' Coleman said over the R/T. 'A hundred plus, sweeping west.'

'Twenty thousand,' John said. 'Take the top, Harry.'

'Will do,' Martin replied, and climbed away above the clouds.

There was, in fact, considerable cloud cover, although the sun was bright and the day very warm. John emerged from the cloud at ten thousand feet and looked left and right as well as ahead. 'See anything?' he asked at large.

'Not a sausage,' Martin replied.

John checked his map. Section G6 was straight ahead and covered the area to the north-west of Newhaven. A large enemy formation flying at any normal height had to be visible. 'Red Leader to base,' he said. 'There's nothing here.'

'They're under the cloud,' Coleman said.

'With no fighter cover?' John was incredulous.

'They don't need fighter cover,' Coleman responded. 'Apparently, there are only fighters, beating up the country-side.'

'Going down,' John told his men, and led them into the clouds.

The pilots assembled around Max. 'We cross the coast at Dover,' he told them. 'And then swing west for half an hour before returning home. Your targets are trains, bridges, port installations, and anything that may be of use to the enemy for moving troops to the coast. Your mission is not to take civilian life, although I understand this may be unavoidable.'

'How many do you want up top?' Gunther asked.

'Our objective is to get in and out. According to the met boys there is extensive cloud cover over south-eastern England.'

'They will see us on their radar,' someone objected.

'Certainly. But in the cloud they will have to find us, and they will be looking for us at five thousand metres or more. When they cannot find us they will come down, but by then we will have completed our mission. Good hunting.'

The various squadrons rendezvoused over Calais and were across the Channel in a few minutes. They made a splendid array – over a hundred machines – and they were not being handicapped by slow-moving bombers. Max turned left as soon as he crossed the coast, dropping down to no more than three hundred metres as he hurtled along. He loosed his bombs over Newhaven harbour and was rewarded with spurts of flame and smoke. Then he was on to open country, saw a train proceeding north and used several of his cannon shells. At least one struck and the train came off the track, spilling people in every direction. He was armed with sixty 20mm shells for each gun, and so had more than a hundred left. He continued west, observing considerable signs of panic beneath him, shot up a bridge, and suddenly saw in front of him a large isolated house.

His heart seemed to skip a beat. Hillside! He flew over it at two hundred metres, could see people in the yard looking up at him. He wondered if his father was there, but then he was at another bridge, and a voice said, 'Babies, twelve o'clock, dropping through the cloud. Quite a few.'

'Climb,' Max ordered. 'Use the cloud to get above them.'

He twisted his own machine and soared upwards. He still hadn't seen any Spitfires and a few moments later emerged into bright sunlight. Then he did see a flight above him, coming down very quickly. He glanced over his shoulder, saw that he was alone. He pulled the stick back and raced at them, unaware of any feeling other than a white-hot concentration.

'Holy mackerel!' a voice said. 'Look at those bars. Who is he?'

'Someone big,' another voice put in.

Max had no idea who was doing the talking, although he understood what they were saying easily enough. He was now closing very rapidly on the three planes, aiming for the centre, but when he was within a hundred metres the Spitfire suddenly pulled up to avoid collision. He went past it, came round in a tight turn, blacked out, and when he regained vision two seconds later he saw that he was immediately behind one of the enemy.

'Shit!' someone said. 'How did he turn like that?'

Max was already firing at sixty metres range. Pieces of fabric and metal clouded the air, overtaken immediately by a cloud of smoke tinged with red.

'Shit!' the voice said again. 'Harry . . .' This time the voice quavered.

One of the planes was also turning very tightly, but Max's reactions, honed on so many aerial combats, were the quicker and another burst had the Spitfire spiralling away.

'Going down!' said a new voice. 'Harry?'

My God! Max thought. That was John.

'Sorry, Skipper, we've a right tiger by the tail. Actually, he has us. Martin bailing out.'

Max was now firing into the third plane, which was trying to get away. That, too, burst into flames. He looked below him and saw a parachute floating earthwards – the man Martin, he assumed.

But now the air was filled with machines, both German and British.

'You know that chap?' a voice asked.

'Yes,' John said.

They had come upon a cluster of the enemy at hardly more than five thousand feet, hurriedly trying to break off their strafing to gain altitude. The fight had been furious but brief, and the Messerschmitts, caught at a disadvantage, had been scattered with some loss. Then had come Martin's call of alarm. Two sections had followed John upwards, and he was as horrified as the other pilots to discover that a lone marauder had brought down the entire Yellow Section.

And what a marauder. For Max, although he must have realized he was hopelessly out-numbered, six to one, was coming straight at them.

'You fool!' John shouted, even as he reset his guns.

The reply was a cannon shot which struck Turnbull's machine and simply blew it apart. John, four hundred yards away, immediately opened fire, but he was premature, and then the 109 was turning again, with startling rapidity, a stream of tracers issuing from its wings.

John was not aware of being hit, but he knew he was being out-flown. He climbed, rolled, regained consciousness, and saw nothing but blue sky. A voice shouted, 'Behind you, Skip!'

John looked over his shoulder, past the iron backrest of his seat, and felt a series of tremendous impacts into the metal. Again he attempted a violent turn, but still the bullets kept coming. Then he felt a deeper impact, and he realized he had been struck by a cannon shell.

The entire machine was shuddering and shaking, and now the cockpit was filled with a mixture of oil and glycol, completely blinding him, and he knew it could only be a matter of seconds before the machine exploded into flames.

He reached up and threw back the canopy, released his belts and turned the aircraft upside down. He dropped into space, pulled the cord, and was then able to clear the mist from his goggles.

The whole thing had happened so quickly and comprehensively that he had not had the time to think of either what was happening to him, or what he could do about it. Now, as he managed to focus, he saw that the 109 had burst through the British fighters and disappeared into the clouds. He found himself shouting, 'Get him!' But he was shouting to the wind.

Jolinda stood in the doorway to watch 833 Squadron return. It was still only ten o'clock, and the sky was clearing, allowing the sun to break through. She counted the machines; there were ten. The only way to tell the Spitfires apart was to count the Swastikas painted on their fuselages. She knew John had seventeen, far more than any other member of the squadron: even Bob Newman only had nine. But the distance was too great to make out any detail. She returned to her desk knowing that as soon as he had reported to Dispersal, John would be over to see her. It was only when she looked out of the window, after reading a couple of reports which she did not actually see, and saw Newman walking towards her office, that she felt a sudden pang of real anxiety, fearing as much for her baby as for her husband – John did not yet know he was to be a father.

She stood up, went into the outer office, reached the doorway as he did. 'Is he . . .?'

'He went in, but I saw him bale out. I'm sure he'll be all right.'

Jolinda's knees gave way, and she sank on to the straight chair beside her secretary's desk.

'It was Max,' Newman said. 'He tore into us like an absolute madman. John was his fourth kill in ten minutes.'

Jolinda raised her head. 'Did they get him?'

Newman shook his head. 'He seems to bear a charmed life. Just vanished into the clouds.'

'When will we know about John?'

'We're checking all the stations.' Newman squeezed her shoulder. 'He'll be along.'

John was taken home, where he was met by Mark and Helen as he was carried into the house.

'It's a sprained ankle, Mr Bayley,' explained the accompanying medic. 'Sustained when he hit the ground.'

'No wounds?' Mark asked.

'I'm all right, Dad, really,' John said.

Mark looked at him, nodded, and indicated the drawing room. 'We'll take it from here, thank you, Sergeant.'

The medic saluted; Beerman and Clements assisted John into the study and placed him in a chair. Rufus followed to lick his hand and Helen poured drinks.

Mark waited for the room to clear. 'So what happened? I know something did.'

'It was Max. He came at us like a bat out of hell, and frankly, Dad, he beat the hell out of us. Me included. He was faster, quicker on the turn, more accurate in his shooting . . . He made me feel like a novice. I have a feeling that if the Luftwaffe had possessed a hundred pilots of his class, Jerry would have landed at Dover by now.'

'So he was on, and you were off,' Mark said. 'It happens.' John lifted his head, and father and son looked at each other. Then Mark raised his glass. 'You're here. That's what matters.'

Tyres crunched on the gravel and Rufus barked. Jolinda came in and knelt beside him. 'Jesus, I was scared. But . . .' She looked at his bandaged leg.

'Just a sprain. And as Dad has said, I'm here, and that's what matters. Third time lucky.'

She squeezed his hand and kissed him. 'I'm so glad of that. And so is Junior.'

He stared at her. 'You serious?'

'The doctor telephoned this morning, but you were already airborne.'

'Well then,' Helen said, 'I think we'll open a bottle of bubbly.'

'At least two!' Mark exclaimed.

* * *

'I have never seen anything like it,' Gunther told the assembled pilots. 'He could have destroyed the entire RAF.'

'I was lucky,' Max said, gulping his fourth glass of schnapps.

The reaction had set in on the way home, slowed for a few moments by his fuel situation which had required total concentration to land safely. But since then . . . He had had every intention of dying this morning. But when he had realized he was opposed by John, his sole ambition had been to avenge Klaus Maartens. He felt he had done that, although he did not think John was dead. But he had been shot down in open combat which meant a great deal, even if he was not quite sure what. And he was alive . . .

'None the less, Herr Major,' Gunther said, 'I – all of us – are proud to have flown with you. Gentlemen, I give you Major Max Bayley, our supreme leader and ace.'

The rafters rang as the pilots raised both their glasses and their voices. Max surveyed their faces and managed a smile. It should have been the supreme moment of his life. Instead it was the emptiest, because his life no longer had any meaning whatsoever.

Except, perhaps, in Erika's arms. They deserved each other.

'Tell me,' the King said as he shook hands with John, after pinning the bar to his DFC on his tunic. 'Is it true that you were shot down by your own brother?'

'It was a family affair, yes, sir,' John agreed. 'But there will be a next time . . .'